D1298116

MONEY *Maker*

TONYA RIDLEY

Life Changing Books in conjunction with Power Play Media
Published by Life Changing Books
P.O. Box 423 Brandywine, MD 20613

This novel is a work of fiction. Any references to real people, events, establishments, or locales are intended only to give the fiction a sense of reality and authenticity. Other names, characters, and incidents occurring in the work are either the product of the author's imagination or are used fictitiously, as are those fictionalized events and incidents that involve real persons. Any character that happens to share the name of a person who is an acquaintance of the author, past or present, is purely coincidental and is in no way intended to be an actual account involving that person.

Library of Congress Cataloging-in-Publication Data;

www.lifechangingbooks.net
13 Digit: 978-1934230695
10 Digit: 1934230693

Copyright © 2010

All rights reserved, including the rights to reproduce this book or portions thereof in any form whatsoever.

Dedication

R.I.P

Nigel Ellison

There was no excuse! We will always love you.

Your smile is truly missed.

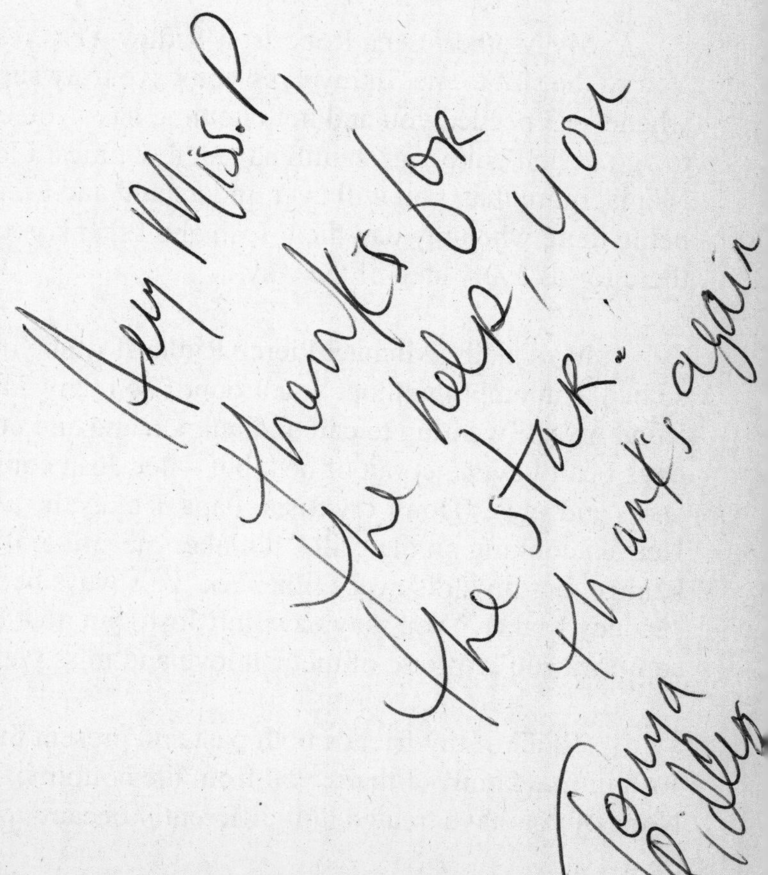

Acknowledgements

I would like to start by saying I've been blessed these last few years. Even though I've been through a lot of obstacles, I've grown as a person and definitely have a stronger relationship with God. P.S. But he's still working on my mouth.

My Mother, Lena Robertson-Ridley-Yes, Yes, Yes! You're the shit to me. In my eyes you have truly supported me whenever I needed you and not one time have you ever told me to "go to hell" like you should have a few times. I love you, Mama, more than you will ever understand and I thank you for being there when my dad died. Josh and I thank you for being there for us every step of the way.

My Daddy, Michael Pierce Ridley-I wish you were here so bad. I'm empty without you around. So many days go by that I find myself wanting to call and talk Obama and politics. Some days I can't even get out of bed, but when Josh comes downstairs and says, "Don't cry Sista, Papa is okay, he and Bud are in Heaven cooking on the grill," it makes me smile. It sounds strange, but it works every time. You've always been my "Money Maker." You may have left Josh, but now he's with me, so I pray you're proud of me. I'll love and miss you forever.

To all of my friends both past and present that have taken Josh in like family- I thank you from the bottom of my heart. None of you have treated him differently because of his disability and I thank you again for that. Nicky Rochelle…Thank you for calling and checking on Josh almost every day.

Azarel, my boss lady-You're the best boss in the world, and I haven't had one since high school. No one could ask for a betta place to be in the book world, besides LCB –What!!! You're truly a good friend outside of books. Thanks for all of our late night talks.

Leslie "Pitbull" Allen-What can I say besides you're the bomb. Thanks for all the help and I do mean ALL your help because without you, this book would not be out. You don't have to put in 110% in all of our books, but you do. So, I want to say thank you from all of us on the LCB roster.

Family- I love you all a lot…even when I go a little crazy. We're truly what families think they are…strong, crazy, loving, ready to set it off and still have each other's back when we know we're wrong. Ruth, Maurice, Sallie and Ed Jr.'s kids – we're the best and the worst, and that's why I love you all.

Derwin and Johnelle Young-I'm so glad you all are in my life. I can't imagine being without you. You two have never let me down. Johnelle, from giving me a bath when I had the car wreck, to you Derwin for paying my bills when I needed you. Now with my Chainsaw here, and the new baby on the way, I can't ask for much anymore.

Sista Andrea Parham and family-I know we do not talk as much as we used to, but nothing will ever stop me from loving you. And let me remind you that you're a lot like your father (smile). To my niece Shanika (Jermey) –you will always be your grandfather's shining star!

To my closest friends thanks for being there for me when I needed you all the most over these past two and a half years. It's been tough, but I made it like I always do. I know that we don't always agree on everything, but let's hope the years to come will be brighter.

Barrett family – I know it's been kinda rough because we act crazy at times, but nothing can keep us down. I love you all so much, and there's nothing you can do about it.

Talk of the Town Hair Salon Family- Where do I begin ? I know you all are sick of me coming to the shop, but somebody gotta wash your towels! Brandi, Chajuan, Allison, Bell, Steve, Trina and sometimes Lee, thank you all for hanging in there with me. I know my texts are crazy sometimes, but so are you. I wouldn't change it for the world. Just wait until I get my *real money*...we're gonna be good.

Jackie Davis and Rhonda Johnson, your boys are in college now, so enjoy and be proud...you deserve it.

Sherry (MF) Richburg – you're one of the strongest women I know. I really couldn't believe (after reading your court papers) that you're still alive. Stay strong, because you deserve the best.

Tam and Dee – It's so amazing how your life can change overnight. Dee-I'm overjoyed that you're feeling much better. My church has been praying for you and I was glad to report that your health is slowly improving. I can't imagine you not dancing to Arab Money (lol). I'll keep you in my prayers. Tam-thanks for all the cute clothes. Shout out to Hush Boutique.

My Godchildren– Shemar, Sherrell and Poobie 32, I love each of you more than you know. Aunt Tonya will always be there whenever you need me. And it's funny that all of you play basketball. When I hit the "Lotto"– you're good forever, trust me!!!

D.J. Smooth – We've talked so much this last year, its funny to me. I just love you and your family (Lula Mae) and your daughter, Shanua. Miss Lady, I understand everything you talk to me about, so understand that I'm here for you. You will always be my stepdaughter and those plans we talked about, let's get them done this year.

Prettydread – I'm glad we're still friends (1988-2010). You're so damn crazy. It's too funny that my boss lady is actually scared of you. Yeah nigga, I know you Jamaican and WHAT?? I can't wait to see you in November. Tell Tophead I said hello.

To my fellow LCB authors-we have had a rough patch last year, but let's put it behind us and make 2010 and 2011 the best ever. Also let's make our newest authors feel welcome. P.S. Capone what the hell are you doing? Lastly, thanks to my cousin Reco for introducing me to Azarel?? LOL

R.I.P. to… Mrs. Ziglar, Mrs. Eloise, Bud Hodges and Rufus Wilson. I can't believe you all are gone. Even though you left a void, your impact in our lives still feels so strong. You all meant so much to us. Grandma Ruth – I still can't believe it's been four years. I miss you so much. The family is sticking together, you would be proud.

To Chanda Ziglar, Carla Johnson, Karen Hodges and Renee Wilson, I know times are tough for all of you, but trust me, it does get better with time. Some people just don't understand, so please cry whenever and wherever.

Shout Outs to all of my prison mail pals. To Kennie Thomas – Khloe's baby shower was nice. "Blac Label"…damn you were my largest customer. People laugh because I get so much prison mail. Just because you're outta sight doesn't mean you're outta mind. Kay Jefferies, Jermel, Raymond, Rhamel, Kiko, Cuz Harvey-Philly, Beefy, G. Hayden, Gutta, VJ, Lil EJ, Country, Face, Jamaican Money, Hardy, DV, Solomn, Rodney, Lil Chris, my cuz Derrick King (Money Maker), Black, Mookie, Paul Streeter and Pepe. The sun will definitely shine again for all of you.

To Black & Noble in Philly…thanks for the support with this new project. To my test readers Ashundria Fisher and Shannon Barnes, and to my longtime friend JD, thanks for all your help.

Lastly to anyone who bought The Takeover or Talk of the Town, I wanna thank you all for your support as well. It's been a while since I dropped my last book, but I'm finally back and ready to grind. Let's gets this money!

Tonya Ridley

One

CLICK.

The cocking sound of Trick's Smith and Wesson shocked everyone around, but especially a frightened Dajon. His face tightened even more as Trick pressed the tip of the gun forcefully into his temple. Dajon laid frozen beneath his sheets panting like an old, overweight dog, breathing loudly through his nose. He had no idea how the trio had crept into his home unseen and unheard in the wee hours of the morning. But he knew the end result. Trick's reputation was known throughout the Philly area, so a save wasn't likely. He watched as Trick gave instructions to his workers who stood guard on both sides of the room, while Trick sat on the edge of the bed close to Dajon's shivering body.

"You want me to bust 'em?" Felony asked in his raspy voice.

Trick nodded slowly as he gazed into Dajon's chubby face. He nodded his head up and down as the street lights shone into the dark bedroom giving Trick a chance to see every fearful expression on Dajon's face. Although the New York Yankees fitted hat hid Trick's scowl, it was clear that his eyes remained focused on Dajon for nearly twenty seconds while his boy's Felony and Polo stared at him in disbelief.

"Yo, like dis taking too long, dawg. Let's go," Polo uttered.

"I got this," Trick countered.

Trick was always difficult to figure out. To most, his calm demeanor was a sign of weakness, but to those who knew him, understood that he was in his most ruthless state when in deep thought... always trying to figure out the best way to take an enemy out. Dajon knew Trick well enough since he'd fronted him drugs on a regular basis. He just didn't know him as well as Felony and Polo did. Suddenly, Dajon's thoughts were cut short. The moment that Trick leaned over, moving closer to Dajon's face, he quickly shut his eyes tightly. Fat boy knew it was over and sadly, there was no escape.

"You see where stealin' gets you?" Trick taunted, pressing the gun even more forcefully into his temple.

Sweat poured from Dajon's face as he pleaded, "C'mon man! I told you what happened…!"

"You must notta heard what happens to niggas who fuck with me, yamean?" Trick said.

"C'mon, man!" Dajon begged even more.

Before he could get another word out of his mouth, Trick withdrew the gun from his head, hitting Dajon across the face with the butt of the gun. Instantly, blood trickled from his face and his eyes ballooned in fear.

"I swear on my daughter, man! Don't do this. Don't do this, man," Dajon ended as tears streamed down the side of his cheek.

"Bitch-ass nigga," Trick sniped.

"Fuck dat shit!" Felony shouted, as he paced back and forth on the right side of the bed. He moved closer to Trick with vengeance in his eyes. "Trick, you know dis nigga lying. Lemme bust'em?" he asked again, only this time he'd removed the .357 that had been stuffed down his loose fitting pants.

Both he and Polo had gotten antsy since they'd been in Dajon's house for more than ten minutes. The plan had called for a quick in and out, leaving Dajon dead. Trick had known for weeks that Dajon's fabricated story about how he'd gotten robbed while in possession of 70,000 dollars worth of Trick's product was all a lie. He'd given him the chance to confess, even offering Dajon a re-payment plan, yet nothing worked. Dajon kept sending messages that Trick should just take it as a loss because there was nothing he could do to get the money back.

Trick finally spoke after minutes of silence. "So Dajon, you know a nigga from the East side name Dre?" He pressed the gun into Dajon's temple once again.

A lump formed in Dajon's throat.

"Ahhhhhhh."

"Huh nigga, you know who I'm talkin' about, right?" Trick jolted the gun a bit. "I got me a sexy lil biddy on the east side so I gotta few friends, yamean?"

"Yeah…I know what you mean, Trick. But c'mon man, put the gun down!" Dajon cried out, while remaining stiffly in place.

"Nah, nigga. You sold my shit to that nigga, thinkin' I wouldn't find out. I know everythin' that goes on in my town," he said with discontent, then grit his teeth. "I own this town. Yamean?" he asked with even more anger in his voice.

Of course, Dajon never said a word. He simply cried like a bitch. Yet none of it phased Trick. He was used to punks and wanna-be hustlers. He'd seen it all his life. In an instant, Trick transformed into what Felony had been waiting for. He rose from the bed like he was being attacked.

Boom!

Trick never even flinched as the gun exploded. But even Felony cringed at the sight of Dajon's blood that covered the crisp white sheets. The sound from the gun left all three men with ringing ears, which of course made Trick realize they had less than a minute to make it to the back of the house where the getaway truck was waiting. Trick had been killing for years so not only was he skilled at murder, but at getting away with it too. It was what he did best. Murder was the name of the game. His whole life consisted of getting money and slaying anybody who got in his way.

Within minutes, Trick had switched into high gear. His

jewels glistened in the darkness as he jetted down the stairs, taking two at the time, then out the back door, following on the heels of Felony. He moved swiftly knowing that someone had probably heard the shots. Trick, Polo, and Felony ran like their lives depended on it, rushing toward Trick's 2010 off white Cadillac Escalade. Within minutes, Polo had hopped in the driver's seat, started the ignition, and sped through the alley way, hopping onto Gratz Street. Trick sighed a deep sound of relief as he laid back in his butter soft leather seats, knowing he'd just gotten away with another murder.

Although his bald head was covered in sweat, he was pleased with how things had gone. He knew that with Polo driving he could rest his eyes for a moment while sitting in his second best treasure. The Escalade with deep black tinted windows was every man's dream. It was fully equipped with everything from 12-inch plasma screen TV's, custom black floor mats and a Bose' system which Polo had now pushed to the limit. Plies song, *Wasted* blasted from the speakers as they sped down Broad street.

Although the music pumped, Trick thought deeply about his life. As strange as it sounded, he was tired of the ups and downs of the cocaine game. And definitely tired of the hatin' niggas in the biz. Everybody he'd ever met was cut throat with the exception of Polo and Felony. It was time for a drastic change, he thought to himself. He'd committed to throwing in the towel and sticking to his new money making business…one that would set him straight for a lifetime. Little did Felony know, but Trick was about to separate himself from any dealings with drugs after their last deal they were headed to make.

"Man, like what time we gotta meet up with Ce-lo?" Trick asked Felony.

"9 a.m." Felony laughed.

"Fuck. That's five hours from now." Trick tugged on his long, full beard showing that he'd already gotten restless. "A nigga need some sleep."

"Dat's your boy. The only nigga in town who gotta get

up at da crack of dawn to get served."

"Like that nigga better be glad his money right," Trick announced. "Yo, stop me by that 24 hour spot....Ahhh what's that jawn called?" Trick snapped his fingers as Felony made a sharp turn, causing him to hold on to the handle above him. "Richies, that's the name of it. Get me one of them egg sandwiches before we go cook up." He closed his eyes. "And good lookin' out back there."

"Always," both men said in unison.

"Now hurry Felony, a nigga hungry," Trick said slouching down in the seat.

"Gotcha dawg."

For several minutes Polo and Felony laughed and talked shit to one another until Trick's cell phone rang. He opened his eyes knowing what was next. The caller ID read trouble. It was Mena, Trick's money hungry girlfriend.

"Talk to me."

"Im'a talk to you alright. Fuck you, Trick! It's five o'clock in the morning and you still not home! Where the fuck you at?" Mena shouted through the phone.

"Takin' care of business. You know what that means, right?" He smirked. "You wanna spend big money every day...well somebody gotta make it, so chill your foul mouth ass out." He paused and put more bass in his voice. "Aye Mena, I told you about disrespectin' me."

"Fuck you, Trick! I bet if I change the locks on your ass, you'll come home at a decent hour."

"Mena, I got shit to do. And besides, It's not like I'm out with some biddy. So I'll see you about ten. And remember, that's my jawn, bitch. You just on a guest pass."

"Ten? Mufucka, you crazy? She screamed like the devil had possessed her spirit. "See if I'm here when you get here, nigga? That staying out all night shit is a no-no for me."

Trick held his breath and gritted his teeth as he often did when his blood boiled. Mena had a unique way of getting deep under his skin. Even though they'd been together for five months, he wasn't crazy in love. He had other women that he preferred to play house with, and Mena knew it. Trick just wasn't the settling down type…just really wanted his dick sucked the moment he opened his eyes every morning. Although Mena's head game and pussy was on point, she was even better for his newly discovered hustle that had been growing more and more by the weeks.

"Mena, if you stop askin' me for new purses, clothes, and jewelry every day, maybe I could come home more often. Man, bye!" Trick spat.

"Trick, Trick, Trick," Mena called out, still holding the phone, but got no answer.

Just as the call ended, Felony startled everyone in the truck. "Oh shit!" he blurted out glaring at the rear view mirror.

By the time Trick turned to look behind, he could hear the sirens sounding from the rear. The blue and red flashing lights sent him into a fast frozen state. In an instant his heart rate sped, wondering what his next move would be.

$ Two $

Five hours had passed and Trick felt like he had conquered the world. He and Felony had been in a fake high-speed car chase, cooked three keys, made the drop to his early morning sale, and now had two large bags of money. It killed him that Ce-lo was his only connection who always wanted to meet early in the morning. Most times, he didn't care. But considering he hadn't gotten any sleep all night this was beyond his limits. He'd killed a man, cooked cocaine like a top chef and was now on his way home to Mena's loud mouth.

After almost falling asleep behind the wheel a few times, Trick finally pulled up in front of his 4,800 square foot home in Gladwyne several minutes later. All he could think about as he turned off the truck's engine was his plush king sized bed that he couldn't wait to dive into. No matter how long he'd been into the fast money drug game, he could never get used to the grueling hours the job required. However, after walking up the driveway his entire demeanor changed as he stopped to gaze at his new prized possession. Gently rubbing his hand across the snow white Bentley Continental GT, he quickly realized that if it wasn't for the work he put in, the new $187,000 dollar car would still be on the showroom floor. He was especially proud of the custom red and black seats and chrome Dub 22 inch rims. As Trick thought about how his new beauty could go from 0-60 miles per hour in 3.7 seconds, the front door to his house flew open. He didn't even have to look up. He knew exactly who it was.

"I can't believe this! Do you know what time it is?" Mena yelled as she stormed outside barefoot in an oversized RIP Michael Jackson t-shirt.

"Yo, I ain't in the mood for this shit, Mena. Take yo ass back in the house."

"I don't give a damn what you're in the mood for, Trick. It's almost ten o'clock in the morning and you're just getting home!"

Trick looked on as one of his white neighbors pulled out of his garage. He waited for the nosey grey haired attorney to drive off before he gave Mena the look of death. "Mena, you better get the fuck outta my face, yamean? Like don't be tryna cause no fuckin' scene in front of my crib. That's all I need is for one of these white mufuckas to call the cops."

"If you stop coming home at disrespectful hours I wouldn't have to act like this." When Trick bent down to wipe a small speck of dirt off the driver's side door, Mena placed her hands on her curvaceous hips and gave him a stern look. "All you care about is this fucking car. Why do you even want me around if you don't give a shit about me?"

Instead of caving into Mena's latest nagging fest, Trick decided to ignore her. Thinking the silent treatment would work, he turned around and made his way into the house. Not one for giving up, Mena followed him like a trained puppy into their two story family room, never missing a beat.

"So, are you gonna tell me why the fuck I'm even here if you don't care about me?" she continued. "I'm so tired of this!"

"Leave then," Trick replied in a nonchalant tone.

Mena's eyes bulged. "Excuse me?"

"You heard me…leave then. All you do is fuckin' nag me, Mena. After all the shit I been through over the last twelve hours, a nigga don't wanna have to come home to this."

Mena finally calmed down. "I'm sorry. I just…"

"You just what? You just run your fuckin' mouth too much. You have no idea the shit I go through when I'm out in these streets, yamean? Me and my niggas were out there tryna outrun some fuckin' cops who weren't even chasin' us and shit. Then I gotta come home to your ass tryna blast me outside in front of the whole neighborhood. Fuck that. It's plenty of other bitches willin' to take your place, so if you wanna leave…bounce."

Even though Trick talked a good game, he really didn't want Mena to leave. She was street smart and good for the business. Plus, she knew too much about his operation. Fighting with Mena every night over stupid shit was starting to take it's toll on him. Trick sat down in his favorite spot on the couch, which had a slight dent from his massive size. At 6'3, two hundred and eighty three pounds, and a tatted up frame, he constantly reminded everyone of the rapper, Rick Ross.

"You know…I shoulda left you a long time ago when you did that bullshit." Mena's entire mood changed. With water welled up in her eyes, she spoke from the heart, "I mean…anybody else with some sense would've left you Trick! But I stayed! In spite of it all!"

"C'mon Mena, don't go there with that shit again. Yamean? Like, we'll neva agree on how it all went down."

Mena went off! "We, my ass! You did it Trick, and you know it. You fucking did it!" she repeated between sobs. "And I'll never forgive you. She paced the floor and let the tears flow. "I got all this shit bottled up inside me still trying to keep this secret from everyone else. And I'm sick of people asking me about it. I'm tired of lying, Trick!"

"I really don't give a fuck what people think, yamean? Like, let's tell the whole story and let your family decide what really happened that night."

"Fuck you, Trick!" Mena shouted to the top of her lungs.

"Let's do it, bitch! Keep talkin' shit."

For some reason when Trick talked to Mena that way it turned her on. She was definitely attracted to men who took control, and dismissed anyone who appeared to be weak. Quickly switching up from bitch mode, Mena walked over to

Trick and sat down on his lap. Even though she was still emotional about all that had been said, Mena managed to push all those feelings aside for the moment. She dried her tears with the back of her hand, and let a slight smile slip from her moist lips. In reality, no matter how mad she was at him she couldn't leave…not yet anyway.

Moving in directly on *his spot*, Mena circled his diamond encrusted ear with her tongue. She knew the minute he realized she didn't have any panties on, her recent actions would soon be forgiven.

"I'm sorry, baby," she whispered in a seductive tone. "You know everytime I think about that horrible night, I get crazy."

"Yeah. I'm tryna understand you. You just need time to heal, I guess."

It wasn't long before Trick's tense body began to relax. No matter how mad he was, he could never deny her sex. If it wasn't for her Beyonce like hips, C-cup breasts, small waist and bomb-ass dick sucking techniques, she would've been gone a long time ago.

"Like you gotta stop that naggin' shit for real."

Mena nodded her head then kissed Trick's full lips. "I know."

Trick pulled his trademark black t-shirt off, then rubbed his hand through Mena's wavy twenty-two inch weave. Instantly, Mena attacked his chest with her hands. He was far from being chiseled, but it always made him feel sexy when she outlined his battle tattoos with her finger. Reaching for his pants, Mena started rubbing on his dick, which started to rise at the thought of her next move. Trick craved her deep throat action, and compared to any other broad she was second to none.

"Oh, so you're not mad at me anymore?" Mena asked with a slight smile.

Before he could respond, she quickly got on her knees, unzipped his Blac Label jeans then pulled out Trick's growing dick. It wasn't long before she began to suck it like it was her favorite lollipop. Trick's eyes rolled to the back of his head while Mena did her best impersonation of Superhead. Once his dick reached it's full erection, Mena stopped.

"Stand up," she ordered.

Happy to oblige, Trick stood to his feet and watched as Mena attempted to grab his wide ass with both of her hands so that he could fuck her face and show off her deep throat skills. Mena's gag-reflexes were sick, which allowed her to take in all ten inches with no problem. Feeling like he was about to bust, Trick backed up before pulling Mena to her feet. With his size, man handling her 5'8 frame was easy.

"Assume the fuckin' position," he said, stroking his dick.

Knowing exactly what that meant, Mena walked over to the dining room table, lifted up her t-shirt then spread her legs for easy access. Doggy style was both of their favorite positions, especially Mena who loved being able to feel every inch of Trick's meat going deep inside her. Not to mention, he was able to reach her spot much easier.

"Yes, baby fuck this pussy," Mena moaned as Trick began to stroke her with a steady rhythm. "Oh, Daddy, I love this dick."

With his ego being stroked, Trick began to dive even deeper into her walls. He really wanted to punish her for all the stress she'd been putting him through lately. However, the harder he pumped, the more he saw her ass bounce up and down, which made him even hornier. Nobody's ass could clap the way Mena's did.

"Oh, shit I'm about to cum," Trick squirmed.

Never missing a chance herself to put it down, Mena hopped up and turned around so she could lick and suck up all her man's juices. Unleashing all of his frustration and energy, Trick blasted every drop that his cannon could produce into Mena's throat. The feeling was unexplainable as she used her jaws to try and pull out even more.

Damn...it's too bad this bitch is always stressing me. She really would be a good broad to keep around, Trick thought right before he made his way to the bedroom and passed out.

$ Three $

Several hours later and after getting some much needed rest, Trick made his way down to the basement where recently only he and Mena were allowed. Back when he first moved in, him and his boys would have several fight parties and watch the Superbowl in his elaborate movie room, but now all that had changed. With his new operation at stake, Trick made sure to keep his friends away. Due to the saturated drug world, he wanted to keep his new scheme all to himself, ultimately becoming a counterfeit king pen.

Walking into what used to be a spare bedroom, Trick turned on the light to reveal a room full of high-end equipment. Since everyone in his occupation knew there wasn't a retirement plan for drug dealers, Trick decided a year ago to come up with a bigger and better plan to maintain his lifestyle. Although the drug money was good, his counterfeiting scheme was just as profitable. Not to mention, the shit carried a much lighter prison sentence if he were to ever get caught. After turning on his computer, Trick walked around to each of his three ink jet all-in-one printers to make sure they were on before pulling out a huge stack of newsprint paper from the closet. With a huge new order to fill for his Columbian connect everything had to be organized before he got started.

It was standard procedure for him to change his computer's password every two days, so it took him a few seconds to think of his newest security measure. After typing in the words, BENTLEY, it didn't take long for Trick to think about how he ended up in the counterfeit game to begin with. Curiosity about the crime initially drew him in after someone tried to give him $10,000 worth of fake bills in exchange for his product a few years back. The bills were so poorly made even Stevie Wonder would've been able to tell that he'd been bamboozled. Thoughts about how bad he punished the dude who tried to play him made Trick smile now because he actually had that fool to thank for introducing him to the business. Trick never forgot how he went home with the fake bills that night, but instead of throwing them away he compared them to a real bill and studied the differences like an exam. From the watermarks to the security threads and color shifting ink, Trick dissected every inch of the bills until the sun came up. It was on that day he decided to take on another crime. Even though several of his first attempts failed miserably, after nearly four months his persistence finally paid off.

When his recent trip down memory lane ended, Trick sat down at his desk, opened a pack of the tissue-like specialty paper then placed several sheets into each one of the printers. Once that was done, he placed a freshly ironed hundred dollar bill on the bed of one printer and closed the top before pushing the scan button. Trick's bills had to be in perfect condition. Wrinkles, or any imperfections would ruin his final product. After clicking the icon for the graphic software on his computer, Trick waited until the bill showed up on the screen before he started to work his magic. During his four months of trial and error, it took Trick a while to realize that after scanning both sides of the bill he needed the software to not only clean up any flaws, but to also make sure his fake watermarks, security strips and bill numbers were in place. With over twelve months of experience, making counterfeit money had become second nature to Trick. His three hour process of making sure each bill was ready to print had now been cut down to minutes. He'd definitely perfected his craft.

Once the front side of the bill was complete, and with just a few clicks, Trick printed out ten hundred dollar bills from each printer before doing the same process all over again with the back side. His ritual was to never start with the back of a bill. Not only was it harder to duplicate, but for some reason it was easier to tear. His eyes lit up like an excited child at Christmas every time he saw the fake bills spitting out. It was something that he never wanted to get used to.

"Mena!" Trick called out after all the printers stopped. "Mena!"

A few seconds passed before she finally answered. Little did he know she was on a secret phone call. "Yeah."

"Get down here. I'm ready for you."

"I'm coming," she shouted, while covering the phone.

Once Trick felt comfortable enough to introduce Mena to his operation, her job was to thoroughly glue each side of the bills together, making sure the security markings lined up correctly. Next she sprayed each bill with a coat of starch, then placed the wet bills into the dryer for approximately three minutes. The purpose of the starch was so the counterfeit pens wouldn't detect the phony money once each bill was cut. Although Mena knew how to make the money herself, Trick had yet to give her a promotion.

Upstairs, Mena ended her conversation, telling the caller that she had to go. "I'll call you when I can get away," she told him sweetly. "Thanks for listening to my problems."

Mena hung up and waltzed downstairs a few minutes later eating her famous sunflower seeds. "Do we have to do this now, Trick ? I wanna watch the Wendy Williams show that I recorded earlier."

"Yo, I don't give a shit about no dumb-ass show. Like, do you know how long it's gonna take me to fill the order I just got? I'm already behind. They want two hundred and fifty grand this time."

"Look I'm not a damn child. Have you forgotten that I'm twenty-four? Don't be talking to me like that," she said with a demanding look. "If you would let me make the money, I could've had some ready. Hell, while you were *out all night*, I could've had several stacks ready to go," Mena replied before spitting a shell inside a red plastic cup.

"How many times do I have to tell you not to touch my computer? You already got your job."

"And I'm tired of doing that shit. Why do I have to keep dealing with the glue and the starch? That shit is sticky. Why can't you do that part?"

Trick's patience was rapidly decreasing. "Because I run the show, that's why. All you do is fuckin' complain. I bet when the latest pair of them dumb-ass Louboutin shoes come out your ass won't be complainin' then, yamean?"

Mena couldn't help but smile because she knew he was right. She was a complete shoe whore. Sucking her teeth, she grabbed a bottle of specialty glue that Trick preferred to use out of the closet, then waited for him to carefully cut the front and back sides of several bills before she started gluing. They worked well into the wee hours of the morning until Trick started rubbing his eyes.

"Man, I'm tired as shit. That's enough for the night. Like it's not nearly enough…not even close to what I need, but I gotta get some sleep." He looked around the room. "The stack in the corner is for the Columbians, but I gotta small stack on the desk that's for my man tomorrow. Make sure you finish sprayin' what's on the desk before you go back upstairs. I'm goin' to bed."

Just as Trick shut down the computer, Mena spoke up.

"Trick, I think I'm gonna go to counseling next month," she said out of the blue.

"Mannnnn, here we go again," he complained. "Not tonight, Mena. You got too many problems for a nigga right now. Just let that shit go. You can't bring him back."

Mena got teary eyed, and clenched her lips together in anger. She quickly changed the subject.

"So, are there extra bills on the desk? You know…besides what your man ordered."

"Mena, you know I always make extra bills just in case I get another order. Why?"

"Because, I already have in mind what I'm gonna get for doing all this shit, so I wanted to make sure you had enough."

"It's amazin' how every time you help me out you want somethin'. Why can't you just do the shit because you're my girl?"

Work for free? Nigga are you crazy? Never, Mena thought.

"You should wanna do nice things for me because I'm *your girl*," she countered. As Trick shook his head and walked out the room without looking back, Mena held a sinister grin and mumbled beneath her breath, "Your payback is near, baby."

$Four$

The next day rolled around with both Mena and Trick exhausted from fucking half the night and most of the morning. They lay in bed ass-naked on crisp, top dollar sheets talking about their future, yet secretly wondering how they'd ever break free from one another. On the surface, the relationship seemed to be stable, but deep down inside neither were sincere about the other. It was all a game; all about a dollar; both counterfeit and real. The game had been played for months, now with Trick two steps ahead.

For Mena, her problems carried more weight. After all, she'd altered her life to be with Trick. The small time job she once held at Peco Electric had been given up the moment he promised to take care of all of her needs. And of course when they first met, Trick started the relationship strong, wining and dining her, and offering a lifestyle change if she agreed to be his one and only. Soon, that all changed, and had been changing for the worse each time a new woman crossed Trick's path.

To make matters worse, Mena couldn't find it in her heart to forgive him for taking away the most precious thing to her. She tried day after day. It just didn't seem to be working.

"Yo, talk to me," Trick said, grabbing his phone off the nightstand on the first ring.

Mena pushed his shoulder and turned the opposite direction. "I thought we said no phones today?" she grilled from beneath the covers.

Trick ignored her and kept his conversation going. “Naw, you got that shit all wrong, yamean?” he told the caller on the other end, while pulling the covers over to his side a bit. Even though he and Mena had been together for months, when they weren’t having sex he was very self conscious about his weight. “Let’s go with the first way I explained. Give me an hour. I’ll meet you on South Street.”

“Stop yanking the fucking covers!” Mena screamed. “And I hate your ass, Trick! This was supposed to be our day.”

“Trick paused, quickly pulled the phone away from his ear, and motioned for Mena to face him. Like a disobedient child she remained under the covers talking more shit than before.

“Man, like my young jawn has lost her fuckin’ mind. But I’ll see you in a hour…I gotta go,” Trick told the caller.

Mena got quiet for a moment as different sets of emotions ran through her mind. She wondered what she really meant to Trick. For her, she knew he was a lottery ticket until she could get herself on top again. At one point she really did care for Trick and wondered if a feeling other than sex would ever resurface for him. Then she thought about what he really meant to her.

“Trick, can we go get my purse today?” she blurted out, while removing the covers. “I worked real hard on that damn order last night.”

Trick glared at her naked body remembering why he was originally attracted to Mena. Her honey colored eyes, long, sexy legs and light complexion was just how he liked his women. He often wondered what life would be like with Mena if he could take away her sarcastic mouth, constant gripes, and love for a dollar. He knew that an extended life with Mena would make him a broke man, but how could he ever tell her that he had no intentions on being with her. For now he needed Mena because she was a good worker, and trustworthy; but knew he’d have to keep laying pipe and spending money to keep her around a while.

Out of the blue, Trick slapped Mena on the ass. "Get up. I'm a take you to get that bag today. But first I gotta meet my man on South Street to make this money."

"Trick, I told you I'm not doing no drug deals. Shit, you think I'ma be in the car with your ass when the Feds come after you?"

"There you go with that fuckin' mouth again. Just get dressed. I'm sellin' the phony stack today, not drugs. Now, go wash that pussy up. I'ma hop in the shower."

Trick got up and rushed toward the shower, showing her every inch of his oversized ass cheeks. Mena just watched from behind, plotting her next move. It wasn't long before she heard the water running, and Trick hollering from the bathroom.

"Mena, get your ass in here!"

"I'm coming!" she shouted, as she grabbed his phone off the nightstand.

Mena got quiet again as she took the next five minutes to carefully creep through Trick's phone. Text message after text message she boiled with envy. *How could he*? she asked herself. She was the one who helped him build the counterfeit business. She was the one who fucked him daily, and she was the one who took his bullshit.

The more Mena scrolled, the more she realized that a few numbers were very familiar. One was her nail tech while another was from their private chef who came to cook for them twice a week. Looking at the messages, she knew they were talking about more than just fried chicken, especially at three a.m. *I knew that fat mufucka was up to no good,* she told herself. Then…jackpot! The Columbians. It was the head guy's number who'd placed Trick's largest order. Mena quickly opened up the drawer, grabbed a small piece of paper and jotted down the digits with her new eye liner. The wheels were in motion as she continued to search like a trained spy.

"Mena…Mena!" Trick yelled, snapping her from her craze.

Her mouth fell open and her voice remained silent. But

when she didn't answer, Trick headed to the bedroom with a towel wrapped around his forty-two inch waist. "Mena...." He paused. "What the fuck?"

"What?" she asked calmly with pain in her eyes. Mena remained stretched across the bed with the evidence in her hand.

Trick looked at her for a few moments trying to figure out if she had completely lost her mind.

"Bitch, why are you goin' through my shit like that?" he screamed.

"What, you got something to hide?" Mena hopped up on her knees. "I can't use your phone to make a call?" Just as she asked that question his phone beeped signaling that he had a text message. Trick tried to snatch the phone from Mena, but she had already caught a glimpse of the name of the person sending the text.

"I knew you were fucking that bitch!" she exploded, as she threw the phone across the room.

Like a provoked monster, Trick grabbed Mena by her feet and pulled her off the bed landing her firm butt cheeks on the floor. "I'm tired of you always bitchin' about stupid shit!"

Mena swiftly pushed herself up off the floor and ran into the bathroom while clutching the Columbians phone number she wrote down into the palm of her hand. Before Trick could make a move, Mena had grabbed a sharp pair of scissors off the sink. "You betta keep your fucking hands off me Trick or I'ma cut your big black ass."

"Oh...so now you pullin' weapons on me and shit?"

Mena could see the anger in Trick's eyes plus she knew a pair of scissors was no match for a skilled killer. Trick had confessed many nights in bed about how he'd gutted snitches and popped bullets into enemies. After several seconds, Mena finally threw the scissors onto the floor realizing it was a weak move.

"I'm so sick of your ass, Trick. Fuck this," she wailed. "Them bitches can have your fat ass." She threw her hands up and backed her body into the countertop.

"I'm sick of yo' ass too, Mena," he uttered with guilt.

"You think you slick, but what goes around comes around baby," she said, pointing his way, while stomping back to their bedroom.

Trick followed, hoping to make things right. He didn't have time for Mena's drama. "You always trippin' about somethin'. If it ain't about another bitch it's about what you ain't got or what you want!" he yelled as he followed her. "Don't I give you what you want?"

"Yeah! You get what you want too, don't you?"

"Like I work for it," he grunted then paused. "But, what the fuck do you do all day, but sit up in here watchin' reality shows all day, then jump your ass up and go shoppin' …and fuck a few stacks of money up when you get ready." Trick stopped to sigh. "Look, I still think you wrong for goin' through my shit, but let's go get your purse. It's the least I can do."

"No. Call the bitch who texted you asking if you coming ova tonight. Tell'er it's ova Trick!" She folded her arms waiting for a response. When Trick's straight face had no emotion, Mena started again. "Oh, I see mufucka!"

"Let's go get your purse," he ended, rubbing his hand backward from his forehead to the back of his baldness.

Mena wanted to throw her clothes in a suitcase and get the hell out of Trick's spot, but she had a mission to complete so leaving wasn't an option. She hopped in the shower, got dressed and made it to the front door within thirty minutes while Trick hurried to the basement to bag up some money. Mena knew it was the perfect time to call her girl.

The phone rang a couple of times before Ronni finally answered, "What it do?"

Mena started to laugh because as long as she could remember Ronni always answered the phone the same damn way. It was crazy how she could always make Mena smile even in the worst situations. They'd met seven years ago when Mena got jumped by some girls at a local club. When Ronni, who just so happened to be walking by saw what was going on, she came to Mena's aid instantly. Not that she really cared, but when she saw that one of the girls was someone she had beef with, she couldn't resist jumping in. Ronni came out swinging like Mike Tyson's sister. The girls were no match for Ronni who although was a little bit on the petite side, had high-quality boxing skills. They'd been inseparable every since.

"What's up Veronica?" Mena knew her friend hated when she called her by her government name.

"Don't call me that shit. My jawns don't even call me that. What up?" Ronni asked again

"Nothing girl. Just tired of Trick's fat ass, that's all. That muthafucka always doing what the hell he wanna do, but that's okay."

"What, he fuckin' some other jawn?"

"Oh, I'm positive he is. Every time I turn around bitches in his face. Then when I checked his phone earlier, his ass was getting text messages from different bitches."

"Girl, why you sweatin' that dumb shit? Get your fuckin' money and keep it movin'. And get you a dick on the side."

"Oh trust me, I'm working on it."

Before Ronni could say anything else, Mena told her she had to go. This was a good time to call someone who would make her feel good inside. Quickly, she dialed. He answered just as fast.

"Yo, you not callin' while you in the house, are you?"

"Stop being so scared. Trick don't rule the world," Mena spat. "I am home, but he's downstairs. So, have you figured out when we can meet up?"

"Yo, why don't you say you going to the mall or something, and call me then. I wanna see you, but you doing this shit all wrong."

Before Mena could say anything else, Trick walked up the steps from the basement. Mena paused trying to figure out if he'd heard any part of her conversation. When he didn't go ballistic, she figured she'd let the caller go.

"I'll call you back later," Mena quickly said.

After hanging up the phone, she strutted out of the front

door with major attitude and waited as Trick unlocked the Bentley with two clicks on the alarm key.

Once in the car, Mena's shitty attitude kicked up a notch. By the time Trick had gotten onto the city streets, Mena had one foot posted up on the dash and the other covering the Breitling clock that Trick loved so much.

"Bitch, are you crazy? Get yo fuckin' foot off my shit. Yo ass don't have no respect for shit, yamean?"

Mena dropped her feet slowly, while rolling her eyes and picking at her freshly polished nails. She had been silent during most of the ride until they hopped onto South Street. "So, who we meeting?"

"My man, Julius. You don't know 'em so don't ask nothin' else about him," Trick snapped.

Mena thought about snapping back but when Trick pulled up in front of Dr. Denim and saw the sexy, confident looking dude standing out front, her entire attitude changed. She sat up in her seat as she watched the man wave Trick down as discreetly as possible. They were parked directly in the front of the store which caused everyone to gawk and comment on the Bentley.

As usual, Trick loved the attention and stepped out grinning, and pimping all at the same time toward his man. Trick's jewelry was always on point, but his diamond studded five karat pinky ring shone extra bright in the sunlight. His matching bracelet was always a showstopper with the ladies, and normally made the nigga's HATE, but next to Julius' jewels he had a touch of competition.

The two men embraced like long lost cousins then moved closer to the window on Mena's side. They chopped it up for a few moments before Trick tapped lightly on the glass motioning Mena to roll down the window.

With glee, Mena hit the button and gave Julius a hard stare.

"Yo, Julius, this my young jawn, Mena. Hand me that stack in the glove box," Trick said to Mena, handing her an Old

Navy bag to slip the money in.

Mena never said a word. She simply nodded, opened up the glove box and stuck the bundle labeled $10,000 inside the bag.

"That's ten, nigga. I need $2,500.00 back by Tuesday." For every hundred dollar bill, Trick's fee was twenty-five dollars.

"Bet," Julius responded.

Trick breathed heavily while resting on the car and tugging at his beard. "I see big things comin' outta this, so don't fuck up, yamean? This is the only time you gonna be able to owe me. The next time I need my money on the spot."

All of a sudden Mena chimed in, "And if you buy more than $50,000 at a time, the prices get better."

"Bitch, shut the fuck up!" Trick snapped. He approached Julius aggressively as if he dared him to respond to Mena. "Yo, get at me by Tuesday. Remember, this could turn out to be huge." He slapped Julius' hand, followed by a bump of the shoulder and a brotherly hug. "I'm out," he ended, rushing around to the driver's side.

As soon as Trick started the engine, he lashed out at Mena. "Mena, stay in your fuckin' place, yamean? That shit was foul. Don't do it again."

Mena ignored Trick and asked, "So, are we headed to King of Prussia Mall or what?"

"Yes, Mena, damn! This shit is crazy…keep pressurin' a nigga over a purse."

"Why not, I deserve it. I already called my girl, Kenya, at Neiman's and told her we were coming today. She knows which bag I want. I just need to let her know we're on our way."

Trick paused for a moment. "You sure you can trust her?"

"Why would you ask that? You been in the store and spent phony money with her before."

Trick shrugged his shoulders. "I'll just use real money today. I think I got enough on me."

"Naw, baby, just use the phony money. Why spend the real money if we don't have to?" She rubbed his back before making sure he understood that everything was okay. "I'm telling you it's cool."

Trick's instincts were telling him not to do it, but he trusted Mena's girl so he brushed his insecurities aside. Once they arrived, Trick pulled up right in front of the store with the intentions of running in and out. Mena didn't want to go into the store, because most of the employees knew her by name so she suggested Trick go alone while she watched the car. Finally, Trick agreed. He grabbed the last stack of money out of the glove compartment, stuck it deep into his jean pockets and got out of the car.

Before he even got to the door, he noticed that Mena had already positioned herself behind the wheel. She knew she was forbidden from driving the Bentley, but used the moment to fuck with Trick. She waved, gave him a fake smile, then blew a seductive kiss.

Not wanting to cause a scene, Trick just shook his head and walked inside. As soon as he walked into the Louis Vuitton section of the store, he spotted Kenya. After making eye contact, she walked over with a huge smile.

"Hello," she said in a professional tone.

"What's up," Trick replied with a head nod.

"Let me show you the bag. Follow me," Kenya suggested.

As Trick followed Mena's friend he couldn't help but notice her phat ass as she switched back and forth in a tight pencil skirt. Normally, when he was in the store Mena was with him, so it felt good to take a free look. When Kenya made her way behind the counter, she placed the embossed leather bag in Trick's hand.

"Mena has great taste. This new messenger bag is from our 2010 Fashion Show Collection."

Trick gave her a look like he could care less. "Yo' I'm in a hurry. How much?"

"It's $3,953.80, and that's with tax of course."

When he handed her the forty crisp hundred dollar bills, Kenya didn't follow the usual protocol of swiping the bills with the counterfeit indicator pen like she was supposed to, so this put Trick's mind at ease. However, that quickly changed when a tall and slim white guy with a cheesy grin quickly walked over.

"Hi, I'm Matt, the store manager. I just wanted to thank you for shopping with us today," he said showing all of his teeth. Trick immediately assumed the guy was gay from all the extra hand gestures.

Trick gave him a head nod. "Yeah, dawg. No problem." *Bitch, take your ass in the back and wrap that shit up*, he thought to himself as Matt stared at the both of them.

"Oh my…you must have one special lady at home if you're buying her that gorgeous bag. Kenya, show this handsome gentleman the new monogrammed Neo bag while I wrap this up."

"Oh no, Matt. I can take care of everything for him," Kenya replied with a nervous tone.

"No, don't worry about it. I'll handle it. Show him some other stuff," Matt said, after taking the money out of Kenya's hand. "Sir, I'll be right back with your receipt."

When Kenya shot Trick a fearful look, he responded with a smile. "Yo, like don't even sweat it. My shit is straight."

He began to walk around to see if any new Gucci sneakers had come in. In his mind, he knew his money had no signs of being fake and would pass any test with flying colors. Several minutes passed before Trick realized that Matt still hadn't come back. When he looked back toward the register, even Kenya had disappeared. Finally getting an uneasy feeling, Trick was about to leave when he felt a sudden tap on his shoulder.

"Sir, we need you to come with us, please," one of the three uniformed police officers said. Trick was used to the police brutality in Pennsylvania so he watched how he interacted with the three of them. He especially kept his eye of the heavy-set officer who was just as large as he was.

"For what?" Trick asked in a hostile tone. He instantly

became nervous, but didn't want the officers to see him sweat.

"We need to ask you a few questions," the heavy-set officer replied. He grabbed Trick by his arm and escorted him to the back of the store.

When they entered the store's security room, another officer immediately took Trick's wallet and other items out of his pockets and handcuffed Trick to the chair.

Pissed, Trick started cussing the officers out and reminding them that he had rights. They all laughed. "We know…we know," one officer said mockingly. "You all always have a story to tell like it wasn't you or this is a big misunderstanding."

Even though Trick was upset, he tried to keep his composure just in case he was able to talk his way out of the situation. Instead of replying, he just looked around the room observing all the cameras and other security equipment. Then his mind wondered to what Mena was probably doing. He wondered if they had her too, until one of the cameras showed his car parked outside. The camera clearly showed Mena sitting in the driver's side applying lip gloss.

I'm about to go to jail and this bitch is putting on makeup, he thought.

"Trent Fowler," the officer said, looking at Trick's driver's license. "Can you tell me where you got this money from?" He held up several bills with black lines going across.

What the fuck? Mena was supposed to spray the money so the pen couldn't pick it up. Did she forget? Trick wondered. *I'ma kill that bitch.*

The officer interrupted his thoughts. "Sir, did you hear the question?"

"I won it in a card game," Trick replied with an attitude.

"Are you aware that it's counterfeit?"

"It is?" Trick said, pretending to be shocked.

The officers all looked at one another. They didn't believe for a minute that Trick had no knowledge of the money being fake.

"Well, whether you knew or not it will be up to a judge

or jury. We're gonna have to take you to the station."

At that moment, his patience had completely run out. It was no more Mr. Nice Guy as Trick stomped his foot and started going off, but the officers just ignored his tirade. As Trick continued to yell, the shortest officer uncuffed him from the chair, placed his hands behind his back, handcuffed him again, and led him out of the store. When Trick passed Kenya she was smiling, which confused him. It wasn't clear until he was outside and saw Mena standing by his car with a big grin on her face waving good-bye to him. It was at that point that he knew he'd been set up. Mena watched proudly as the cops led Trick off in the squad car.

"That's for killing my brother," she said spitefully. "I told you payback was a bitch." She rubbed the hood of her new whip and hopped inside.

$Five$

When Ronni jetted up to the block on Bouvier Street, the harsh look in her eyes told bystanders some shit was about to go down. Her mere presence had always sent chills through every living body in the north Philly neighborhood, but the screw face she wore today told them an ass kicking was near. The weather was unseasonably warm for a mid May afternoon, so Ronni's windows were down on both sides allowing Biggie and Jay-Z's old song, *I Love The Dough* to blast loudly near the garden-style apartment complex.

The wheels screeched and Ronni jumped out of her silver, 3 series BMW strutting like she was gonna murder one of the three girls near the fire hydrant. The veins in her forehead seemed to explode beneath the fitted baseball cap as she flexed in an oversized white t-shirt, long knee-length khaki shorts and Nike boots. Her walk was hard, and her appearance was far from girlie. With long corn rows that touched her shoulders, and a mole on her right cheek, most said she resembled Snoop from the "The Wire," while others simply labeled her a small dyke looking chick.

Without hesitation, Ronni locked eyes with her young worker they called Shiesty and pimped her way looking like a short, angry dude. Shiesty moved with speed, attempting to get loss between the thinning crowd, but Ronni was quick and too witty to get ganked by some hood chick. Before long, she'd made her move, pushed a few people aside, and cornered

Sheisty into a brick wall near the front apartment building.

"Where the fuck is my money, Shiesty?"

"What you talking 'bout, Ronni?" she asked, glaring at Ronni's new tattoo; a sexy silhouette of a woman plastered on the side of her neck. "I'm for real, Ronni," the girl pleaded.

Within seconds, Ronni had reared her hand back and pimped slapped the fearful girl, then followed up with a hard punch to the jaw.

The crowd roared, "Ahhhh, shit!" Then another young voice could be heard saying, "Somebody call Sheisty's brother. You need a nigga for this lil hard bitch!"

Ronni turned slightly trying to catch the culprit who'd called her a bitch, but her real focus was on whipping Shiesty's ass. Before anyone else could say a word, Ronni had already two-pieced the wild-haired girl down to the ground and had commenced to stomping her in the face with her boot. Blood flowed from her face as she tried to shield the blows with her bloodied hands. Shiesty cried out for help but no one would assist.

Suddenly Ronni stopped, looked around, and shouted to the crackheads, "What the fuck ya'll lookin' at? Who got next?"

Ronni then bent down and snatched Shiesty up by her hair and punched her in her face again. All you could hear was Ronni saying, "You betta have all my fuckin' paper by Friday, or you already know what it is."

The moment Shiesty was released she just dropped to her knees crying and screaming, "It wasn't me Ronni, I swear."

Ronni looked down toward the ground where the girl was laying and just stood over her, hawked up some spit from the back of her throat, and spat right in Shiesty's face. Ronni then began to laugh hysterically as she pulled her saggy shorts back up and rubbed her hand over her braids.

It amazed everyone how a five foot three female could intimidate so many people so well. All you could see as Ronni left the spot was the big ass tattoo on the side of her neck and the back of her bloody white t-shirt. Within seconds, Ronni had jumped back in her car and made a quick U-turn in the middle of the street, honked her horn, and sped off like a militant dictator.

As she bobbed in and out of traffic, Ronni's cell phone began to ring. She took her time answering the call especially when she saw Mena's name pop up on the screen.

She finally answered, "What it do, baby girl? You keep callin', everything good wit...?"

Ronni couldn't even get her words out before Mena jumped in and said, "You not gonna believe this shit, Ron. You by yourself right now?"

Ronni took the phone from her ear for a second. She knew something was up by the way Mena seemed breathless. She put the phone back up to her ear and said hesitantly, "Yeah… what's up? You actin' all crazy and shit."

"I got that nigga Trick today. The police just took him into custody."

She waited on Ronni to say something but when she didn't, Mena continued on with how Trick got locked up while buying her a purse at Neiman's. "Girl, you shoulda seen that nigga's face…"

"I don't understand. How did you get the nigga and why would they lock him up?"

"It's more to the story, but I can't talk about it over the phone. Can…" Mena was interrupted when her cell beeped with another call. "Hey Ronni, I gotta get this. Can you come by my crib in the next thirty minutes? I really gotta holla at you about something serious."

"Bet. Gimme twenty."

Ronni agreed like she always did when it came to Mena. Most thought she didn't have a thoughtful bone in her body, but she did value friendship. Ronni had plenty of women that she fucked on a regular, but Mena was the only female who she truly considered family. They were tight…inseparable. So, as Ronni sat back on her headrest and made another U-turn, headed to Mena's she could only imagine what her girl was up to now.

Meanwhile, Mena's head seemed to explode inside with worry. As she waited on Ronni to arrive, she rushed to make herself a strong drink, then headed upstairs where she thought she'd feel safer. As she sipped on a Hennessy on the rocks, the house phone kept ringing sending her into a frenzy. Although the words on the phone said, unknown, she knew who it was. Trick.

A lump of fear formed in her throat as she contemplated her options. It was then that she decided being closer to exit doors was a smarter move. With her drink in one hand, and the other on her hip, Mena swiftly made her way back downstairs when her cell started to play the song, *Div*a by Beyonce.

Mena looked at the phone and noticed it was one of the girls from around by the block that she hung out with sometimes, so she answered the call.

"That fuckin' RONNI!"

"Damn, Tameka! You didn't even give me time to say shit before you started yelling. What did Ronni do now?"

Mena just held the phone while Tameka told her everything that went on at the block.

"You sure?" Mena asked in disbelief. "Cause Ronni been chilling lately."

"Wake up, Mena. With all your street smarts you can be so naïve sometimes."

Mena continued to listen as Tameka told her the entire story about how Ronni beat Sheisty down on the block. She even told her how she thought Ronni was unstable.

Mena listened half-heartedly as she began to pace the floor. "Okay Tameka, I'll talk to Ronni about that shit cause she know how the game is when it come to getting money."

Mena thought to herself, *we don't need no extra shit to jump off with the plan that I got for us.* "Alright girl, I gotta go," Mena said, ending the call abruptly.

As soon as she hung up, the house phone started to ring again. Without thinking twice, Mena just picked up the phone because she already knew it was Trick and that he wouldn't stop calling until she answered.

"Yeah," she answered in a fucked up kind of way as if Trick had done her wrong.

"This is A.C. Communication from Montgomery County jail with a collect call from…."

There was a long pause on the phone before Trick finally spoke, "BITCH! It's me."

The operator went on with directions; press 9 to accept and 5 to disconnect. Mena slowly took her sweet ass time once she heard Trick say, "Bitch," but she knew she had to answer before he sent Polo and Felony over to the house. And she knew the whole Felony situation was about to get complicated. She finally pressed 9 and said hello in a dry tone. She already knew Trick was truly onto her bullshit.

"So Mena, like tell me what the fuck happened today? And like you better have a good fuckin' answer."

Silence filled the air.

"Do you hear me talkin' to yo ass?"

Mena remained quiet.

"You know I'll kill you, yamean?"

At that moment Mena downed the rest of her Hennessey, then began pacing the floor as Trick shot out one threat after another. She was scared shitless wondering if Trick was positive she'd set him up.

When the mental abuse finally stopped, Mena asked, "What are you talking about, Trick? What did the police say, and when are you getting' out?"

Trick never said a word back to Mena because he realized she was the mastermind of the shit from the beginning, something he just didn't want to believe. He played it cool and told her, "When I get out, I'ma find your ass, BITCH. And I'ma gut you like a fuckin' pig! I saw that fuckin' look on your face!"

"Trick, don't say that honey," she pleaded. "I was just mad at you. I waved because I wanted you to think I would be driving your baby. You got this shit all wrong."

"Oh, do I," he countered unconvinced.

Mena knew from the tone of her ex-boyfriend's voice that she had to act quickly. "Look, I'ma work on getting' you out."

Trick continued on with question after question. Before long, their ten minute call was almost up. Right before Trick hung up he added, "Mena, you got some serious explainin' to do. I'ma send Felony ova to pick you up."

Shit! I got to get the fuck outta here before this nigga has me killed, she thought.

Once the call ended, Mena still held the receiver in her shaking hand. Her daze continued for several minutes as her heart raced. She knew what Trick was capable of and she knew she had to go. Finally, she dropped the phone and fell back onto the couch. She knew these were truly her last days in Philadelphia, the land of what was supposed to be brotherly love; a place she had called home since she'd left South Carolina fifteen years ago. Thoughts of South Carolina instantly got Mena slightly choked up. Sadly, she thought about how her mother just one day up and rolled out on both her and her younger brother, Donte. With Mena being nine at the time, and Donte only six, she couldn't even fight the decision of the state to send them both to foster care. It hurt her deeply that her mother never came back to look for them, or even cared about her whereabouts. If it hadn't been for an aunt in Philadelphia who decided to take them both in when she was sixteen, Mena wasn't sure where she'd be at the moment.

Over the years, family members who still lived in Charleston told Mena that her mother was alive. Mena tried to make contact on several occasions, but after never getting a response she fell back. She hurt many nights trying to figure out why her own mother never tried to reach her. It was hard. And the empty spot in her heart was deep.

Quickly, Mena snapped out of it. She knew she needed to focus on business. Her thoughts then switched to each machine in the basement. She thought about how she would build clientele in the south; then it hit her. At some point she'd have to call the Columbians. After laying there for a while, and thinking things through meticulously, Mena's plan was finally all put together.

She knew deep down that Trick really wasn't the one to deceive. It was clear that once he got out, he would want revenge, and would get it if he ever found her. Before another thought could infiltrate her mind, the doorbell rang sending Mena into cardiac arrest. She jumped up and rolled along the carpet like she was a part of Philly P.D.'s SWAT Team. Her heart beat rapidly while she squinted to see from the floor. She gawked toward the door hoping to get a glimpse of the culprit but couldn't. Instantly, Mena hopped up, stooped as low as she could and made her way up the steps taking two at a time. Once in the bedroom, she ransacked the room searching for Trick's gun.

Nothing.

Then the doorbell rang, again.

And again.

All sorts of thoughts flooded her mind. Mena inhaled, then exhaled praying for her life. She knew if she didn't answer, Felony or Polo would soon kick the door in.

Then the ringing became more consistent. Back to back it rang like an antsy child on Halloween. Quickly, Mena darted over to the bedroom window suspiciously, then slowly pulled the curtain back. She sighed at the sight of the BMW. Indeed it was Ronni.

With sweat covering her body, Mena stomped back downstairs and snatched the door open. "Bitch, you scared the fuck outta me! Bring your ass in here. We got shit to talk about."

Ronni looked at Mena as she entered the house and noticed her good friend's worried facial expression. She turned to give her girl a cold stare, then pulled her in for a quick embrace. "You did something. I can tell. It's that shifty look you get in your eyes when you fucked up. What is it?"

"Shut the hell up, Ronni!" Mena shouted. "My nerves are bad. Look, I'ma tell you all this crazy shit one time, so listen good."

Ronni looked at Mena as if she had lost her mind.

Mena breathed heavily and looked at her friend as if she was about to confess to murder, "I got Trick fucked up today with his counterfeit money," she admitted.

Ronni had a stunned look on her face. "What? Counterfeit money. What the fuck are you talkin' about?"

"That's how Trick got locked up today. He got caught with some fake money."

Ronni covered her mouth with her hand. "Get the fuck outta here. You lyin' bitch. Where he get that shit from?"

"Downstairs," Mena said, pointing her index finger toward the floor. "He's been making it for a while now. And I been helping him make it."

"Oh, shit. So, this nigga slingin' and makin' fake dough. Why the fuck didn't you tell me!" Ronni shouted.

"Because, I didn't want you involved until everything was straight." Mena went on to tell Ronni her role in Trick's operation and how she'd switched the stack of money that he took into Neiman's.

"I can't believe you set that fat nigga up," Ronni replied.

"Hell yeah, I set him up, so stop staring at me like I did you wrong or something." Mena was beyond frustrated but she kept focusing on Ronni's outfit. "It's spring, almost summer, Ronni, and you got on Nike boots. And please stop wearing all them hard looking boy clothes all the time. Remember, you are still a girl, Veronica."

"Bitch, tell me what happened, this shit is not about me," Ronni said, taking a seat on the couch near the window. Ronni wasn't afraid of Trick, but she wasn't stupid either. She wanted a clear visual on anything or anyone coming to the house.

Mena began giving every detail of what happened at the mall and every threat Trick made on the phone before she got there. It took nearly five minutes to lay it all out. Mena seemed to perspire more as she told Ronni that she'd been planning something like that for a while.

"Damn, Mena," Ronni chuckled, "you got balls, and you slick, too."

She liked that about Mena, though. All of a sudden Ronni stood up as if she was about to leave. "Trick locked up so you good." She kissed at Mena. "Look, I gotta date, so I'll holla later tonight."

"Wait a minute! I'm not finished with you yet. Why did your ass go by the fucking block and beat the shit outta' Sheisty today?" Mena stood with her hands on her hips. "Damn Ronni, she can't owe you but so much money. You collect almost everyday from the girl anyway."

Ronni looked at Mena as if she had nerve to be talking, after all she just told her about how she betrayed Trick.

"Fuck that! I beat the shit out her ugly ass, so next time she get a package from me she'll know how to act wit' my shit." Ronni laughed. "You feel me on that?"

"Yeah, yeah," she said, trying to appease her hyper friend. "We got some real shit to talk about. Sit down," she ordered after checking the surrounding area again from her front windows.

"You got ten minutes. So let's hear it," Ronni said, taking a seat again.

"Okay, when Trick called I could tell from the sound of his voice that me and him are over. So, I wanted to run this by you to see what you thought about this plan. Trick is onto me so you know I can't be around when his crazy-ass touch down, so I called my favorite cousin DJ in Charleston, S.C. about coming through to see him."

"Anddddd," Ronni asked, checking her watch. Her expression showed her disinterest.

"Well, you remember him, don't you? The one who owns the barbershop, Blazin' Kuts."

Ronni shook her head. "Get to the damn point, Mena."

"A smile appeared on Mena's face for the first time. So, what better time to go than now?" she told Ronni with confidence. “I don’t want you to rush into anything, but I know how you like making that paper. This counterfeit thing was getting big for Trick. So, I was thinking, let’s go down to the country and make some real paper. Run this counterfeit shit down there.”

“Ronni hit Mena with her trademark gesture; she banged one fist into the other as she thought deeply. Then a grin appeared on her face. “How much we gon’ be makin’?”

“A shit load of money.” Mena smiled, showing her perfect set of teeth.

“You think we can pull that shit off?”

“Hell yeah.” Mena got excited. She hopped up from the couch, rushed around the room, talking one hundred miles a minute. “You know I already know how to make the money so it won’t be shit for us to set up shop in South Carolina. We can do this, Ronni!”

“They got any country biscuit eatin’ bitches wit’ good pussy down there?”

“Stop playing Ronni, this is serious.”

Ronni looked into Mena’s stern eyes and knew she was ready, so she had to say yes to getting that paper and getting the fuck out of town before Trick really got out. They both knew they couldn’t afford to be around once he got released. As Mena poured Ronni a drink, ready to go over the details, her cell started ringing again, but it wasn’t her normal ring tone. Mena glanced down at the phone a little harder this time wondering why a name didn’t pop up.

She didn’t sweat it. She flipped open her cell phone like nothing was really wrong. The deep baritone voice of a black man said, “Hello, Mena, my name is Grover James. I’m handling Trent’s case for you.”

Mena looked so confused, wanting to say, *you can’t be handling shit for me*. But decided to say nothing at all.

“He called me as soon as he was booked. I’ve been calling, but couldn’t get a hold of you.”

Mena remained silent.

"Are you there, Ms. Austin?"

"Uh huh."

"Trent has his first court appearance in the morning and I will make certain he gets a bond. But I would prefer Trent stay in custody at least two days until I see the judge I need. Trent says you can handle getting the money so, we'll need to post bail."

"Uh huh," was all Mena could say.

She stood in the middle of the floor looking dumb-founded and thinking, *I loved Trick but shit happens, and I'm getting the fuck out of town, cause I know he put this lawyer up to placing this call to me.*

"Thanks, Mr. James, for the call. Keep me informed please."

As Mena slammed the phone down, all she could do was look at Ronni with glassy eyes and say, "Fix me another drink along with yours, cause that was Trick's attorney telling me all the bullshit that's about to happen with him over the next two days." She stopped talking and cupped her face with both hands as if a breakdown was near. Her voice trembled as she spoke, "Ronni, we need to be out of this fucking place in the next hour or so."

"Word. It's that serious?"

"Look, I know you a bad bitch, but we're no match for Trick's boys. If you down with this South Carolina thing just say so." Mena's eyes begged Ronni to say yes. "Trust me…we're gonna be the shit, Ronni. We're gonna take over South Carolina with this counterfeit shit. Just say yes."

Without hesitation, Ronni said, "Hell yeah. I'm already the shit…just need a lil' more paper behind my name, so fuck it, I'm in. Like my man Jigga said, "Fuck rich, let's get wealthy!"

Mena's wild movements with her hands showed her excitement. "Okay, so here's the deal. I'ma call and rent us a small hitch, cause we gotta take all the equipment with us. You go home, pack your shit, then pick up the hitch on your way back over. And Ronni, we don't know what Trick got up his sleeve so be back within an hour and we'll go stay in a hotel for the night. I'll have all the equipment in the living room by time you get back, and we'll be ready to jet from P.A."

"Sounds like a plan. But hurry the fuck up, Mena. Don't be packin' all that make-up, booty shorts, and weave supplies." Ronni had to laugh at herself.

"If I wasn't nervous as hell, I'd curse your boy-looking ass out. But I'm already stressed. I'm just running upstairs and throwing some shit in the bag and I'll be back down stairs waiting on you."

"Remember, the equipment is the most important shit," Ronni instructed putting more bass into her raspy voice."

"I got this, Ronni. I'm the brains of this operation, *remember that*," Mena snapped, ushering her new partner to the door.

Ronni calmly opened the front door, and looked both ways before stepping onto the walkway. She stopped and turned to Mena who was nervously peeping from the door, checking both ends of the street for any unusual signs.

"Hey, Mena." She paused to look back over her shoulder and shot her girl a devious smile. "We takin' the Bentley, right?" Ronni slid her hand across the roof as she passed.

Mena froze as her eyes ballooned. "What? Bitch, are you crazy?"

"Hell yeah, we gon' ride in style, baby. Fuck that sloppy nigga, Trick," she said, hurrying to her car. "Let it do, what it do, baby girl. See you in an hour."

Six

Exactly one hour and thirty minutes later, riding along the overpass headed south, Ronni and Mena gasped when they saw Felony in his black Charger pass beneath them. As they drove equally fast and in silence, they each thought about their demise. Although the darkness had set in, Felony drove wild and speedily as if he had a perfect view combined with the perfect scowl, destined for revenge.

Luckily, he didn't see them or the fact that Mena had her feet kicked up on Trick's dash. Mena thought about calling Felony's phone. But the conversation would get too deep and Mena hadn't come clean with Ronni yet about *everything*.

Suddenly, Ronni picked up speed as she laughed loudly knowing they'd gotten away. There was more traffic than anticipated on the bridge for nine o'clock at night which pissed Ronni off. She drove like a mad-woman, dodging in and out of traffic as she cursed like a penitentiary hoe. She also didn't seem to care that they were pulling a small U-Haul hitch behind them.

"These fuckin' tolls!" she shouted, while making a b-line toward the E-Z pass lane.

"Ronni, what the hell are you doing!" Mena yelled while lifting her body toward the dash. "We don't have an E-Z pass!"

"And…" Ronni said, still driving through the lane without traffic. "I don't sit in traffic!" she yelled out the window crazily to a male toll booth worker holding his arm out. "Bill us!" she screamed as the chrome rims on the Bentley sparkled under the toll booth lights.

As soon as the Bentley rolled through the unoccupied lane a flashing red sign read, *not paid*.

"Are you crazy? Stop driving like that before we flip over. Did you forget that the equipment is in the damn hitch!"

Ronni smiled. "I got this, bitch! Stop whinin'. I been drivin' since I was fourteen."

"Look Ronni," Mena fussed as she looked behind them for any sign of the cops. "Don't start this stupid shit. We got money in the car, crazy. Plus, what if Felony got to the house and called the car in stolen?"

Ronni hunched her shoulders and turned up the music. She danced as if she didn't have a care in the world. "We'll be in D.C in two hours and in South Carolina in eleven if we don't stay in D.C. Just sit back and chill. Well, first count that money," she instructed.

Mena saw the look in Ronni's eyes so she wanted to get things straight....and fast. "Look Ronni, I'm going to go ahead and call the Columbians to see if they wanna meet first thing in the morning to take this loot off my hands. So, get all your crazy thoughts out of your mind," she added, while glancing at the duffel bag full of the money that Trick had printed for the Columbians.

"What?" Ronni questioned with a devious grin. "I'm just sayin' count it, so we'll know what we workin' wit'."

"Oh, I know you well Veronica Grimes. You thinking about ballin' with this money. But fuck that," Mena said, whipping out her cell.

Mena yawned, then slipped the folded up piece of paper from the side pocket in her purse and commenced to dialing the Columbians 202 number that she'd taken from Trick's phone. She knew that Trick was working on printing up enough money to fill their large order, she just had no idea exactly how much he'd made. Before she left home, she didn't count it. She'd decided to just stuff it all into the black duffel and jet before getting caught by Felony.

The phone rang as Mena attempted to think. Suddenly, her jaw dropped. Mena was shocked that the voice on the other end had answered on the first ring. "Hello…hello," she repeated. She was unsure about how to begin the conversation since she didn't even know of a legitimate name she could ask to speak to.

"Yes. How can I help you?" the voice sounded in a deep Brazilian accent.

"Yes, I'm calling on behalf of Trick. This is his girlfriend, Mena."

Silence filled what were supposed to be words on both ends of the receiver.

She hesitated. "Hello, are you there?" Mena asked.

"Tell him we gon be at the Ritz Carlton at Pentagon City right outside of D.C.," Ronni interjected with base in her voice.

Mena flashed Ronni off with her hands hoping she would shut the hell up. "This is Mena," she repeated, "Trick's lady."

"Ah yes, we've heard the name, but what can I do for you, Miss Mena?" The voice sounded a bit warmer which put a slight smile on Mena's face.

"Trick told me to call. He's gotten into a little bit of trouble, and doesn't really wanna use the phone, so I'm helping him out."

"Oh, yeah."

"Yeah. So I just want to let you know that I'll be in D.C. until tomorrow. I'm about an hour away now. I've got some of the money you ordered. You wanna meet me to collect?" Mena asked, getting excited.

"Ahhhhh," he hesitated. "I'd bettah not. I should wait for Trick to call."

"What he say? Tell me, Mena?" Ronni yelled out as she swerved across the road.

Mena gave Ronni a look that said *shut up* before she continued.

"No need to wait for Trick. You can trust me," Mena told the man with confidence.

"Trust?" He laughed. "No dear. I'll need to talk with Trick."

Mena couldn't believe what she was hearing. "Trick?" she questioned slowly. "Well, he told me to make the call. So, it's either deal with me or nothing," she said sweetly.

"Fuck that shit!" Ronni shouted. "Give me that damn phone. Tell his ass the truth. We the only ones wit' this green shit so he gon be ass out if he don't link up wit' us."

"I'm sorry about that," Mena said into the phone while giving Ronni the evil eye. "My sister is drunk," she said calmly, trying to move closer to the door where she could cover the phone. "I think we should at least meet. Tell me your name, and the best way to reach you, and I'll call you when I'm close to the hotel."

"My name? I don't think so my dear. Just have Trick call me when he can talk. Then we can meet and I'll take the baby."

The baby. Yeah, I understand, Mena thought to herself. Mena kept thinking *oh shit; I'm missing out on my first sale.*

"Well, what about…" she finally said.

CLICK.

The phone line fell dead and so did Mena's spirit. "Fuck fuck, fuck!" she shouted out in frustration. She leaned back into the soft leather seats with a salty attitude as Ronni talked shit about how the Columbians would be calling them soon.

"They're gonna wanna be our fuckin' best friends," Ronni joked, doing her best impersonation of Al Pacino in Scarface.

Mena knew none of it was true so she grabbed the bag full of money and commenced to counting. "Just drive, we got a long ride," Mena commented. The more and more she allowed the fake money to rub the insides of her fingers the more irritated she became.

"I just need for us to hurry up and get down south with DJ and make us some real money. We don't have to worry about anything down there cause I'm gonna find us our own customers, and you know it won't take too long to get on the grind," Mena said.

"Did you tell DJ what was up?"

"Nope. Not yet. Just told him I got something good that will get us all paid. He know everybody," Mena boasted, as she counted with one hand, and dialed digits on her cell with the other.

Ronni looked at Mena like she didn't believe how connected DJ was in the south. She'd bragged on several occasions about how DJ's barbershop was the talk of the town, but Ronni still considered it to be all talk. Ronni thought about how Mena always put her few family members on a pedestal, but in her eyes none of them were worth shit. She thought about saying some out of pocket comments about DJ and her unknown siblings until she turned to see Mena leaving him a message on her cell.

"DJ, it's your cuz. I'm on my way, baby!" she exclaimed. "Just like I told you, we gonna get shit popping. Call me when you get this."

Mena hung up and finished counting. "Fifty grand," she reported with half a smile. "Trick normally gets one-fourth in real funds, so this fifty won't get us much if we selling it off for real loot."

"Yeah, but we can spend that shit, too," Ronni announced, putting more pressure on the gas.

"Fuck no, Ronni! I got plans. My whole life is going to change soon, so don't think about fucking things up for me."

In less than two seconds Mena's demeanor had changed. The jolly person she pretended to be on the phone was now a woman with a worried expression.

"Hey Ronni, can I ask you something?"

"Shoot."

"You think if I went looking for my mother when I get to South Carolina, I can find out why all this happened to me?"

"Mena," Ronni gave her friend a hard stare. "Do yourself a favor and go to sleep. "I'll wake you up later when we stop for gas."

"Fuck you then, Ronni," Mena said as she turned over to rest her head against the window. "I *will* find her. And I *will* get answers as to why she left me and my brother," she said softly.

Ronni's curiosity got the best of her. It was a good time to ask what everyone wanted to know. "So, have the police come up with any new leads on who killed your brother?"

"Nah," Mena answered dryly, with closed eyes.

"So what do you think really happened?"

"I don't know, Ronni. I told you I was asleep," she lied. "Plus I don't want to talk about that right now. I think I'll take your advice. I'm taking a nap," she ended, pressing her face against the glass.

$Seven$

The next morning Mena jumped up in fear at the sounding of her cell. She looked to her right only to see woods and no sign of Ronni in the driver's seat. Her heart raced and her veins seemed to pop from her head, as her feet wrestled below to locate her flip flops. Suddenly, her neck twisted to the far left as if she were the exorcist. At that moment, Mena realized that she was at a rest area off the highway. Without looking at the clock, she figured it was somewhere in the neighborhood of 7 a.m. The air smelled of morning dew and the sun had not yet shown it's face. With no one in sight Mena opened the door slowly and hopped out, hoping to find some answers.

Each frightful thought flooded her mind as she thought about the possibilities of Ronni's whereabouts. Had Felony found them and had taken Ronni off somewhere to kill her? Had Ronni double crossed her and taken off with the fifty grand? At that moment, Mena plastered her face against the car window to see if the duffle bag of money was still in the back. Then the ringing of the phone startled her. Mena rushed back inside, flipped open her phone and realized it was a call she needed to get.

"Yo, what kinda games you playing?" she shouted into the phone.

"I was just about to ask you the same thing. So tell me, Mena, what's this all about? Trick callin' me from jail. He says you put him there. Then I go to the house and it looked like somebody robbed the place. You puttin' a nigga in a bad situation."

Mena's heavy breathing slowed. "Listen, we just gotta talk. I shoulda told you everything the other night at the hotel. I knew at some point I was leaving him. I told you that, you just didn't believe me," she explained. "But it's just so much more to tell you. And me and you…this complicates things more."

Just as her nerves were about to explode, Ronni came rushing across the grass with three bags of chips in her hands.

"Why in the hell are you lookin' at me like that?" Ronni asked.

"Look, give me a couple of hours and I'll call you back."

"You betta. Cause Trick gettin' out tomorrow and you know he gone come after you. That's my boss, so what am I supposed to do?"

"Okay," Mena ended.

As soon as the line went dead, Mena started in on Ronni, "Why would you leave me in the car sleeping?"

"Bitch, I didn't know I was a babysitter. I been drivin' all night while yo' ass been sleepin'." Ronni threw the keys into Mena's chest. "You drivin' now, since you talkin' shit. We only got two more hours to go."

Mena played in her hair, twirling it around her fingers like a small child would do. "I'm sorry Ronni." Her eyes pleaded for forgiveness. "I just woke up in a panic and felt like we shouldn't have been parked way over here… away from everything."

"Well, I got sleepy…needed an hour nap, so this was the best spot. Besides, we almost died twice last night when I was up alone," she smirked. "So, a nap saved both of our lives. Just be glad we already crossed the South Carolina line."

Mena smiled. "That's cool. But you drive," she said tossing the keys back to Ronni, and hopping into the passenger side.

"Damn bitch, you gonna at least go pee?"

"I guess you're right," Mena said, noticing that her phone was ringing again. She grabbed her phone and rushed off toward the bathrooms, wondering what was so important with DJ.

"What's up, cuz?" she answered with a wide grin.

"Where you at?" he chimed.

"In hot ass Carolina," she joked. "It's not even ten o'clock and already hot as hell. We should be there in a couple of hours though. Ronni is a road dog, she's been driving all night," Mena bragged.

"Bet. Come straight to the shop. I'll be here waiting on you."

"Damn, you start early don't you?" Mena asked, entering the bathroom.

"Damn right. I open up at seven o'clock. I can't stand to let even twenty dollars get away from me. Besides, it's Friday. Everybody gonna be out early today." He paused. "You remember where it is, right?"

Mena laughed. "Yeah, I remember. You still the same DJ." She shook her head at the thought of her crazy cousin. "Alright, so let me use the bathroom, and I'll see you in a bit. Oh... wait until you see what we driving. You're gonna trip out."

Mena hung up, used the restroom and stopped off at the vending machine for two bags of Cool Ranch Doritos. As soon as she got back in the car, Ronni sped off like she had a mission to accomplish. Instantly, the sounds of Lil' Wayne filled the car as the ladies made their way down the highway. Mena sat up tall, feeling refreshed as she munched on her chips and played with her hair.

"Ronni, I got a good feeling," Mena exclaimed.

"What? About your weave, or this counterfeit shit?"

"I really do hate you sometimes, Ronni."

"You and every other jawn," Ronni commented as she displayed a wide grin.

That one comment led Ronni into one of her long confession sessions with Mena where she bragged about how many women she'd turned out for the month. Most times Mena didn't want to listen, but on a long journey, Mena felt it was a comical way to pass the time.

Soon the sun rays had gotten stronger, hours had passed and the Bentley had finally pulled up to the El Cheapo Mini Mart on Dorchester Road in Charleston. Mena looked around at the mini-mart and realized hadn't much changed since she was there a few years ago. She pulled out her cell to call DJ to let him know she would be out front in less than two minutes. She had a smile on her face as she thought about DJ cutting hair by day then leaving his shop quickly to go sell his weed after they closed. Mena liked the fact that she would be spending time with him and his girl, Camie. He and Camie had been together for years. Mena really liked Camie. She came from a good stock, was family oriented and would make a good mother to DJ's kids someday. She hoped they would marry soon; the same dream she had for herself.

When DJ answered Mena screamed into the phone, "I'm hereeeeeeee!"

Mena got excited and began fixing her booty shorts and fastening her bra back up while Ronni pulled out the parking lot of the store, headed to the other end of the street to see DJ. However, just as she pulled out, she nearly crashed into three dudes driving a S550 Benz that caught her eye. As they both looked up, the guys stared at Ronni like she was crazy. That's all it took for her ADHD to kick in. Out of the blue, Ronni sped up and cut them off as if she were the police.

Quickly, she pushed the button for the window to roll down and shouted in rage, "You should'a got the fuck out the way!"

As Mena looked on, she shook her head because she knew it was about to be on from there from the gangsta-looking faces that stared back at her.

Mena screamed at Ronni, "Please don't do that shit. Damn, we just got here."

"Fuck that! You see how them niggas looked at us." Ronni looked in the rearview mirror as the Benz sped up and inched toward the U-Haul hitch. "I wish y'all would hit my shit!" she screamed. "Do you see these niggas?"

Mena nodded. "Yeah, but what the fuck do you expect? You just cut them off, fool."

"I see these country mufuckas wanna play games," Ronni said before applying more pressure to the pedal.

No one even noticed that the closer they got to the barbershop the Bentley was riding up on the curb with the Benz right behind them. When the car suddenly screeched then stopped, Mena jumped out and started going off on the guys while trying to keep Ronni from acting out at the same time.

"Are y'all crazy? You almost made us run off the road!" Mena yelled.

Before she could say another word, Ronni pulled out her 9mm and aimed it toward the guy's car. Nobody moved. Seconds later, DJ rushed out the shop begging Ronni to put the gun back in her pants. By now it was all out war. Several guys jumped out with their own guns in the air, scaring everyone in sight, except Ronni. With the help of DJ, she lowered her gun, but kept her grip tight as she stuffed it into her pants.

She stared intensely until one guy screamed, "Ya bloodclot bitch."

Another guy looked directly into Ronni's eyes and said, "Me not fear of you pussy clot."

By this time all the barbers started pouring out. All they could do to help DJ was rush in front of Mena.

DJ shouted to one the Jamaicans, "Yo Skully, be easy man. These my peoples. They from Philly. Just chill. It's all a misunderstanding."

DJ walked his tall, linky frame toward the guys and talked for minutes in a low-key tone while Mena and Ronni looked on without saying a word. Mena looked up and couldn't believe DJ actually knew them well enough to calm the situation.

It took him a minute or so to get shit under control, but it was much harder to control the rasta they called Skully. You could tell he was the craziest of the crew. It was obvious he'd been in a lot of shit because he had several battle scars to prove it, especially the long gash that ran across his nose and ended up on his cheek. If it wasn't for DJ, Mena and Ronni would've been six feet under. I guess that was their welcome to the Carolinas.

Mena had a funny feeling that she'd see the Jamaicans again. She tried to smile hoping to end the beef, but the Skully guy was still pissed when they made eye contact.

"Tis won't end up like this the next time," he warned.

Ronni eyed him back like she wanted to say, "Fuck you rasta, but Mena pushed her toward the shop. After the Jamaicans finally got back in their car and sped off, Mena looked at DJ with relief in her eyes as Ronni hopped back in the driver's seat to pull the car off the curb. After she parked, the three of them walked back into the barbershop like nothing had ever happened. Mena spoke to the all barbers while Ronni looked around the shop like she had a gripe.

"Can I get a hair line shape up?" she asked one of the barbers.

"You got braids," the barber replied.

"Nigga, I know. Just line me up," she shot back. "I should'a shot one of them muthafuckas," Ronni finally blurted out to Mena as she hopped in the chair.

"No, you shouldn't have. We can't get caught up like that anymore. We're only here for one reason." She shot Ronni the evil eye. "Not to start a fucking street war," she added.

"Oh, trust me it won't happen again, unless I'm bustin' some shots off," Ronni replied real tough-like.

Mena thought to herself about all the shit that had just gone down. They didn't need any bad blood. They needed money.

DJ went back to cutting his customers when one of the barbers on the far end of the shop said, "This got to be yo' cuzin' Mena."

"Yep, this is my fly ass cuz. And she got sexier too since the last time I saw her. She looking like a model now…hair all down her back, tall and slender. Damn, Mena!" He smiled at his first cousin. "You didn't tell me Ronni had a Bentley. But what's up with the hitch on the back of the car though?"

Everybody in the shop burst into laughter because DJ had already told them all about how crazy Ronni and Mena were back in the day so nothing would've shocked them. They all chatted for a while talking about old times and crazy shit that happened in the south. Soon, somebody ran out to get the girls two of *The Barbeque Joint's* famous pulled pork sandwiches with macaroni and cheese. They ate, sat, and talked for a while longer until Mena told DJ that she and Ronni wanted to leave and go to his spot. They couldn't wait for him to finish cutting hair.

"DJ, I need to get freshened up and rest up a bit," she told him with a serious face. "Camie is home, right?"

"DJ stopped cutting for a second. "Yeah, she home. Let me walk you out front. I shouldn't be too much longer."

As Mena and DJ stepped out of the barbershop a black Aston Martin was coming to a stop at the sign right in front of them. Mena immediately zoomed in on the driver. She looked at her cousin and didn't say a word, when a tall, dark skinned guy with long dreads down his back rolled his window down, looked at them, and smiled.

"Jay, ya got time to shape me face up?" the dread head asked.

"You know it, Khadafi. Just park. You always good around here. Give me a minute to talk to my cousin and I'll be right in," DJ responded.

Mena looked up at him and they locked eyes instantly. As he parked and got out, Mena's juices began to flow. He was just what the doctor ordered.

As Khadafi walked by, he immediately said, "Come to me pretty gurl."

Mena couldn't believe he was talking to her. She looked around and then back at DJ, before focusing her attention back at the heart stopping man and his deep voice. Her panties got moist instantly, just standing there in front of him.

Khadafi looked at Mena like a precious jewel under a microscope. “What’s a beautiful gurl like ya doin’ around here? Me never seen ya before.” From his accent, she could tell that he was Jamaican...although he did dress very American.

“I’m here to get paid like you,” she boldly stated with a smile, referring to his car. “What’s your name?”

Not even Trick had ever made her feel like that, so she knew there was going to be trouble if she ever stepped in front of him again.

He smiled again, exposing six teeth that had been coated with platinum and diamonds. “Khadafi.”

She liked that he wasn’t too flashy, only sporting an icy diamond bracelet. Before she could take the next step Khadafi walked up, grabbed her hand and pulled her close to him. There was nothing Mena could do but allow him access in her personal space. They stood there until Ronni’s loud- ass walked out and started laughing.

“You found you one already, huh Mena,” Ronni said with a smirk.

Mena ignored her friend and chose to keep her eyes glued on Khadifi.

“A’ight, well let’s get the fuck outta here cause I need a shower,” Ronni said, starting up the car.

Mena laughed because she knew how crazy Ronni could act at times. She decided to head toward the car before she drove up and down the sidewalk.

“I’m gonna see you another time,” Mena said to Khadifi as if she owed him an explanation.

DJ gave Ronni the directions to the house while Mena tried to get one last look at the new love of her life. After looking in the direction of Khadafi for several seconds, she gave him a wink as Ronni sped off with the hitch almost turning over.

Mena did a good job ignoring Ronni as they drove toward DJ's apartment. All she could think about as the car pulled back onto Dorchester Road was Khadafi. His bright smile and seductive eyes had her mesmerized. She couldn't believe the chemistry they seemed to have in such a short period of time. Mena thought about how she'd play things when she saw him again, and how good she'd fuck him on their first date. She smiled. Khadifi's sex appeal seemed to consume her mind…so much that she decided she would ask DJ to make the call hooking them up once she got settled. The more she thought about her life, the more Ronni cursed loudly as they rode through the hood.

"These broke-ass mufuckas!"

Ronni frowned as she looked out the window. The streets began to change for the worse; looking more run-down by the minute. Most people either walked up and down the street looking for a crack sale, or sat around hoping to get a taste of some crack. Some even had the nerve to run up on the Bentley as their oohs and aahs could be heard from inside the car.

Ronni looked around and smiled. "We gettin' ready to get paid out this mufucka! You hear me, Mena?" Her voice got louder and more boastful. "Look where I brought us, baby girl." She held her fist up, waiting for a pound from Mena, but got nothing.

Mena simply shook her head at Ronni's self-fulfillment and made sure her door was locked. She prayed that Camie and

DJ didn't live in the hood or anywhere near the block they were on. There was too much at stake.

"Damn, Ronni, we got this money and equipment…we might have to get a hotel room if DJ lives near here."

"Damn straight," Ronni replied, swiftly turning the corner and running a red light in the process.

No sooner than Ronni turned onto another road, Mena's prayers were answered. She watched her good friend slow down drastically, looking for the name on the outside of the apartment complex in front of them. It was mediocre, of course below standards that Mena was accustomed to; but all for good reason.

"This is it, Ronni finally uttered. "Orleans Gardens. It's not the best, but it'll have to do for now."

"Yeah, it's okay, better than where we were before," Mena added. "Park the Bentley close," she suggested, "over there." She pointed to her left near a huge dumpster in the back of the development. "They live in building five."

"Bitch, I know where to park *my* shit." Ronni laughed loudly.

Mena didn't think it was funny. She was tired, sweaty, and was dying to clean herself up. "Ronni, look, we got a job to do. Park the car, and let's get this hitch off of here so we can turn it into U-Haul tonight."

"I know this, Mena," Ronni said sarcastically, "let it do, what it do, baby!"

"You still pumped up after driving for almost thirteen hours?" She looked on in disbelief. Her girl was really starting to get on her nerves.

"Hell yeah," Ronni answered while backing up speedily. Within seconds, she had parked cattycornered as if she owned the parking lot, hopped out, and opened the back door, grabbing the duffle bag of money.

Without hesitation, Mena snatched the bag with force. "I got this, Ronni." Her eyes rolled to the back of her head. "Get one of those printers out the hitch."

Ronni made a loud huffing sound, but marched toward

the hitch quickly.

Mena waltzed through the parking lot at a snail's pace and climbed the stairs headed to the second floor with Ronni dead on her heels, still talking shit from behind. By the time Mena made it to DJ's front door, Camie was standing there waiting with a smile on her face and right hand on her hip . Camie's Double D's greeted them both well before her timid sounding voice did.

"Mena!" Camie bellowed. "So glad you came girl. Your cousin has been talking about you coming all night. Look at you, girlllllll. You look gooooooddd... and fly as usual." Camie was one of those fast talking, southern girls that gave off good vibes as she talked with speed. "Y'all come on in," she ended as she stepped back to let them both into the apartment.

"Ronni, this is Camie. Camie this is Ronni," Mena stopped to introduce.

"Nice meeting you." Camie waved in her normal southern greeting.

"What up."

Ronni spoke, then glared for a moment before she walked all the way inside. Camie was naturally beautiful, with freshly, honey-colored, shoulder length hair, accented by perfect bangs cut across the front of her face. As soon as Ronni passed by Camie, it was clear that she had her eyes on the southern woman. Her figure was petite and tight just like Ronni liked, all except her complexion. Camie was extra light, almost pale, and her face was adorned with what seemed like millions of tiny freckles.

Ronni watched Camie walk all the way into the apartment until she looked at her ass, realizing she didn't have one. *Damn,* Ronni thought to herself, *I need Mena to show me how to make me some money so I can buy Miss Camie an ass. Then maybe when that's done, I'll take her from DJ.* Ronni began to laugh to herself as Camie talked swiftly, showing the girls around the modestly decorated three bedroom apartment, and then finally the room where they would be staying.

Ronni peeped inside as Camie walked around the tight, undecorated bedroom like Vanna White on The Wheel of Fortune. She kept extending her arms gracefully as she showed off the walk in closet and queen-sized bed; the only piece of furniture in the room.

Finally, Ronni shouted out to Mena. "I'm runnin' back downstairs to get our equipment out the hitch. Can you see if Camie can bring us a card table or somethin' in here to sit this shit on? You know…show us some southern hospitality."

Mena quickly cut her eyes at Ronni. She was heated that Ronni was talking as if Camie wasn't standing there. "Camie, do you have anything we can use?" Mena asked coyly.

"I'll think of something." Camie made sure she didn't look Ronni's way.

"Bet. I'll be right back," Ronni announced.

As soon as Ronni stepped out of the room, Camie began.

"Mena, okay you know I don't like starting trouble…but is your friend gay? I mean she acts like a dude."

Before Mena could say anything Camie continued… "And why are you with her, Mena? Ahhhh… I don't think I like her too much."

Mena smiled. "Well, she obviously likes you."

They both laughed slightly.

"I got a man, Mena." Camie snickered lightly.

"She's cool, Camie. Really she is. She's been a good friend to me…you just gotta get to know her."

"I don't think so."

Camie left the bedroom and rushed into the living room noticing that Mena was on her heels. "Help me pull this old table into your bedroom. You can use this for now to set your equipment on. It's wide enough. What kind of equipment is it anyway?" She paused to hear the response.

Without a response, and avoiding Camie's stare, Mena lifted the other end of the table and they proceeded back into the room where Camie restarted her investigation. "So, how long are you guys gonna stay? And why did you leave Philly again?"

"It's a long story, Camie. I told DJ I would fill you guys in."

Luckily, the sound of Ronni's voice cut the conversation short.

"I got time."

"But I'm tired, Camie."

Ronni made her way back into the apartment with a computer and a scanner, and asked Mena to go back down with her to get the rest. Mena happily rushed off to help Ronni. It was the only thing that would save her from Camie's numerous questions. For some reason, Camie wasn't street smart and probably wouldn't understand what Mena was about to do, or why. Therefore, she felt like keeping her out of their business plan was the best option for the moment. Camie told Mena she would give them some time to get settled and if they needed any help to just ask.

An hour later, the hitch was empty and the ladies found themselves cooped up in the room with the door locked. Finally, everything they needed was set up in the room as if they'd been in business for weeks. Boxes of well-needed paper and glue covered the table along with Trick's prized Sony computer. With the three printers, two rulers and paper cutter on the floor, a mini office had been created. They were open for business.

Soon, the door flung open and Ronni made her way to the kitchen as if she owned the place. Mena followed hoping to ask Camie for a washcloth and towel, but instead found Camie with her face bawled up at the kitchen table as Ronni blurted out another insane comment.

"Damn Camie, you didn't fry us up no southern fried chicken, or nothin'? A bitch hungry," Ronni said with a smirk. She reached for a strand of Camie's hair until Camie ducked like she was in a boxing match.

Camie refused to smile back. "I can tell DJ to bring some food home," she uttered in her softest voice. She closed the magazine she'd been reading on the table and asked Mena if everything was okay so far.

Mena began to speak but Ronni cut her off. "Forget about it," she told them both. "I'll get something while I'm out. I need to see what the good city of Charleston has to offer." She rubbed her hands together speedily. "Mena, give me some money."

Mena's neck snapped back like the chick from the exorcist. She knew that Ronni was out of pocket saying those words so openly in front of Camie. "Ronni, I'm tired," she said, moving sluggishly toward the couch in the living room.

"So, give me the money and take your tired ass to sleep."

"Stop it, Ronni," Mena snapped. She took a seat on the big, cocoa colored sectional and searched for the remote.

"So, what's the problem?" Ronni had her arms spread wide, still standing closer to the kitchen, but just a few yards from Mena. "What a bitch gotta do, beg you or somethin'? I mean you got plenty of money, Mena." Ronni moved closer to the living room area, ready for a beef while Camie's eyebrows crinkled as she listened on.

Mena ignored Ronni, hoping they wouldn't fuck up their living arrangements so early in the game. "Ronni, I said I'm tired. I need a shower and some sleep."

"Well, I need some money and some pussy," she said sharply, then gave Camie the once over.

Camie turned her head completely, almost afraid to be near Ronni. Within seconds, she jetted into her bedroom, knocking down a few pictures by mistake along the way. As soon as Mena heard her door slam, she hopped up and got deep into Ronni's face.

"Oh, so this is how you're gonna act?" Her finger moved speedily like an angry parent.

"Mena, you had me drive all the way the fuck down here to South Carolina and now you don't wanna give me some of the money in the bag? At least show me what's goin' down wit' the money and how to make it. It's not like the shit is yours." Ronni's voice deepened. "I mean…."

"Fine!" Mena shouted, stomping like a two year old.

"Follow me, big time. I can see now that you're going to mess up our whole operation before it even gets started." Once in the room, Mena slammed the door. "Now, I'm not giving you any of the other money. I put that up for safe keeping. I'll make you a small amount of cash to last you for the week, but that's it."

Ronni just glared without emotion. She wanted to slap Mena down to the floor, but she needed some play money at the same time. "Are you gonna stand there and talk me to death, or are you gonna start producin' some green?"

Ignoring Ronni's sarcasm, Mena began the money making process the exact way she'd been trained. After placing a crisp, but old, one hundred dollar bill on the bed of the printer she hit scan, clicked on the graphic software and waited for the image to appear.

"Trick always uses older money," Mena commented.

"Why?" Ronni asked like a curious student.

"Because older bills have easier security marking to duplicate," Mena replied while moving her mouse. "Even the printers are older models and the software too. New printers and software have more advanced anti-counterfeiting codes, so you have to stay away from those."

"So, you really gotta know what the fuck you doing, huh?"

"That's right. So pay attention."

"Bet," Ronni said, staring at the computer.

"See when you scan the bill, the markings are not gonna be there, so you gotta make them. That's where the software comes in," Mena said. After that process was complete, she asked Ronni to put a piece of the paper in the printer, saved the bill's image as a pdf document, then hit print.

Ronni was amazed as the green hundred dollar bill made it's way out of the printer. Once Mena turned the hundred dollar bill over and repeated the same process, Ronni couldn't contain her excitement.

"Damn, I can't believe you were holdin' out on me."

"Well, like I said, I was gonna tell you when the time

came," Mena replied.

"Yeah, sure."

Once the two sheets were done, Mena showed Ronni the gluing and cutting process before finally spraying the bill with starch. "The starch is used so that when people in the stores use those counterfeit detector pens, the money will turn yellow and not black."

Ronni held up the fake bill. "Oh shit. I can't wait to try this out."

"And that's it. Once we put the money in the dryer for three minutes, we're all done," Mena continued. "The key to this shit is to go slow. When you rush and don't do every step right, that's when you fuck up."

"Well, you don't have to worry about that," Ronni said, turning the bill back and forth.

When nine more bills were complete, Mena prepared for one last lecture on how they didn't need to be flashy while in the new town. But out of the blue, Ronni jumped up and almost knocked Mena down as she leaned in and snatched the small pile of money that had just been printed. Mena gave Ronni a hard stare, but nothing was going to stop Veronica Grimes from doing what she wanted to do.

Ronni was almost to the front door before Mena even made it out of her new bedroom. She started to scream just as DJ came in and Ronni brushed pass as she held onto the front door.

"DJ, I'm out for the night, looking for a South Carolina jawn."

"What is a jawn," he asked with a frown on his face.

"It's a noun. It can be anything…a girl, a car, a house….anything. It's Philly talk. But yo' country ass wouldn't know shit about that. I wanna go see what this thousand dollars can get me tonight. Any suggestions?" Ronni inquired.

Camie peeped from her bedroom after hearing Ronni's voice. "Uggh," she said to herself. "How long will she be here? DJ!" Camie called out.

Ronni kept yelling, "I'm going to the club, baby! Let it do, what it do," she sang. "You want to go, Camie?" She stopped her performance and turned to DJ again. "You got any weed?" she asked him slyly.

"You paying?"

She gave off a foul smile until DJ returned with a crazed look that said, don't fuck with me Ronni.

"Ronni, where are you going?" Mena asked, finally making it to the front door. Her hands were folded as she grilled her girl with DJ looking on. "You don't know your way around this place."

"I'm straight," Ronni grinned. "I'm takin' my Bentley and goin' to find some weed, some bitches, and possibly some new contacts."

The door slammed, leaving Mena speechless. *Why does Ronni think the world is hers*, she wondered?

DJ saw the look on Mena's face and offered one piece of advice. "Mena, I know that's your girl, but you better be careful … she's dangerous."

"That's just Ronni," she told DJ with confidence. "She's crazy, but that's my girl… always had my back." Mena gave up a half smile. "Just like you, cuz. No worries, okay. I'm headed to take a shower."

"Wait! Mena, what's the new business we about to get into? You said you'd tell me as soon as you got to town." DJ's face begged to know the answer.

"Just let me take a shower, then we can talk."

Mena walked away pretending not to be frustrated. But half of her heart told her that her cousin was right about Ronni. But Mena knew she had bigger problems. She wasn't sure how she would deal with the Felony situation. She had promised to call him back and knew he was waiting.

Inside the bedroom, she dialed Felony's number thinking about how she would explain that she couldn't give her whereabouts.

"Felony, It's me," she said when he answered.

"Mena, what the fuck is going on?"

"Look, I left... couldn't take his bullshit anymore."

Felony expressed frustration in his voice. "C'mon Mena, he cheated, you cheated...we all cheat."

"Look, on the real, you and I had fun…but you can't protect me from Trick. I have no one else so I bounced."

"Where are you?"

"You know I can't tell you that."

"Why, I would neva hurt you. I just wanna love you."

"No, Felony. You wanna keep fucking me. It was good while it lasted, but we can't do the long distance relationship. Plus, you still work for Trick."

"Yo, I gotta go…but I'll call you in a few days or so."

"That's cool," Mena said, hanging up. She knew that was the end of their secret relationship.

$ Nine $

Hours had passed and the good times rolled. It seemed strange for Mena to be so cheerful, and hanging out with such good company. She and DJ had been sitting closly to each other, chopping it up like old times just as they'd done as kids. Hours had flown by since Mena had showered and gotten comfortable in a pair of gray, Juicy Couture sweat pants and a rhinestone tank top. She sat Indian style on the over-sized couch banging out yet another bag of sunflower seeds. She began flipping through old photo albums that showcased many missing elements from her younger life; pictures of her grandmother who was now deceased, and the many cousins who had moved away and hadn't kept in touch. For Mena, it was like a mini-family reunion on paper.

So many missed moments popped into her head. So many Christmas' had gone by without her presence. Although she'd remained in contact with her older aunts and a few cousins in Charleston, there was always a sense of detachment. Was it because her mother had forgotten about her completely? Even though she had taken on her aunt's last name she still wanted to be considered as a Joyner, the family name. In her heart, she knew that she was an outsider. Someone who no one cared too much about. DJ and his mother seemed to be the only family members outside of the aunt who'd taken her in when she was sixteen that even considered her family.

"DJ, look at you here." She pointed to an old photo with DJ riding his bike with his mother, Mena's aunt at his side. "Oh my God! Look at that shirt," she exclaimed.

"Oh, you think that's funny, do you? Well, look at this."

Mena was shocked to see a picture of herself when she was six years old with two long ponytails sitting in her aunt Catherine's lap. "Whoa…we're gonna have to burn this biddy."

Mena tried to remove the picture from behind the sticky film until DJ slapped her hand. Together they laughed as the pages flipped to more emotional pictures. One by one, they discussed DJ's father, his jail-bird brothers and finally his aunt Sonya, Mena's mother. Of course, the raggedy photo of Sonya ten years prior brought instant pain to Mena's heart. As her finger rubbed across the plastic, DJ tried to change the subject.

"So Mena, are you gon' tell me this hair-brain scheme of yours? I mean this shit brought you all the way to South Carolina." He attempted to take the photo album out of her hand. "I've been waiting to hear it."

She snatched it defiantly. "DJ, how is she?"

He could tell from the sound of her voice that her soul needed to know. "Mena, please don't start. We all know how your mother is. I mean… Sonya hasn't changed at all," he said lifelessly.

"Does she still live near?" Her face had a concerned look.

DJ hesitated. "Yeah, she does."

"Do you see her a lot?"

"C'mon, Mena." DJ placed his head into the palms of his hands. "Cuz, we were having a good time. Now, you gonna go mess things up." He reached out for Mena's large bag of ranch sunflower seeds. One by one, he cracked pretending to be a sunflower eater, all in an attempt to avoid eye contact with his cousin.

All of a sudden Mena began talking as if she were in front of a therapist. "I thought about all those empty holidays where everyone else had their family around and Donte and I had no one. Well, no one until Trick came along," she corrected. "On the surface, things seemed good for me." She paused with a smile.

DJ sighed. He wanted to ask about Donte's death but decided against it since Mena still spilled her guts.

"I always had nice clothes, nice jewelry, sorta whatever I wanted financially, but on the real, DJ, I want to make amends with my mother." A flood of emotions ran through her bones as she said the words *my mother*. She wanted badly to have that mother-daughter relationship that she'd been missing out on.

"That might be a little scary," DJ admitted.

"Why?"

"She's still on drugs, Mena. Heroin," he said matter of factly.

"So, she's still my mother. And I want to see her."

"Not a good idea."

The photo album dropped to the floor ending with a loud thump onto the hardwood. "Listen, I need this. I really do. It seems that I'm always searching for answers no matter how hard I try to forget. I just want to make things right."

"But you seem to be doing good for yourself, cuz. And what about your dude? Y'all gon' tie the knot, right? That's all you need…you and your man."

"Hmmmph." She breathed heavily. "Well, that's another story for another time. Take me to see my mother, DJ. Please," Mena begged.

His mouth fell open and silence filled the room. Luckily, Camie barged through the front door talking a mile a minute, and rushed over toward the television set. "I can't believe y'all still sitting here. It's almost 8 o'clock." She stopped and checked her watch. "I forgot to take my portfolio down to Angie."

Mena looked at her like she was crazy. "Camie, you always speed ballin'."

"Girl, I'm trying to get this job as a stylist in North Charleston. The owner of the salon be having her work all up in magazine's like Black Hair and Upscale, so I gotta make sure she know what I can do. Gotta get this money," she announced then smiled at DJ.

"That's my baby." DJ smiled back. "We trying to move up outta here soon. Get us a nice house maybe in Summerville somewhere…over there where the white folks live."

"That's right." Camie blew kisses through the air and rushed back out the door.

As soon as the door slammed, Mena sat up as if an epiphany had hit her. "So, cuz, I know you sell weed, but are you really making any money?" Her eyes glistened.

"A little." DJ shrugged his shoulders. "Why you ask?" He was just happy that she'd gotten off the subject of her mother.

"'Cause I want to talk to you about why I'm here."

DJ got excited. His eyes lit up as he moved closer to the end of the couch. "It's about time. I've been waiting to hear this. What, we gon' open a boutique or some type of t-shirt shop?"

Mena choked on one of her sunflower seeds. "You're funny." She chuckled a bit, then began. "Well, your cousin has lucked up on something big and I want you to be a part of it."

He grinned widely as Mena began to give the details blow by blow of how Trick ran his counterfeiting business and how she planned on doing the same in the south with his help. She briefly explained how she'd make the money and he'd find her the right people to sell it to.

DJ listened intently then hit her with question after question. "So, how you make a profit?" he wanted to know.

"Easy. We take one-fourth of the money. So if somebody wants to buy $1,000 in bills, we make $250.00. It's simple. Find the big ballers in town…you know the big spenders and we'll make a killing."

DJ sat with his chin rested on both knuckles while he calculated hard. "Ummmm," he uttered.

Mena confirmed what he was wondering. "Yep, you got it." Her grin intensified. "If we get enough customers who buy at least two hundred grand a month, we'll make fifty thousand a month off each customer. You do the math baby."

"Damn Mena, you on to something." DJ hopped up and began pacing the floor as if he was thinking of people to call. "This is fly. Real fly."

"No, this is unique. Nobody is doing this kinda shit out here…I'm almost positive." Mena continued as if they were having their first board meeting, without Ronni of course. "Just think, our overhead is low, we simply buy the paper, glue, ink, spray, and other supplies….that's it. Our biggest job is printing the money and getting the customers who will buy. People who are used to spending big money," she reiterated.

"I got it. I got it. I'm all in," DJ announced, stopping in the middle of the floor.

"I figured you would be. Follow me." Mena hopped off the couch.

DJ followed excitedly like a trained puppy trying to figure out what person in the family Mena could've inherited her plump ass from. Luckily, he wasn't into incest, because Mena was a bad broad, he thought to himself.

Mena opened the door to the back bedroom so DJ could get a good look at what they were dealing with. His eyes bulged as he saw the transformation.

"Damn cuz. …" He cleared his throat. "This is for real, huh?"

"Yep. Come inside and close the door," she whispered, even though no one was in the house but them. "Now, I know Camie's your lady, but I think we should keep this under wraps for a while. Just in case anything kicks off we don't want her in any unnecessary trouble."

DJ thought for a second before speaking. He figured if they kept things quiet then no trouble would come. He'd been selling weed on the side for years and nothing bad had ever happened. Camie had known about that since day one. Besides, they never kept secrets from each other. "That's cool, cuz. But how you suppose we keep her out of this room."

Mena smiled. "A lock."

DJ hunched his shoulders. "Do as you please." He wasn't

in full agreement about not telling Camie, but being that he was so mesmerized by Mena's set up and the potential money they were going to make, he was willing to say anything.

"We gon' get paid!" he said excitedly as he moved around the room.

"We sure are. If we do this shit right, neither of us will ever have to worry about working another day in life. So you got any folks in mind for our first set of clients?" Mena folded her arms and leaned against the wall.

"Hell yeah. Just give me until tomorrow. I'll make a list and a few calls."

"Well, don't say too much," she instructed, "Just ask if they're interested in an opportunity. If they are, tell them to meet us at the shop tomorrow at seven. Cool?"

"Cool."

"Hey, Mena. There's only one bed in here. You and Ronni dyking?"

Mena stared at DJ hoping he wasn't serious. She started to respond until he burst out laughing.

"No seriously, you know you welcome forever, but how long you plan on sharing this bed with her?"

"Like I said, if this all goes as planned, we'll all be paid in no time. I say a month at the most."

"This is gonna be one long, hot summer." DJ shook his head as he ran his fingers across a hundred dollar bill that lay on top of the printer. His face seemed to crinkle a bit.

"Confused, huh?"

He just shook his head.

She picked up another bill from off the table and handed it to DJ. Mena moved in closer. "I tell you what. Let's bet. If you can tell me which bill is fake and which is real I'll show you how to make the money. If you can't tell the difference, you take me to see my mother. Tonight," she added in a strong, sincere voice.

DJ looked at Mena intently before saying … "Bet."

$$$

Exactly twenty-five minutes later, Mena found herself in the darkness of DJ's black Chevy Avalanche, headed back through the run-down neighborhood that she and Ronni had talked about so badly earlier in the day. It was clear that DJ had lost the bet and desperately wanted to know how Mena could make such perfect counterfeit money. It had been wearing on his mind the entire ride over to Sonya's, but he said nothing…just computations swirled in his head. On the other hand, Mena had gotten what she wanted; a chance to see the woman who gave birth to her for the first time since she was nine.

Everything seemed to move in slow motion as DJ gave his best account of what Sonya had been doing. He'd heard recently that she had two other children, but hadn't met them. They were potentially Mena's full siblings and a part of the missing puzzle she so badly wanted to pull together.

As soon as DJ mentioned two kids, Mena got antsy. "Boys or girls?" she asked.

DL shrugged his shoulders. "Mena, I hate to ask this, but what happened with Donte? I mean why is it such a secret?"

"It's not, she explained. We just don't know all the details so instead of starting rumors, I just remain quiet."

Mena tilted her head onto the window and closed her eyes. She hated going back to that dreadful night. The night that would haunt her forever. It still seemed like yesterday, even though it was over two months ago.

She remembered being drunk, out of her mind. It was a party just for two, her and Trick. She danced for him on top of their expensive dining room table. Trick stood on the side throwing dollars as the music pumped and the alcohol filtered through her sweaty body. Mena remembered dancing seductively in three inch pumps, and a black lace panty and bra set. The champagne bottle held in her hand was half empty, as she drank straight from the Dom Perignon bottle. She was on bot-

tle number two while Trick was on number three.

The night had been going well and Mena felt good. It was clear to her that she had thrown her hands above her head moving to the music. She had just put her right foot forward and pivoted in slow motion when Donte walked in. Seeing his face had ruined the twosome's mood, since they weren't expecting company. but when the other two faces appeared, Trick went for his gun.

Mena knew Donte was forbidden to bring anyone to the house, and from the looks on their faces, it was clear it was more than a visit. It was a robbery. Trick shouted at the two guys who had drawn their guns too, and barked at Donte asking who the fuck they were. And what did they want. Mena remembered jumping from the table and stumbling toward the kitchen in hopes of grabbing one of the many guns Trick had stashed around the house.

Gun shots went off. And everything happened too quick for her to remember. The intoxication took over Mena's mind as she rushed back to help Trick and her brother. More shots fired and before she knew it, sirens sounded, and two people lay in a pool of blood on the floor. Everything else was a blur. She could never remember for the life of her. It seemed like Trick grabbed her to save her, but she wasn't quite sure. The only thing that was clear was the paramedics had entered the house, and Donte was pronounced dead.

The sound of DJ's voice brought Mena back to reality. She didn't want him to know that she'd zoned out, so she responded to what he'd said. "Cause I do want to get married, do you?" he asked.

"Yeah , I do."

DJ listened as Mena rambled about how she wanted children, at least two or three depending on how soon she got married. The conversation had gotten good, but cut short as DJ pulled into the drug infested parking lot where tons of people walked along the cracked cement sidewalks in the darkness, and sat around the run-down apartment complex cursing and talking loudly.

"We're here, cuz. Welcome to Bayside Manor. Section 8 at it's finest. Well, that's the old name, now it's Bridgeview Village," DJ announced with a frown as he yanked the key from the ignition and got out. "Let's go. The later it gets the more violent it gets. Chucktown is the murder capital of South Carolina and I'm not trying to be on the eleven o'clock news."

"Damn," Mena replied.

She looked around intently at the broken silver chain fences, the trash that covered the walkways, and the needles that could be seen covering the pavement beneath her feet. Mena lifted her eyes long enough to notice DJ five or six steps ahead of her and decided to pick up the pace. She wasn't afraid. She'd been in the hood. She grew up in one of Philly's hoods, but everything seemed so foreign to her. It wasn't the place where she lived as a child, but seemed several steps beneath. What had really sent her mother downhill?

DJ stopped at 105A and began banging on the door while Mena kept checking over her shoulders. Soon, a loud, light-skinned woman snatched the door open and immediately began cursing like a sailor.

"What the fuck do you want Donovan Joyner? You stingy mufucka," she said, with a dingy looking toddler clinging to the bottom of her right leg.

The woman appeared to be in her early fifties which made Mena question if it was really Sonya. Her mom had her when she was sixteen which would've put Sonya at forty exactly. The woman looked beat down, like she'd lived a hard life, but still held her shapely figure; one similar to Mena's. Goose bumps rose all over Mena's body as she smiled, hoping Sonya would recognize her as she cursed at DJ. Mena wanted something about her to seem familiar to the woman who'd given up her parental rights years ago.

"I came to visit." DJ stuck his hands deep into his pockets. "I brought my cousin to see you."

"Your cousin?" Sonya zoomed in on Mena. "She yellow

as hell, and don't look nothing like your ass. Anyway, who the fuck is she?" She paused. "Mufucka, you brought a social worker to my damn house?"

Mena's heart began to filter toward her stomach. She was hurt and DJ could see the pain in her eyes. There was nothing he could say or do. Sonya had done it again. She'd managed to fuck her life up as usual and now had included Mena in her attempt to destroy the world.

"I told you we shouldn't have come here," DJ whispered.

"It's okay," her voice trembled. She tried to put on a plastic smile. "It's okay…really. I wanted to come here. I mean…I needed to come here."

"For what?" Sonya's voice was harsh. "You bring a housewarming gift? Some drugs? A little change? Something!" she badgered.

"Because I need to talk to you about the past, mother." Mena's tone was soft. It exposed the hurt.

"Mother?" Sonya's eyes drew blood. "Oh, so you think I'm yo momma. Girl, don't come around here looking for no hand outs. I got enough children to take care of and you not one of 'em."

"C'mon Mena," DJ urged, noticing the tears welling up in her eyes. "I told you this wasn't a good move."

"I need closure, DJ." Mena moved away from her cousin letting him know she still wanted to talk to Sonya.

"Oh yeah," Sonya spat. "Here's your closure."

Mena didn't even get a chance to blink before the heavy door was slammed in her face. As she fought to dry her falling tears, nothing could console her, not even DJ's compassionate arm as he nudged her along the walkway. Mena walked briskly behind DJ as he fussed about his aunt's behavior.

"I'm sick of her shit," he fussed. That's it. I'm not fucking with her no more."

"Don't say that."

Mena hoped Sonya would rush behind with a made for T.V, I'm so sorry story. Unfortunately that never happened, but her cell did ring. Without hesitating, Mena answered, hoping it was a call to erase the past or start a new one.

"Hello," she sniffled.

"No sense in cryin' now! Bitch, you took my mufuckin' car!"

Trick yelled into the phone loud enough for DJ to know that it was a male voice going ballistic. His voice roared like thunder telling Mena that there was no turning back.

"What? Why you acting like that?" Mena asked meekly, climbing back into the truck.

"Felony said my jawn was gone. And you, too. All my shit is gone, Bitch. ALL MY EQUIPMENT! You scandalous-ass hoe! I'm callin' it in stolen. Mena, if you not up here at this jail to see me by tomorrow and explain all this shit, consider yourself dead!"

"Oh, I didn't know," she answered mildly, hoping DJ couldn't sense what was going on.

"What the fuck are you talkin' about?"

"I'll be there Friday," she said, before Trick could say anything else. She hung up quickly but kept talking. "Oh, I love you too, baby."

Mena removed the phone from her ear and turned it completely off. She then looked over at DJ and began crying. "Take me home please."

Ten

Shortly after midnight, Ronni staggered through the dark, narrow hallway that led to the entrance of Club Fantasy. Due to her baggy Rock & Republic jeans that she refused to pull up, Ronni had already shelled out an extra twenty to get past the bouncer so she wasn't in the mood for anymore bullshit. No one ever questioned her fashion sense in Philly. After hours of show-boating around town, drinking and smoking weed, it was clear to those who passed her that she was feeling good. Especially from the two-step dance move she did as soon as she walked inside. She'd heard from a few cats that she'd met earlier in the day that Club Fantasy was the hottest strip club in town; the place where freaks gave dancing a new name and held the crown for having the baddest nude bitches in the game. Now, it was time to test their theory.

When the last set of black double-doors opened Ronni's temperature rose. "Good gracious!" she hollered, "let it do, what it do!" she shouted loudly after eyeing a big butt stripper on the huge stage in the middle of the dimly lit club.

"Now, that's what the fuck I'm talkin' 'bout! Booty shakin' all around!"

Ronni's eyes darted to the L-shaped bar where she spotted an empty bar stool to the right of the stage. She strutted that way with her usual cocky-like walk and landed on the bar stool where she eyed the thick bartender for seconds then switched her focus back to the stage. Several guys had crowded around for the finale where the stripper held a firm hand stand with her legs wide open and dollars were being placed into any available opening.

"That ain't shit!' Ronni announced to everyone assembled around the bar. With a smug expression, she reached into her pocket regaining her focus on the shapely bartender.

"Gimme all one's, beautiful," she announced, throwing the only seven hundreds she had left onto the counter. "And gimme a Ciroc wit' a splash of cranberry. Get yo'self somethin', too."

Unenthused, the bartender snatched up the money, turned her back, and rushed over to the heavy-set gentleman at the end of the counter who made the switch, handing her back seven hundred one dollar bills.

While Ronni waited she turned her attention back to the stage where the crazy talking DJ was announcing the next act. The whole scene reminded her of Jamie Foxx in the movie, *The Players Club*, how Jamie talked shit in between spinning records.

"This is it, baby!" he shouted on the mic. "The one we've all been waiting for. Dig deep and pull everything but the lint out your pockets cause this lady's gonna get it all. And if you're hungry, don't fret." He slowed the pace of his words and spoke passionately. "Miss Reece's Pieces is here and got plenty to feed you!"

As the crowd went wild, and men clapped from every area of the club, Ronni couldn't help but laugh. "Reece's Pieces, what kinda damn stripper name is that? What happened to Peaches and Cinnamon? That must be some country shit," Ronni joked to no one in particular.

However, when Ronni looked toward the stage she had to admit that Reece was doing a hell of a job. Ronni stood up in awe seeing Miss Reece hit the stage grinding to, Ciara's sultry song, *Ride*. Her moves were hynoptic and had Ronni wanting a closer view.

She turned, collected her drink off the counter, scooped up her ones and rushed toward the right hand side of the stage.

There were about three other guys up close, but no competition from where Ronni sat. *Corn ball ass niggas,* she told herself.

Ronni examined Reece's bronze body from the top of her firm shoulders to the bottom of her thick thighs. It was obvious that Reece had sprayed herself with some type of glitter or shiny paint because it looked as if her entire frame had been dipped in caramel. Ronni assumed the multi-colored wig she wore also added to the whole candy themed idea.

"Oh yes, South Carolina, baby," Ronni chanted to herself. Her juices began to flow as she watched Reece work her thighs and caress her breast all in one seductive motion.

Ronni sat with her legs wide open, front and center, trying to play big as she sipped her drink. When they finally made eye contact, Ronni had her attention for what seemed like hours. As soon as Reece got close enough to the edge of the stage, three stalkers to the left rushed to her, ready to shell out one dollar bills as soon as she came their way. Ronni wanted first dibbs on Reece but saw the bouncer with the bald head sending fire eyes her way as he stood nearby.

"C'mere," Ronni motioned with her finger.

She stuck a stack of one's out in front of her, but Reece slithered over to some chump with a weak fade and acne all over his face.

"Oh, so it's like that?" Ronni expressed loudly. She spread her hands into the air showing her anger. The bouncer gave Ronni the evil eye again and in return she flipped him the finger.

Reece was obviously playing hard to get. Ronni laughed at how women always faked like fucking with another girl was next to criminal. When they fell hard and finally got a chance to feel the tongue they changed their tune. Ronni sipped her drink and tried to remain calm, but Reece's sex appeal had her about to commit an orgasmic suicide right there in the club.

Before she knew it Reece had bent all the way over, grabbed her ankles and allowed every patron of Club Fantasy to explore every crevice from her cleanly shaven pussy down to her ass-hole. Suddenly, the DJ played some unknown Luke Campbell song with a fast beat that made Reece go crazy. She started jiggling her ass and slithering across the front of the stage while dollars were being tossed her way.

Some guy called out, "Work that body Miss Reece."

Ronni shot him a mean stare as if Reece were her woman. Reese did a few more snake-like moves then stood up in a hurry. Moments later, she started making her butt cheeks clap which damn near sent Ronni into cardiac arrest. She stood up like she owned the place, dug deep into her pockets and pulled out some twenties.

Real ones, shit, she thought to herself. But it had to be done if she wanted to overshadow every other guy in the room.

Ronni looked on with jealous eyes as Reece bent down low to allow the dollar bills a smooth entrance into the garter belt on her thigh. But when she made eye contact with Ronni once again that all stopped.

Ronni coerced Reece with eight real twenties swaying them in the air from side-to side. They made eye contact and Reece swirled over to the end of the stage where Ronni sat drooling.

"Oh so, we got a real baller in the house tonight, ladies and gentleman," the DJ announced.

Reece had her going. She'd managed to summon Ronni close to the stage where her eyes were leveled with Reece's pussy; pussy that was now two feet from Ronni's face. Reece held her position for minutes like an acrobat working in the circus.

Reece had knelt down to the ground, had her legs wide open and had her back arched backward to the ground. If it weren't for the wig that nearly touched the ground it wouldn't have been clear that her head still existed. All of a sudden *Get Low* by Lil Jon came blasting through the speakers and Ronni started rubbing twenties in between Reece's crotch.

The bouncer headed Ronni's way until Reece put up her palm giving the *it's okay* signal. Ronni was mesmerized as she studied the inside of Reece's thighs like she was studying for an exam. Ronni considered herself one to always play cool, but nothing could stop her pussy from thumping inside her jeans.

Finally the song ended, but not the real show. Reece finished her stage performance, hopped off stage, and straddled Ronni in front of everyone. Although a surprise, Ronni welcomed the chance. As Reece grinded, Ronni pushed back, wishing she had her strap on dildo. She'd taken all of Ronni's twenties but wanted all she had. Her thick nipples stood at attention as she dipped Ronni's face into the middle of her perky breasts. Ronni obliged and took two licks before tossing some of her ones into the air.

"You never seen it rain like this before," she bragged to Reece before allowing all seven hundred ones to shower them from above. Instantly, two bouncers rushed over and began scooping up the money while Reece pretended to be in deep love.

Before long, Reece got up, walking away slowly giving Ronni the goo-goo eyes and blowing kisses as she made her way to the back. Ronni finally came back to reality and realized everyone in the club had been watching her make it rain. She was on cloud nine getting the attention she always craved when a familiar face shot her a wide grin. It was weird since it was the guy she'd seen earlier at DJ's shop.

The stranger sat across the room in what was supposedly VIP. The section sat three inches off the floor surrounded by a red velvet stanchion rope and two bouncers on each side. Ronni knew she belonged with the big dogs so she raised her glass high in the air as a sign of camaraderie and began walking toward the VIP.

As Ronni got closer she realized it was Khadafi, the guy Mena had fallen for in such a short amount of time. Khadafi nodded and gave a signal for the bouncer to remove the rope so Ronni could come inside. But once inside the ropes Khadafi gave off a cold stare leaving Ronni unsure about how he really felt about her being there.

"What's sup, Philly gurl," Khadafi said. He spoke slowly just as he did earlier in the day as if he was always thinking about his words carefully.

"You do your homework, huh?"

"In me town…of course." He paused then offered Ronni an intimidating look and a seat.

Ronni took a seat two chairs away from Khadafi. "Just came out to see what South Carolina has to offer. No what I'm sayin'," she joked then took the last sip of her drink.

"Another round," he whispered to his personal waitress who stood a few feet away.

"What you drinking," she asked Ronni.

"Ciroc, wit' a splash of cranberry."

Khadafi smiled. "Ciroc? Ya look like a Remi or Patron gurl."

Ronni couldn't help but stare into his iced out mouth. "Been down that road. I usually drink Ace of Spades back home, but I knew they didn't have that up in here." Ronni looked at the waitress. "Right?"

"No, but we have Moet."

"See, just cheap-ass Moet. I only fuck wit' the best," Ronni bragged.

When the waitress walked off Ronni seemed a little uneasy. Khadafi had a serious entourage sitting behind him; like eight deep watching them as they connected. However, the gruesome dude with the scar going across his face stood out the most. A face that looked as if he'd just committed a murder or two before arriving.

Oh shit, I think that's the nigga with the Benz. The one who almost popped my ass earlier in front of the barbershop, Ronni thought as the two made serious eye contact.

Under normal circumstances, she would've said some foul shit causing a scene but ole' boy gave off a hostile stare and Ronni wasn't packing. *Damn I hate that I had to leave my shit in the car*.

"Wa ya lookin' at? Ya waan tess me?" Skully asked in his

thick Jamaican accent. He looked at Khadafi. "This da blootclot me tell ya about earlier. One who damn near run us off da road."

Khadafi looked at Ronni. "Oh, so ya da one."

"Yeah mon. She even pull a gun...she try and fight 'gainst me!" Skully yelled. "Nobody tess me!"

He appeared to be getting hyped until Khadafi came to her defense. "Calm down Skully. Ya two just got off to a bad start, but I'm sure it was just a misunderstanding. It's ova. Right, Philly gurl?"

Ronni stared at Skully for a few more seconds then turned her head. "Yeah, whatever." She put a few ice cubes in her mouth then continued. "You always travel deep like that?"

Khadafi shrugged his shoulders. "Occasionally."

"I see you got good taste," Ronni said, eying the thirty thousand dollar Audemars Piguet watch on his wrist. "So, what a girl gotta do to get one of those?"

"Oh, so ya are a gurl," he joked, but with no laughter.

"Very funny." She nodded like he had one up on her.

Off the break, Ronni was ready to ask Khadafi to buy some counterfeit money, but moved a little slower than usual since Khadafi's personality couldn't be figured out easily. One thing for sure was that he was a weed head. Out of the blue, he fired up the largest blunt she'd ever seen and puffed right in the middle of the club like the shit was legal. The ganja-like smell stunk up the whole place causing both Ronni and two of his boys to start coughing.

"Yo, what's that shit you smokin'? That shit is potent," she managed to get out between coughs.

"It's me own creation. Here." He passed the blunt Ronni's way. "It's southern hospitality," Khadafi said firmly.

Ronni held up her hand. "I'll pass this time."

"We consider dat a sign of disrespect."

"Well, from one baller to another, I've had enough for one night. I'm here to make moves."

Khadafi took another huge puff before speaking, "Ahhh. So, dat's what brought ya all da way to Charleston? Business moves."

"Yep. Business. That's what I'm about. Makin' money." She looked at Skully who was staring right in her mouth. *I wish this serial killer lookin' muthafucka would try me. Gun or not, I'm not goin' down wit out a fight,* she thought.

"I hope ya intent is not to be an addition to da drug trade." He frowned. "We have dat covered around here."

"Naw. Not interested in that juvenile bullshit anymore," Ronni belted with the intent on insulting him. "My shit is way more classy. Unique, too. Won't have po-po always on yo ass."

Khadafi's eyes widened. "Is tis profitable?"

"Everythin' I do rings money," she boasted, "But see for yourself."

"And how me supposed to see."

When the twenty-something old waitress walked up, Ronni slapped a stack of money on her tray. "This round's on me," she bragged.

The young girl smiled and walked away. "Thanks!"

Ronni leaned in closer to Khadafi. "So you see just like that I covered that bill, right."

Khadafi nodded. But wasn't enthused.

"Well, that was my money… not the U.S. government's money."

His eyebrows crinkled.

Ronni continued, "I printed that money. It's counterfeit baby, but spends like the best Lincoln, Jackson, and Benjamin you've ever had."

Khadafi's interest seemed to be peeked. "So counterfeit, ya say?"

"Yes. I got the whole game covered. I'm just lookin' for some players in the area to get down. You feel me?"

"Tell me more."

Ronni leaned in further, giving step by step instructions on how she wanted things to flow and at what cost. Ronni played big…real big as if she were the mastermind and had been making money for years. Of course there was no mention of

Mena at all. Or the fact that she had a partner. Before long, Ronni had flipped out her phone, done some calculations on the calculator for Khadafi and decided on a meeting time for the following day. Everything had run smoothly until Reece walked out and leaned against the ropes waiting for Ronni to end her conversation.

"So tomorrow it is," she told Khadafi as she stood and gave a firm handshake.

"Tomorrow," he confirmed.

"You know what they say….never leave a horny bitch waitin'."

$Eleven$

The next morning rolled around with Mena scrambling to the left side of the bed wearing an oversized white t-shirt that read- Bootylicious. The sun shone brightly for 8 o'clock in the morning, but she strained hard to identify the small pair of hands that had been tugging at her panties. Mena hopped up, pulling her sleep mask from her eyes and stood near the side of the bed with her arms crossed.

"Have you lost your fucking mind, Ronni?"

"Why you so hostile so early in the mornin'?" Ronni kept her eyes closed hoping that the bright sun would disappear. "Keep your voice down and close those fuckin' blinds. I need some sleep."

"I guess you do," Mena snapped. "Nobody told your lil'ass to stay out all night."

"Oh, so you jealous?" Ronni laughed as she slapped a pillow over her head to block the rays from the sun.

"Look, our sleeping arrangements may not work if you think you're gonna be all touchy feely with me." Mena removed the two scarves from her head allowing her weave to fall perfectly onto her shoulders. "I can't believe you." Her stare should've meant something to her friend, but it didn't. "You've never tried no shit like that before."

"I never seen you in those black lace panties before either," Ronni joked.

"That shit ain't funny."

Ronni removed the pillow from her head and lifted her

body just enough to make Mena feel like they were having a real conversation. "Naw, seriously Mena, you know I don't want you, girl. I was just dreamin' about Miss Reece's Pieces from last night." She kissed at her three middle fingers as if there was some sweet smell left on the tips. "That bitch was phat and her booty was real juicy. Umph, umph, umph," Ronni bragged. "Pussy so good make your knees buckle."

Mena shook her head. "I'm not trying to hear this nasty shit."

Ronni smiled. "Don't be scared. Let's just say that I had a blonde moment…thought you was her." She laughed wildly before laying back down and tossing the covers over her head.

"Ummm, huh," Mena mumbled. "You know I don't do that dyke bullshit!" she snapped, while walking around the room showing that she was seriously disturbed by Ronni's antics.

"Bitch, stop trippin'. You my dawg. It won't happen again."

"It better not!"

When Mena threw one of the extra pillows at Ronni, she didn't even budge from beneath the covers. She pretended to be sleep until she finally spoke.

"I'm sorry. Come to bed, Mena," Ronni stated like a compassionate husband, still buried beneath the pillow.

"Hell no. I need a new roommate," Mena mumbled before heading to the shower. "You need to get your dirty lil' ass up," she snapped, grabbing her towel from the back of the door. "I know you hate to bathe, Ronni, but at some point you must wash. Besides, we got a business meeting at one p.m."

"Fuck you with a big fat dildo, Mena," Ronni mumbled, while falling fast asleep.

"In your dreams, bitch!"

When the door slammed shut, Ronni dozed off for some well needed rest.

$$$

Five hours later, things seemed to be in full swing. Mena sat silent in the living room with notepads and pencils ready for the first board meeting of Counterfeit LLC. She had notes written everywhere; from topics to discuss, goals, targets and dates. Everything seemed to be organized down to a list of things to do. The only problem was that she was the only one in attendance.

Ronni was still asleep at 1:15 in the afternoon and DJ was late. He'd told Mena that he would leave the barbershop in well enough time so that they could get down to business as planned. Thursday's weren't considered a busy day, so he said, which meant that it shouldn't have been a problem.

Mena put a check mark next to the #1 on the yellow legal pad that read-*Locate some stores to make purchases and get back change*. Her mind raced as she thought about Belks, and Dillard's, two major department stores in the area. Her plan was to hit the stores daily, making small purchases; less than $2,000 and then collecting the change. That was a long, drawn out process which consisted of hitting at least twenty stores per day to make $1,500- $1,700 dollars. It wasn't a long term goal, but in the short term it would bring in some funds until clientele got good.

Mena was becoming frustrated with her new partner's lack of time management. She was just about to jump up when DJ waltzed in the door with an overly ecstatic expression.

"What up, cuz?" He jumped over the couch and landed perfectly on the cushion with a huge smile.

Mena returned with a half-ass grin, then peeped at her watch.

"I hope you got good news since you showing all your teeth."

"Indeed I do," he replied. "We 'bout to get paid!" DJ clapped his hands several times high in the air.

"What the fuck you yellin' 'bout?" Ronni asked, standing a few feet behind the couch. She began rubbing her eyes and thick eyebrows as if she still needed more sleep. "What time is it?"

Mena cut her eyes at Ronni. "Go brush your damn teeth, then come out here so we can discuss our plan. Did you forget about the meeting?"

"Oh, I'm ready," Ronni announced, smoothing out her gray wife beater. With plaid printed boxer shorts and tattoos covering her entire arms she looked just like a boy.

"No, you're not. I refuse to have you sit here blowing funk in my face."

DJ was amazed. "I can't believe you wear boxer shorts. You don't have a dick do you?" he joked.

"I got a few strap on's in my suitcase if you wanna see 'em," Ronni suggested.

DJ quickly shook his head. "Naw, I'm cool."

When Ronni turned toward the bathroom, Mena gave DJ step by step information on how her short term plan would work with collecting real money from the stores. He listened intently for what seemed like hours as she gave him names of the stores that she thought would work. DJ seemed to nod more than he talked. It was clear that Mena was in charge.

Before long, Ronni was back out in the living room rubbing her hands swiftly together as if some money was coming her way. Mena went over anything important that Ronni had missed and then began asking for suggestions on how the business would run. She knew that both Ronni and DJ were watching her closely to see if she really knew how to run shit so she was careful with her words.

Deep inside, she knew she had a good business sense, but was sometimes afraid to let loose. College had never been a reality for her, always just a dream, but she was determined to make the money making business work. Most of her life, men seemed to take control once they got to know her. It was a trait she possessed, one where she was attracted to domineering men. But she knew she was smart enough to handle things.

"So, here's the deal. There's money to be made out here, so I got it all planned. We just gotta work hard at building the clientele," Mena said to them both.

"So, what, we workin' on commission or some shit?" Ronni frowned. "Cause I'm not clear on how we splittin' the money? If we're going to be counterfeit distributors, let's be the best damn distributors we can be."

Anxiously, DJ sat up. "I got three people lined up. I got this nigga named Shu who live on Flood Street. He like that…got a lot of cash. Got his own little territory selling cocaine. Not sure how much shit he really moving, but he spends a lot of money. I told him everything. Oh, and the other two niggas on point as well."

"Good, that'll work," Mena replied. "So…"

"So, I got an even better connect," Ronni interrupted.

"You do?" Mena asked with a confused expression.

"Yeah, you only been here overnight," DJ added.

Ronni threw up her hands. "Nigga don't underestimate me. Like I said I got an even better connect."

"And how do you know this?" Mena questioned.

"Because the nigga had on a thirty thousand dollar watch, that's how. Mufuckas rollin' like that are definitely caked up," Ronni said.

DJ seemed curious. "Who is it?" He knew everybody in town, so he couldn't figure out how Ronni could've gotten to someone before him.

"That nigga Khadafi," Ronni stated proudly. Seconds later she jumped up and started pacing the floor. "See, I was in the strip club last night tryna scout out some new pussy, right? You know, tryna see who gon' be on my team down this mufucka. That's when I seen the dude Khadafi in VIP. So, I go up in there, we kick it, and before you know it, we talkin' business."

Mena was pissed. "Why would you do that, Ronni? We just got here. You don't know who that nigga knows. That shit was stupid!" She stood up off the couch with an evil scowl.

At that moment Ronni stopped dead in her tracks, ready for whatever. "Bitch, what the fuck you standin' up for? Are you tryna go there wit' me?"

"I'm just saying, Ronni. You always running your fucking mouth. You were just supposed to hang out last night, not tell a complete stranger about our business," Mena spat. "You should've left that up to DJ."

Ronni shook her head. "See, this is why I just fuck bitches then send them on their way. Y'all never satisfied, never appreciative. Here I am tryin' to expand our shit, and you complainin'."

DJ finally intervened. "Not to take up for Ronni, but she did get a hell of a connect. I tried calling Khadafi today because he was on my list, but he didn't answer. He's paid, and got a lot of power around here. It don't get any better than that."

"See," Ronni said like a five year old child.

Mena finally sat back down. "I still don't think you should've talked to him without telling me first, but let's just move on. Who's gonna be our first customer."

"Well, my people said to give them a day or two and they'll be ready," DJ informed.

"Well, my shit is on this evenin'," Ronni announced. "That nigga Khadafi is…"

Before she could finish, Camie walked into the apartment with a huge smile. Looking like she couldn't wait for summer to arrive, Camie made her way over to DJ sporting a long floor length maxi dress, and gladiator sandals. She seemed happy as usual when she planted a huge kiss on DJ's thick lips.

"Hey y'all," Camie spoke.

"You got one for me?" Ronni asked. When DJ and Camie both gave her a look of death, Ronni smiled. "Damn, I was just jokin'. Lighten up people."

"What are you doing here, Camie?" DJ inquired.

"Well, I went to the barber shop and they said you'd left. So, I came here to look for you. I tried to call, but your phone keeps going straight to voicemail," Camie replied.

"So, why are you stalking me? Can I not leave the shop without you needing to know my every move," DJ snapped.

Camie's eyes bulged. "Excuse me. I can't believe you're talking to me like that in front of guests. For your information, I went to the barbershop to pick you up for our lunch date. We always have lunch on Thursdays. It's your slow day."

"Tell 'em girl," Ronni said, egging the situation on.

By now Camie had tears in her eyes. "Shut up, Ronni," she said just before storming off into the master bedroom and slamming the door.

"I'll deal with her later," DJ said. "Now, where were we?"

"Does she know about all this?" Ronni inquired.

When DJ shook his head, Mena spoke up. "Ronni was just about to tell us how Khadafi is ready to do business."

Ronni clapped her hands. "Oh, yeah…right. Now, as I was sayin', Khadafi is ready to start right away. But he wants to see if the shit is legit first."

"What do you mean?" Mena questioned.

"He wants to see if the money is straight. He don't want no Monopoly type shit. Know what I'm sayin'? He wants *you* to hand a cashier some fake money while he's watchin', just to see if *you* can get away wit' it." When DJ and Mena nodded their heads Ronni kept talking, putting emphasis on the word *you*. "He wants *you* to meet him at Citadel Mall, seven o'clock sharp inside the Foot Locker." She pointed at Mena.

"Me? Why me? This is your deal," Mena said with a frown. "Why Foot Locker?"

"Well, he made it very clear that he wanted the *pretty girl* to meet him, so I know that nigga wasn't talkin' 'bout me," Ronni said with a smirk. "The Foot Locker shit, I suggested. Since you goin' to the mall you might as well pick me up some sneaks or a Sixer's jersey."

As Ronni continued to talk, Mena zoned out of the conversation for a moment. A part of her was slightly nervous because she couldn't believe that this was finally happening.

However, the other part was just as exciting. Her first potential customer…first potential order was hours away. Although she knew she'd have to train Ronni on her business tactics, Mena had to admit, her unruly friend had come through for them. Not only that, the person she'd pulled in was someone Mena definitely wanted to get to know a little better. Any thoughts about Trick and her life in Philly were becoming nonexistent. This was going to be her new life now:CEO of Counterfeit LLC and possibly the girl of a South Carolina baller.

$Twelve$

At exactly 6:58 p.m., Mena sashayed through the Citadel Mall on her way toward the infamous sporting store. It had been a while since she had butterflies in her stomach when it came to a man, but she couldn't deny how anxious she was. Dressed in her True Religion skinny jeans, Alexander McQueen python pumps and a beaded tunic, every man she passed turned to get a second look. Some of them even had the heart to try and get her attention, but Mena wasn't the least bit interested. She had an agenda and socializing with the local flunkies wasn't part of the plan.

As soon as Mena walked into Foot Locker, the first thing she did was scan the store for Khadafi. Even though she'd only seen him one time, as fine as he was Mena knew she could easily pick him out of a crowd. She wanted him to know how professional she was when it came to business by being punctual. One thing she had learned from Trick was to have good time management skills. She could remember the countless times he'd cursed his friends or workers out for being even a minute late. He thought it was thoughtless, inconsiderate and always preached the same gospel, "You fuck wit' my time, you fuck wit' my money." It was a motto that Mena had learned to appreciate.

Realizing that Khadafi still hadn't shown up, Mena began to browse the store to see what she was going to purchase with the fake cash. Since she hadn't worn tennis shoes in over two years, she knew whatever she decided to get had to be for Ronni.

"Can I help you beautiful?" one of the referee uniformed salesmen asked her.

"Ah…yeah. Do you all have any Sixers jerseys?"

The employee shook his head. "No, I'm afraid not. But we do have Lebron's new Miami Heat jersey. Number six, baby. It's a replica, but we still can't keep them in the store."

At that moment, something told Mena to turn around. When she did, Khadafi's 6'3, two hundred and fifty pound frame stood a few feet away from her. He looked good in his oversized Polo shirt, baggy jeans and Prada sneakers. Seeing him made her wet all over again as she tried to keep her composure.

"Where you from? I've never seen you around here before," the salesmen said.

She turned back around. "Oh…umm I'm from Chicago." *Come on Mena, get yourself together. You can't act like a rookie in front of this man*, she thought to herself. "Actually, I'll take the Lebron James jersey. Give me a small," she instructed.

"It's for your son, huh?" he asked.

Mena couldn't help but chuckle. "Yeah."

As the salesmen went to grab the jersey, Mena wanted to turn around and look at Khadafi so bad, but knew that wasn't a good idea since they were supposed to act like strangers. Instead, she walked up to the counter to pay.

"Thanks for shopping with us. She'll ring you up," the salesmen said pointing to the evil looking cashier with the multi-colored hair.

"Thank you," Mena replied as the cashier scanned the tag, still giving her an evil stare.

Just as Mena wondered how Khadafi was going to monitor everything, he walked up to the counter acting as if he was interested in a hat. "Ya have a fitted Yankees hat in 7 ½?" he asked.

"I'll look when I'm done with her," the cashier responded dryly.

"Tanks, me can tell dat ya really like tis job," Khadafi shot back.

Mena wanted to laugh, but didn't want to risk pissing the cashier off any more than she already was. She needed the transaction to go as smoothly as possible.

"Your total is $59.11," the cashier stated before stuffing the jersey in a bag.

However, instead of paying attention, Mena was so intoxicated by Khadafi's Yves Saint Laurent cologne that she didn't even hear her.

"$59.11," the cashier repeated.

"Oh, yes right," Mena said coming out of her trance.

Her nerves were completely shot. Not only from Khadafi, but also from the fact that this was her first time ever using the fake money in a store. Her hands shook slightly as she reached for her Gucci wallet and pulled out a phony hundred dollar bill and handed it over. Putting the money in her wallet made the scam seem more believable; another lesson she'd learned from Trick.

As the cashier placed the money in the light to look for the security markings, Mena instantly felt lightheaded. At that moment, she began to doubt her money making skills and hoped like hell she hadn't forgot to coat the bills in starch. She didn't need to go out like Trick…not right now.

"Ma'am is this a…" was all the cashier said before Mena started coughing uncontrollably. Next came the shortness of breath and the chest discomfort. It felt like she was about to have a heart attack. "Are you okay?" the cashier asked.

"Yes, are ya okay?" Khadafi repeated.

Mena managed to nod her head. "Yes, I'm fine. I just swallowed my gum, and I guess it went down the wrong way. Now, what were you saying?"

The cashier took out the counterfeit pen detector. "I was just about to ask if this was a gift," she said, taking the pen and marking the money near Benjamin Franklin's head. When the bill turned yellow, Mena felt as if a boulder had been lifted from her shoulders.

"Yes, it's for my son," Mena replied. She decided to keep the lie going.

After finally receiving her $40.89 in change, Mena grabbed the bag from the cashier and made a swift exit out of the store. She hoped like hell the test was enough to prove to Khadafi that the money was legit because after this experience she wasn't going through that agony again.

"Ronni and DJ need to do this part. I'll just make the money," Mena said to herself as she walked back toward the main entrance. "That job is made for the employees not the CEO," she joked.

By the time she made her way through the food court, her phone began to ring. After looking at the caller ID and not recognizing the number, she took a chance and answered it anyway. *Damn, I hope it's not Trick.*

"Hello."

"Well done."

Mena's eyebrows crinkled. "Who is this?"

"It's me. Khadafi, baby."

Her frown immediately disappeared. "Oh, hi. How did you get my number?"

"Ya gurl Ronni gave it to me. Or shall I say, ya boy?"

"You're funny."

"Me don't really do phones so let's meet at da Red Lobster right outside da mall in ten. Okay?"

Mena wanted to say she didn't do anything less than the Oceanaire when it came to seafood, but decided not to act like a bitch so soon. She couldn't help it though. Next to sex, all she and Trick ever did was eat.

"Sure. I'll see you there," she said before hanging up. "Who am I fooling? That sexy muthfucka could've told me to meet him at Taco Bell and I would've graced the opportunity," she said out loud.

$$$

When Mena walked into the restaurant, Khadafi was surprisingly already sitting at the bar with a drink in front of him. As she made her way toward the bar, the same butterflies from before quickly reappeared. Whatever it was about him, Mena just couldn't seem to shake.

"Hey you," she said, taking a seat beside him.

"Hello, pretty gurl."

The moment Mena placed her purse down, she couldn't help but stare at his dreads that almost touched his stomach. With skin the color of brown sugar, he reminded her of a true Rastafarian.

"What ya eatin'?" Khadafi asked. He motioned for the bartender to come over.

"Nothing. I'll just take a Sangria if she can make one."

He smiled. "Are ya sure? Ya watchin' ya figure?"

Mena shook her head back and forth. She wasn't a huge fan of his platinum grill, but his dimpled smile gave her butterflies.

Khadafi ordered her two Sangrias along with another Hennessey and coke for himself. "So, Philly gurl, ya got a good head on ya shoulders, huh?"

"So they say. This industry is for real. Some serious money can be made. You just gotta trust me."

"Trust?" He let out an enormous laugh. "Me trust no one, especially someone as beautiful as ya." Khadafi reached and grabbed the tip of her chin slightly.

Mena grinned widely. She loved the way his voice always accented the letter *t* so strongly. "Why would you say that?" she blushed, losing focus on the business at hand.

"Ya know 'bout Adam and Eve, right?"

Her expression quickly changed. "Look, I'm trying to do you a favor…you know… put you on to something good. Either you down or you not." She crossed her arms.

Khadafi finally backed off realizing Mena had skills. He couldn't resist complimenting her. "Damn, ya sexy."

"Thanks." Mena hunched her shoulders, pretending not to be excited. All along, her hormones had been raging ever since he touched her chin. "So, you said well done earlier. Does that mean you're gonna do business with us?"

Khadafi waited until the bartender placed their drinks down before he continued. "To be honest, me don't normally do business wit' strangers. Me don't trust too many people. Ya understand? Plus ya gurl Ronni is too much of a wild ting."

At that point Mena thought she'd gone through all of this for nothing. Like the deal was over before it even began. She took a huge sip of her drink.

"But me gonna try it out. Ya seem like a good gurl and me like dat," Khadafi said after downing his drink. "I can't lie though it seems to be very profitable."

Mena downed her drink as well. "Trust me, it is. We're gonna be some very wealthy people."

"Seems like ya already wealthy. Me saw what ya was drivin' at the barber shop. Anybody drivin' a Bentley can't be broke." Mena couldn't think of a lie fast enough before he continued. "Me wanna ask you how ya get into tis counterfeit ting, but I'm gonna trust dat ya know what ya doing. I'm gonna do business wit' ya, but understand tis." Khadafi leaned toward Mena and spoke soft but stern, "If tis ends up jeopardizin' what me got goin' on now, there'll be a price to pay."

Anyone within earshot would've probably been intimidated by Khadafi's threat, but Mena's reaction was just the opposite. Dealing with all of her crazy drug dealing ex-boyfriends in the past, she was used to people talking shit. She wasn't worried.

"Ya understand?"

"Completely," Mena said, starting on her second drink.

Two hours and several drinks later, Mena and Khadafi were joking with each other as if they'd gone to the same high school. Although neither went into details about their pasts, they managed to keep an interesting conversation going. Mena enjoyed the fact that he made her laugh; something that Trick could never do…probably never wanted to do. Not to mention, he was extremely attentive to what she had to say, which was another attribute none of her past boy toys seemed to have.

Things appeared to be going well until a tall Amazon-like girl walked up on them without being detected. When Mena eyed her enormous Nikki Minaj booty and fake silicone breasts, her demeanor screamed, 'stripper with a little bit of money hungry bitch on the side.'

"So, you can't call me back, but you can take some hoe out to eat," the girl said in a sassy tone. Everyone in the bar area gasped and immediately looked in their direction.

"Who the fuck you calling a hoe?" Mena yelled.

From the look on Khadafi's face it was obvious that he didn't care for embarrassment. "Fatima, ya got tree seconds to get da fuck outta here."

Apparently his threats didn't bother her either because she didn't budge. "I'm not going any damn where. How you gon' stop calling me for her? You know what, fuck you…"

It only took one second for Khadafi's fist to make contact with Fatima's face. She hit the floor instantly like a boxer who'd just simply had enough.

"What me tell ya about disrespectin' me? Ya don't disrespect Khadafi. Me will bury you, ya know!"

Mena's eyes widened. She'd had her fair share of brawls with dudes, but no one had ever knocked her out in public. *Maybe I do need to take this nigga seriously*, she thought.

Just as Khadafi was about to start on round two, Mena jumped up and pulled his arm. "No, don't!" She quickly went into her purse, pulled out three fake hundred dollar bills and yelled for the bartender to keep the change."

Realizing he'd lost his temper, Khadafi quickly followed Mena outside. As she was about to head toward her car, he stopped her. "No, let's take me car. We come back for yours."

Mena seemed hesitant. "Ahhhhhhhhhh…"

"Don't worry, me not gonna hurt ya."

After contemplating for a few seconds, Mena took him up on his offer. All she could do was hope that his ass wasn't a psychopath as they drove off in his black on black Mercedes CL Coupe. The ride was nothing like Mena expected or dreamed. Her heart was set on pretending like it was their first date. Instead, she listened to Khadafi take three different phone calls, making threat after threat pretending to be Nino Brown from New Jack City.

"Take da .357," he badgered someone through the phone. He banged against the wheel as he took a curve on two wheels. Mena held on tightly as she cut her eyes Khadafi's way. At no point did he think his behavior was strange or that he needed to explain. "We'll see about dat when da nigga is six feet under!" he roared. "Take care of it! Take care of it!" His voice got louder as he accelerated with speed.

With each corner Khadafi took, he cursed violently and gave instructions on who to shoot and when it should get done. Mena sat back fearfully in the speeding car, texting DJ the entire time. Khadafi was beyond mysterious.

What the fuck have I gotten myself into? she asked herself. *Why me? Why do I get all the murderers and the dope dealers*? She began to think about her past relationships with men and what line of work they were in. None of them proved to be worth a grain of salt. They never respected her, never truly cared about her happiness, and never intended on making her wifey.

Her hope was that Khadafi was different; that he would treat her like a woman needed to be treated. DJ had told her that Khadafi was a true businessman. He dabbled in a few illegal activities, but overall nothing extra shady about him. But then she thought about the new call that had just come in and the words he spoke to someone named Skully, she thought otherwise.

"Yo Star, let me talk to tis lovely lady." He paused slightly to listen to Skully talk shit about Mena. "Nah, Star, she's a good gurl. Me know y'all just got off to a bad start." He paused again. "What! So we gonna have to get da guns ourselves now, huh? Me kill dat bloodclot nigga!" Khadafi spat.

Apparently, she was looking for love while he was looking for guns.

As soon as Khadafi got off the phone, he glanced over at Mena. "Me wanna apologize for all of dat, pretty gurl. Every ting just got carried away." He reached over and grabbed Mena's hand. "Don't tink me some type of animal."

"I don't. I guess you had to do what you had to do, right?" She shot him a half of a smile.

"Exactly."

Khadafi continued to drive for a few more minutes until they stopped and parked at what looked like a park. Looking around, Mena hoped that he wasn't there to dump her body in some abandoned field. "Why are we here?" she asked with concern. She could care less that her favorite song by Usher, *There Goes My Baby* had just come on the radio.

"Me just wanted to be around ya for a little longer before ya go back home. Me had a wonderful time until dat bloodclot Fatima ruined it."

She let her guard down a little. "Yeah, that was crazy, but I had a good time, too." Silence filled the car for what seemed like forever until Mena decided to end the awkwardness. "So, the only time you talk a lot is when you're telling someone how to kill." She let out another forced smile.

"So, me see ya have a sense of humor."

"We all should. Do you?" she asked, still a bit fearful of his intimidating demeanor.

"Somewhat." He stared directly into her eyes. "So, tell me Mena, why aren't ya married?" He caressed her wedding finger and shook his head the entire time he talked.

"I never found anybody who set me on fire." She giggled with a school-girl laugh.

Khadafi stared her up and down as if she were a piece of meat that he was preparing to devour. "Me know somebody came along who was good for ya." He grabbed her hands and pulled her close.

"Yeah, but I want what makes me happy. Somebody who'll nurture me…Makes me tingle inside. Someone who is good for me."

"Oh yeah. Ya tink me good for ya?"

"In some ways. I guess."

"What about in bed?"

Mena's bashful expression showed that she was shocked at how direct Khadafi was. And it seemed as if he'd leaned in more and held her hand tighter. She cleared her throat hoping to say what she wanted to say gracefully. "I…"

"If me ask ya a question ya promise not to slap me?"

Looking at what you did to that girl, you don't have to worry about that shit, Mena thought. "Go ahead…ask me."

"Can me have a kiss?"

His question had thrown Mena completely off guard. Even though she wanted to kiss him all night long, she didn't want to seem too easy. "Yes," she finally answered.

With eyes full of excitement, Khadafi slowly made his way toward Mena's lips. Once they made contact, what probably started off as just a peck turned into a deep passionate tongue wrestling session. Moments later, Khadafi began to kiss her neck, then her chest. Mena could tell he wanted something more. So did she.

"We're not gonna be able to do this in the front," she said.

"Me get us a hotel room, ya know," he managed to say as his tongue dove in and out of her bra.

"No, I want you now," she replied with a devilish smirk.

Not having to convince him, Khadafi quickly hopped out the driver's seat and into the back with Mena right behind. After pushing the driver and passenger seats up as far as they would go, it wasn't long before her shirt and bra were completely off. With soft, featherweight touches Khadafi kissed her shoulders and then lowered himself down to her breasts. He kissed each one lightly, and then licked her nipples, savouring the taste of her skin.

"Ya sure ya wanna do tis?" he asked all of a sudden. "Maybe we shouldn't mix business with pleasure."

"Yes," Mena moaned, "I need pleasure."

That's all Khadafi needed to hear before he gently pushed her down on the backseat. They didn't have much room, but in the heat of the moment who cared about accommodations. After removing her clothes, he stared at her body for a quick second before kissing her smooth stomach. Moments later, he slowly slid his tongue down between her thick thighs, quickly finding his way toward her protruding clitoris. When Khadafi started to suck her hanging lips, the juices from Mena's pussy ran down her leg. It was the best oral sex she'd ever had. The more his tongue dodged in and out of her nest, the hornier she got.

"I want you," Mena purred.

Her body shivered as Khadafi yanked his pants off, and exposed his rock hard dick. Because it was so dark she couldn't get a real good look, but she knew it had to be at least ten inches or more.

He rubbed the head up against her clit slowly, before finally inserting it inside. At that moment, there was no time to take it slow. Khadafi went all out. Mena clinched her teeth, then began digging her nails into his back as he pounded her walls. With each thrust, she moaned even louder sending him into overdrive. His hands gripped Mena's calves, while he dove his manhood in and out. By this time, the soles of her feet were completely flat against the ceiling. Khadafi's dick felt so good, Mena could've cared less about the fact that her head kept hitting the door panel. Khadafi took full control over her pussy, sending her into complete ecstasy.

"Fuck me harder!" she demanded.

Happy to oblige, Khadafi pushed his swelling dick as far as it could go. At that point both of them began to moan, bringing on a climax at the same time. "Oh, shit! Me about to cum gurl," he said before quickly pulling out.

Mena didn't even care where his sperm was headed as

she reached her own orgasm. While trying to control her breathing, she looked over at Khadafi who was breathing just as hard.

"Damn, if you fucked me like this in the car, I can only imagine what you'll do in the bedroom. I guess what they say about Jamaicans are true."

Khadafi couldn't help but laugh.

$Thirteen$

After twenty-four hours of no sleep, Mena finally cut the final stack of bills, then coached DJ on the detailed process of gluing both sides of the bills together. She wanted him to be able to construct the money from start to finish in case of an emergency. In her mind, she knew Ronni wasn't the right person for the job. Drake played lightly in the background as DJ worked and Ronni sat off to the side on the computer messing around on Facebook. The more Ronni laughed and degraded people's photos, Mena kept working. She made a few comments from time to time but focused on closing down her part of the money-making process. Once the starch and dryer procedures were done, Mena handed thirty grand off to DJ and had the rest set aside for herself.

"Where the fuck is my stack?" Ronni asked with a hard stance.

Mena sighed. "Where are your clients?"

"Well for one, bitch, the nigga you fucked last night is *my* client."

Mena huffed. She couldn't even respond. DJ's eyed widened, realizing that keeping Ronni from getting money wasn't going to be easy. He also questioned if Mena really fucked Khadafi the night before. Ronni continued to look at Mena sideways. She hated the way she took control.

"And two, Miss Loose Booty, I got people I'ma go see tonight," Ronni badgered, circling Mena like she was ready for a fight. "Don't go makin' decisions for me. I run this shit just like you do." Her voice thumped throughout the bedroom. "Is that me ova there?"

"That stack isn't done."

"Well make it done, bitch!"

Mena kept rolling her eyes as she moved quickly around the room, attempting to ignore Ronni. There was thirty-five thousand dollars on the bed exactly, bundled up into two even piles. She thought about giving Ronni one stack then decided against it.

"Look Ronni," Mena said, grabbing a Dick's Sporting Goods shopping bag from underneath the bed, "Khadafi got a sale for this money, and the rest of the money we brought down from Philly."

"The fifty grand?"

"Yep. And DJ already got people lined up. So, I'll make some more tomorrow." She hunched her shoulders as if it was nothing more to say. "I'm tired and don't feel like arguing with you."

"Tomorrow?" Ronni asked in a hard tone.

"Yep, tomorrow."

Ronni bucked, moving closer to the bed. She was becoming more and more frustrated by the minute. She thought about snatching the money off the bed and leaving without a care. She knew DJ wasn't tough enough to stop her. He had height, but in her eyes he was a punk, just knew a lot of people. Then she caught herself. It wasn't right to get crazy with Mena, she was obviously just dick whipped.

"Look, this shit not gonna go down like this. Now, somebody gonna give me a portion of their money until we make some more."

Suddenly, a horn beeped from outside causing Mena to smile.

"Ronni, I'm going to handle some business tonight, but I'll definitely make plenty more tomorrow. I love you, girl. You know I got you," she grinned while speedily stuffing the three stacks into her Gucci duffle bag.

Ronni started kicking unused newsprint paper across the floor, then played soccer with some of Mena's clothes. Her anger was intensifying, yet both Mena and DJ remained in their own world.

"We created the perfect American Dream and now you on your way to ruinin' it over some dick!" Ronni threw a can of starch into the wall. "Business is business, Mena!"

Just then, Camie burst into the room with a puzzled look on her face. She gazed at them all crazily. Quickly, her eyes scurried the room. She gawked at DJ, then Mena, and finally Ronni.

"What the fuck is going on in here?" Her arms spread wide and eyebrows crinkled near the edges. "DJ, is there something you forgot to tell me?"

Everyone assumed he would try to sound submissive since he'd been holding out on his girl. They were known to share everything, money, problems, and especially secrets. It was evident she was pissed.

"Not really," DJ replied.

"Not really? Are you serious?"

"Now's not the time, Camie."

"Okay DJ, let's do dinner away from the house." Camie held both hands in the air as a sign of surrender, knowing they had some things to work out in private. "We need to talk." She turned, expecting him to start walking behind. But he stood frozen with the money glued to the palm of his hand.

"Ahhhhhhh Camie, C'mon, chill baby. I'm working on something big."

"So when was you gonna tell me?" Her hands graced her hips then her eyes bounced from Mena to Ronni again. Of course Ronni egged her on giving her a look that said, *get his ass*.

"Now's not the time, Camie," he said not even giving her eye contact. He played around with his stack, separating the money into three separate piles. He then typed into his blackberry.

Mena gathered her things and left within seconds.

"So, you leavin' me behind to clean this shit up?" Ronni barked.

"Do whateva you want, Ronni. Just put the lock on the door." Mena looked over at Camie on her way out the door. "Well on second thought. I guess the lock is not needed anymore."

"I'm out, too," DJ told them all, leaving Camie standing in the room with Ronni.

"DJ, DJ," Camie called out repeatedly.

Several seconds later the front door slammed. Both Camie and Ronni stood in the middle of the room with hard, scolding faces. "I can't believe this bull shit. You know we just got played, right?" Ronni asked.

"I see," Camie said softly. "I don't know what's gotten into him."

Ronni composed herself long enough to pick up the mess she'd thrown across the room during her temper tantrum. Strangely, Camie helped by picking up a few pieces of paper off the floor. Ronni gazed at her thin, pale looking legs wondering how far she could get them above her shoulders. Then she laughed at herself.

"So Camie, you really want to know what's going on here?"

"I sure do. Whatever it is, it's changing DJ."

"You deserve to know," Ronni said, sounding like a marriage counselor. "You're a good girl. I mean I know you don't like me too much, but I know you good people."

The plan was to get on her good side in hopes of a relapse. But Camie wasn't going to be an easy fuck. But she did seem surprised as Ronni softened a bit.

"You a family woman, aren't you? I can tell by the way Mena said y'all spend time together...you know…actin' like white folk."

Camie laughed. Meanwhile Ronni was like a dog in heat. Camie's sweet fragrance had filled the room and was now already in the nasal tube of Ronni's nose.

"So Camie, I have a question….you in love wit' DJ?"

"Ahhhh…yes, of course I am." Ronni caught her off guard.

"Just because you love him doesn't mean you have to let that nigga talk to you like that," Ronni replied. "You ever had a woman make love to you?"

"Ahhhh hhh, Ronni, let's stop here." Camie clammed up again and began backing her way out the room. Her warm smile began to fade. It was good having someone to talk to about DJ, but Ronni was moving in the wrong direction.

"Girl, I could do some things to you to make you forget...what's his name, again?" Ronni snapped her fingers jokingly.

"No thanks, Ronni," Camie said, backing completely out of the door. But thanks for listening."

"Damn," Ronni whimpered. "You're one hard nut to crack."

Camie grinned. "I'll catch you later, Ronni."

At least we're friends for now, Ronni silently cheered.

$ Fourteen $

For the fifth time in less than an hour, Mena laughed, blushed, and almost cried. She and Khadafi sat side by side at the Italian restaurant, *Mercato* with his right arm wrapped around her waist and feeding her fried calamari from time to time with his left. Besides the fact that Mena had hips for days, he really was enjoying her company. They talked about everything from her childhood, to wanting to reconnect with her mother, to him wanting to open up his own Jamaican catering business. They seemed to fit like a glove even though Mena thought his long term goal was odd. Most of the drug dealers she knew up north went into real estate, which made Khadafi a rare, but interesting breed.

It was weird. Every time Mena even looked his way a funny feeling came over her. He was powerful, yet attentive and sweet all at the same time. Although her hormones were raging, it wasn't just about sex with him. He was the type that made you want to change your whole life, throw all your extra emergency numbers away, and start looking for a white dress.

As Mena finished up her shrimp scampi, her phone rang two quick times signaling that she had a text message. Thinking it was DJ, she grabbed her phone hoping her cousin had good news about the five grand he was supposed to make. Mena's face frowned instantly once she read the message.

I still can't believe ur ass left wit' out leavin' me my fuckin' share! That shit was foul. Bitch u betta have my money from what u sold when u come back or else!

Mena didn't take too kindly to Ronni's threat. She started to text back, but decided to take the high road.

"Is every ting okay?" Khadafi asked. "Dat wasn't ya boyfriend, right?"

Mena smiled. "I told you I don't have a boyfriend."

"Just checkin'. Me don't like liars."

"Me either, so I hope Fatima is really out of the picture," Mena shot back.

"Me don't deal wit' dat bloodclot anymore. Me heard da people at Red Lobster wanted her to call da police, but she told them no. Me would'a buried her if she did. Trust me."

Not wanting to get Khadafi in a bad mood, Mena decided to drop the subject. Besides, they still had to meet up with two of Khadafi's connections and the last thing she needed was for Khadafi to change his mind.

An hour later, Mena held Khadafi's hand as they drove steadily through Moncks Corner, a small town thirty-three miles west of Charleston. Mena had no idea who they were going to meet, but Khadafi insisted during the forty minute drive that the guy was cool.

"Me didn't used to deal wit' white boys back when me first started me career, but tis guy has earned his stripes," Khadafi joked as he made a right onto Lakewind Drive.

While Mena eyed the nice custom built homes, she thought to herself, *I'm not used to dealing with white boys either, but I don't have a choice but to trust your judgment.*

Pulling up into the driveway of the thirty-four hundred square foot suburban home, she continued to survey the perfectly manicured lawn, two-car garage and unique double front porch that Charleston homes were famous for. It didn't look like someone up to no good would live there.

"Are you sure we're in the right place?" Mena asked.

Khadafi smiled. "What were ya expectin', pretty gurl? Some rat infested neighborhood wit' crack heads walkin' around?"

Just as Mena was about to speak, a loud and dirty Ford F-150 pulled up behind them. Breaking her neck to look in her side view mirror, she watched as a tall white guy with ripped jeans and a green John Deer hat walked up to the car. He looked like he was going to a red neck convention more so than doing business with them.

"Dafi, what's going on brother?" the white man spoke in a country accent. He tried to give Khadafi a brotherly hand-shake, but just couldn't seem to get it together.

"What's sup, Dillon?" Khadafi replied.

Dillon looked in the car. "Who's this? What happened to Fatima?" It was obvious he didn't care about fucking up Khadafi's love life.

"Fuck dat bloodclot. She's history. Tis me new gurl, Mena."

Dillon nodded his head. "Hello Mena."

"Hello," Mena answered. She was flattered at what Khadafi said, but had no idea they were claiming each other al-ready.

"Mena, get da bag," Khadafi instructed. "So, ya got da money? Is it all there?"

Dillon pulled a white envelope from under his dingy t-shirt. "Yeah, here it is. Are you sure about this Khadafi? I mean, maybe I should test it out first."

Khadafi got hype. "Have me ever steered ya wrong? We been doin' business a long time and I've neva fucked ya ova. How dare ya question me?" His nostrils flared.

"Oh no, I wasn't trying to insult you. It's just that I've never known you to deal in this kind of business before," Dillon said turning red.

Khadafi grabbed the bag from Mena. "Well, tis is me new business now." Once Dillon handed him the envelope, Khadafi passed the shopping bag back to his client. "Trust me, ya be back for more. That's twenty grand."

At that moment, Mena's phone went off again. It was an-other text message from Ronni.

Bitch, what's takin' u so long? Hurry up wit' my money!

Turning off her phone at this point, Mena listened as Khadafi and Dillon wrapped up the transaction. Seconds later, Dillon walked back to his truck, backed out of the driveway and took off.

Khadafi didn't waste any time opening up the envelope. After quickly counting out ten thousand dollars, he handed Mena seventy-five hundred. "Tis me fee," he said, taking the other twenty-five.

The smell of real money gave Mena an instant high. "So, you charged him half?"

"Yes. Is someting wrong wit' dat?"

"No, not at all. It's just that we were supposed to do, one-fourth, remember?"

"Me remember, but decided to change policy. Ya okay with that?"

She shrugged her shoulders first, then said, "More money for us, I guess."

"Good, then let's go," Khadafi said, getting out of the car.

Mena looked confused. "Where are we going? I thought this was Dillon's house. He just left."

"No, it's mine."

As Khadafi made his way to open her door, Mena couldn't believe that he was taking her to where he laid his head already. *Niggas in Philly don't wife you this soon,* she thought. *Maybe it's a country thing.* Whatever the case was, Mena was glad that he'd decided to fuck with her. It was almost as if they were meant to be together.

$Fifteen$

Hours passed with Ronni still spread out across the bed catching the tail end of the movie, *Training Day*. It seemed strange that she would be spending a Thursday night alone. But that's what her life had come to in Charleston. Let Ronni tell it; everybody was out making money, fucking, or splurging, while she was being sabotaged by Mena and her controlling personality.

Suddenly, Ronni hopped up to watch herself in the mirror imitating Denzel as he said, "Who the fuck you think you fucking with? I'm the police! I run shit here…y'all just live here! Yeah, that's right you betta walk away. Gone walk away cuz I'ma burn this muthafucka down. King Kong ain't got shit on me!" Ronni banged her fist against her chest like an erratic woman, then rubbed her hand across the black doo-rag that covered her frizzy cornrows.

She suddenly stopped, then allowed her eyes to roll to the back of head for several seconds. Out of the blue Ronni laughed wildly just as she did whenever she watched that scene. It reminded her so much of herself; especially the cockiness. By the time the credits rolled, Ronni was pacing the room. Just that quick her temperament had changed again. The movie had psyched her into wanting to fuck Mena up for leaving her high and dry. And the fact that Mena hadn't texted her back angered her more.

"Oh so bitch, this how we playin', huh?" she asked herself, real rowdy-like.

Instantly, Ronni became enraged. She threw the phone across the room then twisted her neck toward the closet. It was time to make Mena pay. With quick, steep strides, Ronni rushed the closet yanking out Mena's favorite possessions onto the floor. She knew her girl loved clothes and shoes more than anything. The intent was to make her feel what she was feeling at the moment. Disrespected. It was payback time.

Piece by piece, she began ripping Mena's two-hundred dollar Hudson jeans like a jealous boyfriend who'd been waiting on his cheating woman all night. The sound of sturdy denim being ripped echoed throughout the room. Christian Louboutin, Gucci, Dolce Vita… you name it, it got fucked up. Ronni tossed things about until she stopped abruptly. She paused, out of breath, while eyeing the white plastic bag with crisp, green bills hanging from the sides. Her breathing pattern finally slowed a bit as her thoughts played ping pong inside her head.

"Oh, this whore stashin' money now," Ronni said to herself. Swiftly she grabbed the bag, opening it in a hurry, and estimating with the intensity of a calculator.. The count…about twenty-five grand.

"This bitch, Mena!" she uttered.

Ronni allowed the crisp bills to glide through her fingertips as one of her hair-brained ideas popped into her head. One that she assured herself would be a sure bet. Although it was Mena's idea to hit up the south with counterfeiting… that game was moving a little too slow for Ronni.

That's when it all came together. She needed to get back to what she did best. Ronni was a dope dealer by trade; had been since she was seventeen. So, if Mena thought she was going to hold her hostage, she had another thing coming. The money was just what she needed to buy product and attract customers of her own to a different industry.

Quickly, she threw on some oversized basketball shorts and a lightweight jacket, to cover her tank, never removing the doo-rag, and headed for the door. Her swagga seemed to intensify even though she hadn't made moves yet. But that was just

Ronni, overly confident and conceited. By the time she hopped in the car and drove over to North Charleston, a place she'd hung out a bit her first night in town, she'd mapped everything out in her hand. What better place to start than Forest Park, where some fake baller she had met said he worked the neighborhood.

When the white Bentley pulled onto Playground Road minutes later, all eyes moved in that direction. The Philly tags were an instant deterrent and those nearby doing wrong scattered. It was a strange car to see in that hood and one that hadn't been welcomed there before. So, no ooh's and aahs sounded as Ronni expected. She parked in a slanted position then stuffed her gun underneath the seat as she surveyed the area from inside. Aside from the many children running around, most of the adult activity seemed to take place near the basketball courts.

Wall-to-wall niggas lined the gates wearing low-hanging jeans and plain white t-shirts, all except the few bare backs who lifted weights like they were on the yard at Leavenworth Penitentiary. Ronni hopped out of the car boldly and approached the first person she saw. He was a tall boy who looked like he needed to be in the NBA.

"What up?' he greeted in a southern tone.

"I'm tryna spend some money," Ronni told the young boy who appeared to be in his early teens.

"I'll take it."

"Fuck you, lil nigga."

He grinned and pointed toward a concrete slab about five yards away that sat at about five feet off the ground. Within seconds, Ronni noticed two guys on top of the concrete slab and headed in that direction. She picked up the pace while eyeing them all, wondering if she'd made a mistake by leaving her pistol in the car. It wasn't for the niggas, it was for the two big pits who were losing control the closer she got.

It wasn't her surroundings she feared. Ronni never feared the hood. She was the hood; Philly hood at that. She'd been around the projects all her life and it was where she felt most comfortable. With the pit bulls barking like crazy, she moved past all the bystanders with confidence wondering who to approach on the slab first.

It became some oh 'eeny meeny miny moe' type shit as they all had dreadful scowls across their faces. There were two guys standing on level ground, and one leaning, who was smoking a blunt and looked like he smoked just as much crack as he sold, and two sitting up high on top of the concrete stoop, one acting like he was the Prince of Whales. No one said a word, only stares.

Eventually Ronni walked right up on the guy who looked like he was the man and whose face looked just as gruesome as the pits who were tied up and barking nearby. It tripped Ronni out that he sat like he was the shit, in a fold-up picnic type chair. Although his face was nasty-looking, he was super cut up like Debo from the Movie, *Friday*, and his muscles bulged from beneath his t-shirt that had a picture of Tupac on the front. He had a huge platinum chain with a dollar sign swinging from his neck that seemed to catch Ronni's attention as she spoke.

"Who slingin' the good shit out here?" she asked boldly, then pulled the white plastic bag from the corner of her jacket.

The man's eyes squinted. He didn't quite understand how to process Ronni's boldness. None of the guys smiled back or even attempted to speak. The only sound that could be heard was the cocking sound of someone's Smith and Wesson.

"This bitch 5-0, Noble?" the scrawny guy who quickly stumped his blunt into the ground asked. His face had that, *we're all about to get busted* look.

Ronni never flinched. "Do I look like 5-0?" she asked with a sly grin. "I'm offended," she told them all with her hands in the air. "So, Noble," she continued, letting the guy with the chain know that she now knew his name. "I didn't come here on no bullshit. I'm 'bout business," she added, while pulling out the money. She looked around making sure to watch her back, seeing that the guy to her left still had his gun out. "I'm from Philly, the real hood," she bragged. "Just down here for a while wit' my fam. But I need to buy some shit, and some folks tell me you the man," she lied.

Noble raised his chin up with interest but kept his face balled up. "You got I.D. ?" he asked, speaking for the first time.

"I.D.? What the fuck?"

"Yeah, I.D. That's what the fuck I said!"

Ronni slipped her hands into her shorts and took two steps toward Noble only to get stopped by a heavy-set bald guy who appeared out of nowhere. His right hand was tucked into his jeans insinuating that he was either playing with his crotch or had his hand on his piece.

"Lemme see that," he told Ronni as he took her driver's license and handed it up to Noble.

Noble studied it for minutes before asking, "What you lookin' fo'?"

"A half of a key if the price is right." She shot him a look asking if he could produce.

"What would make you think a mufucka got that kinda weight out here. We don't even know you. But I know somebody who know somebody," he told Ronni in his Barry White voice. "Give my little man right there twelve grand and he'll get it to the right person."

"Twelve?"

"Yes, twelve thousand," one of Noble's workers chimed in.

Ronni twisted her lips and turned her head in frustration. When she turned back around to look at Noble again she stole a chance to study him deeply in the face. His profile appeared to be permanently bawled up and he reminded Ronni of his pit bulls. She thought the shit was comical but didn't want to piss Noble off.

"Look here Noble, I'm not 5-0, I assure you. I don't give a fuck if somebody's grandma get the shit. Just don't fuck wit' my doe. I'm not used to working like this. After all, I just met you."

She took a few seconds to count out the twelve grand

and handed the money off to the little dude who bounced a ball back and forth between his legs. As soon as the money was passed, the sounding of the ball stopped and two of the four guys disappeared, leaving Noble and the bald guy with the gun behind.

Ronni stood a few yards back feeling like she'd just visited royalty and couldn't get close enough to him for a basic conversation. Noble clearly wasn't a talker so Ronni stood with her hands stuffed in her pockets looking for the right words to break the ice.

"You know I can bring some real dro down here if you got the right clientele, right?"

Noble said nothing.

"No really. I make shit happen. You need to ask somebody 'bout me."

Noble laughed slightly and shook his head as if he couldn't take it anymore. "Ask who?" he wanted to know.

Ronni started name dropping as she felt like she'd taken a few baby steps with Noble. "You know DJ from Blazin' Kutz?"

His face scrunched up. "Who the fuck is that?" His voice roared over the loud noise of the hood.

"He got that shop on Dorchester Road. Everybody know'em. Those my peoples," she bragged.

Noble looked at his boy and they both had a shared moment. "Why the fuck would I know a damn barber?"

"I guess not," Ronni fired back after taking a second look at Noble's unkempt fro and the nasty looking hair that was growing all over his face. "What about Khadafi or Skully," she added.

"Oh, you know Skully?" Noble questioned. All of a sudden he seemed interested.

"That's my man." Ronni smiled. "Me and Khadafi real cool."

"I 'on know shit about Khadafi personally…heard the name before but that nigga Skully I know. He a bad dude...put his work in on the murder scene."

Ronni got extra happy. "See you thought I was on some bullshit. I'm bringin' some shit down for Skully next week. Here, take my number, and get at me." She took two more steps forward, close enough for Noble to reach out and grab the piece of paper. "I'ma sell this shit then I'll be back if it's some good," she said as she saw the young guy approaching with nothing in his hand.

Things seemed leery but Ronni remained calm. "Get up wit' a bitch," she told Noble. "Let's break bread tomorrow or something. Let it do, what it do, baby."

"We'll see."

She frowned when the guy who'd taken the money was close to where she stood. She then glanced from Noble to the guy. "Where my shit?" she barked.

"Yo, my man gone walk you to your ride. I got yo number, and he'll give you one to get in touch with me. Aye, one last thing. If I find out you set me up or you 5-0, static comin' yo' way." Noble stood up showing that he was built like he lifted weights for a living.

"Aye, lil nigga, where my shit?" Ronni said, again figuring she was about to get played.

"I got it, right here." He patted his jacket to let Ronni know everything was on the up and up. "We not gone do this shit out here in the open," he said as if he was schooling her.

Ronni looked at the young guy with hatred realizing he was walking her to her car like a little kid. But before she could even turn back toward Noble for goodbyes, he'd disappeared off the platform and someone else was untying the dogs to leave the area too.

"Everything betta turn out a'yite," a voice sounded from behind. "Or it's rock-a-bye baby," another one of Noble's goons said with the cocking of a gun.

Ronni could hear the threats from behind while walking to the car, but she wasn't worried about shit. She'd sell Noble's shit and be back for more by the end of the week.

$Sixteen$

Everyone knew time was Mena's pet peeve, but no one seemed to give a shit. The meeting was scheduled to take place at 8 o'clock sharp just one hour after Blazin' Kutz had officially closed, and DJ still hadn't arrived. The streets were nearly bare with the exception of a few people walking on the opposite side of the street bombarding the Koreans for chicken wings and mumbo sauce. Mena, Khadafi and Ronni all stood out front choosing not to exchange words, only evil stares. It was turning out to be a jealously issue where Mena had abandoned her friend to give love another shot.

Two days had passed since their last unfriendly encounter where Ronni was denied any access to money and Mena left with Khadafi in a hurry. Why? Ronni couldn't understand. But it was clearly the sex. That was the real reason why she hadn't been back to DJ's …48 hours of good loving. Mena knew she'd had a few wild ones in her day, but nothing compared to Khadafi. And nobody was going to fuck up her chances of being his lady.

For Mena, things had blossomed into full swing, both sexually and financially. All the money she printed for her and Khadafi and the money she brought down from Philly had been sold. And over ten people had placed decent orders with them to be delivered by Monday. The fact that Mena hadn't been back to the house or even called angered Ronni most; not to mention the phony personality she carried while Khadafi was in her presence.

Ronni eyeballed her girl who stood close to Khadafi like she was paid to do so. The fact that Khadafi palmed her ass and held it firmly like it belonged to him didn't sit well with Ronni either. But she had to admit, Mena appeared to be happier than she'd seen her in years. And she looked good, too. Her three inch Sergio Rossi peep-toe heels and her short, black Theory skirt showed off her thick thighs and the sleek cut top that stopped mid-way past her belly exposing her sexy navel.

"Mena, Mena, Mena," Ronni repeated.

"Where the fuck is he?"Mena asked out loud while checking her watch and blatantly ignoring Ronni. "I can't believe he's doing this," she added, hoping to get a budge from Khadafi who was handling business and never even took his eyes off his phone.

Ronni didn't care about DJ being late. She simply hated the site of her girl clutched up with someone who looked like he had her on lockdown. While Khadafi typed messages back and forth into his phone, Ronni encircled them both, pacing the sidewalk continuously.

"My girl Mena, baby girl will always catch her a big fish wit' some bread," Ronni badgered.

Mena disregarded her comments the best she could. She was like a schoolgirl smitten by her new boo. She kept a firm hold on Khadafi's elbow as her hand remained interlocked between his arm and his one hand still planted firmly on her ass. Every now and then she'd roll her eyes in Ronni's direction.

"Damn bitch, where's your pride?" Ronni blurted. "I mean go ahead and bark like a dog. Jump on one leg," she mocked while acting like Eddie's Murphy's bride-to-be in *Coming to America*.

Ronni continued to joke while Mena twisted her lips and kept a watch out for DJ who was now twenty minutes late. It seemed as if they were all getting restless. The sun had gone down, and dusk was quickly approaching. Out of the blue Ronni noticed a strange looking Dodge Charger creep up the street, but turned onto one of the alleyways belonging to a business across the street.

"Oh, so Chinks driving Chargers now?" Ronni laughed until she saw that no one else thought her joke was funny.

Mena never even looked her way. It seemed that her complete attention focused on Khadafi who held his Blackberry to his ear, meticulously spitting words to Skully that obviously troubled her.

"Me not tinkin' about dat. She just tryin' to start trouble. She has noting betta to do," Khadafi said, as Mena listened like a nosey neighbor. "Dats a problem," he said in a very stern tone. "When me finish here, we can meet up."

Mena placed her hand gently on his chest and snuck a soft kiss on his cheek hoping that he wasn't interested in a new woman or that Khadafi wasn't having problems with another old love. At this point she was ready to fight for her man. Once he hung up, she started to drill Khadafi about what she'd heard but when DJ's big, tall frame whizzed past them, stuffed in a turbo Porsche Panamera truck with paper tags, all eyes ballooned and jaws dropped.

DJ quickly parked the silver machine curbside in front of Khadafi's Benz and hopped out like he was the man. "You like?" he asked, pimping over toward the shop. The excitement showed on his face as he greeted everyone. "What up people?"

"What's up, my ass!" Mena belted. She stood with her hands on her hips as DJ pulled out his keys and bypassed them all to unlock the door. "So, you buying new cars already? You haven't made any real money yet, crazy?"

"I sold all my shit," he bragged. "And why you hating Mena? If I want a new ride, I want a new ride." DJ laughed as he unlocked the door and held it open for everyone to pass through, waving his hand downward like a high-paid doorman.

"But, you've only been doing this biz for two days," Mena fussed as she entered the shop. "And I only gave you 30k which means you made $7,500." Mena's anger showed as she spoke rapidly in the middle of the barber shop's linoleum floor. "And all the money you made is not yours to keep," she blasted.

"You do realize that wasn't a part of the deal, right?" Her voice deepened with concern.

DJ rubbed his hands together with the same wide smile plastered across his face that he had when he first pulled up. Apparently nothing Mena said could upset him. "Look cuz, I sold all my shit. All of it," he boasted. "And I got folks lined up to buy a lot more over the next few days."

Mena's tight cheeks relaxed a bit as she turned to see what Khadafi and Ronni thought. The two of them both sat on opposite sides of the room in the black leather barber chairs that lined the wall doing their own thing. Ronni had an XXL magazine held up to her face and a few Source issues in her lap. Her head remained deep in the printed pages while Khadifi showed his disapproval of DJ with silence and a mean grimace on his face.

Mena continued with her raving as DJ turned on a few lights and opened the blinds slightly, "DJ, I'm just not understanding why you think you can go out and buy a fucking Porsche. I know that car is an easy $135,000. You're doing too much too fast."

"Mena, why are you so concerned?" DJ laughed then walked over to the soda machine and slipped a dollar through the slit. "Cuz, I got credit. The money I'm about to make is gonna be crazy. I'm gonna be mad paid, so I got me a car. Plus, I'm headed to ATL on Wednesday for some folks who ordered 50k. Khadafi, you got folks out there, right?"

Khadafi just nodded. "Maybe. We'll see. You know me don't do too much talkin' in the open."

"Right, right," DJ repeated, grabbing his Pepsi from the bottom of the machine.

Mena's frustration showed but she knew it was time to get down to business. "So DJ, where's the real money you made from the counterfeit I gave you?" She took a few steps in his direction holding her hand out.

DJ pulled two stacks from his back pocket, handing them to Mena with pride and took a seat next to Ronni with a sly grin. As Mena thumbed through the cash, DJ tried to come out the mouth real slick. "So, what you pull in this week?" he asked Ronni with sarcasm.

"An AK 47, you wanna see it?" Ronni's face showed she was serious.

"Damn, Ronni, a muthafucka can't even play with you no more. I guess since you back to slinging powder it has changed you. You all uptight," DJ said, taking a swig from his Pepsi bottle.

Ronni's eyes lit up. *How the fuck did he find out*? She wondered. She knew DJ was trying to dry snitch on her so she went at him hard. "Fuck you, country boy. What you know about powder? Or anybody who sells it."

"No, fuck you, girl-boy," DJ quickly shot back.

"Okay, okay stop it," Mena told everyone after seeing that Khadafi was irritated by all the craziness. He was interested in making money only and had made it clear to Mena earlier that he had no interest in either Ronni or DJ.

"Me want you to come sit rych here," Khadafi told Mena, patting the bar stool that sat next to his chair. "Let's get dis meetin' on a role."

"Yes, Mena sit by your ruler," Ronni added. "As a matter of fact, go ahead and suck that nigga's dick right here."

"Fuck you, Ronni," Mena called out, taking a seat next to Khadafi.

Ronni's head moved from right to left with pity. "Isn't that sweeeet," she mocked then became enraged. "This is bullshit," she erupted then tossed the magazines on the floor. "What's this whack-ass meetin' about anyway?" Ronni asked loudly. "Get on with it."

Mena began with an overview on how much she'd printed and how much they'd sold within the past two days. She then talked about what she expected over the next few weeks and wanted to know if anyone had experienced any problems.

"So, I'm going to spend the next few days printing about $300,000," Mena exclaimed proudly. "That's based on what

Khadafi needs, and what DJ says he needs, about 50k, right?" she turned to ask DJ. "And Ronni, I'm printing you twenty grand."

Ronni finally became semi-interested in what Mena was saying. "That's cool," she responded not wanting to seem too pleased. It wasn't a lot, but enough for now to keep her happy.

"Printing three hundred thousand will take some work, so I'll need some help," Mena explained.

"Look, bitch I'll help, but I'm not in kindergarten so I want to do more than just glue," Ronni advised.

Mena rolled her eyes. "Ronni, cut it out, I'll need help with the meticulous parts. Why you always gotta complain?"

"I'm not complainin'. I'm just expressin' an opinion. You need to show me how to make that money so while you out fuckin', production is still on the move." Ronni paused. "I mean does anybody agree? How we gon' run a successful operation if Mena is the only one who knows how to make the money perfectly from start to finish?"

"You right about that," DJ chimed in. "I did it once from start to finish, but I'm no pro. But for now, I'm good. I'll need my money first though, I leaving for Atlanta tomorrow."

"Well me and Khadafi got one customer who's tryna see us tomorrow, too. He wants 45k, so we gotta get busy as soon as we leave here," Mena advised.

Ronni was about to comment but the front door opened quickly, too fast for anyone to react. Gun shots blasted and the deafening sounds of bullets ricocheting off the walls was all that could be heard above Mena's screams. Two men had filed in wearing all black, shades, and black doo-rags that stopped beneath their foreheads, each toting Desert Eagles and .357 Magnums, one in each hand.

It didn't take long for Khadafi to spring into action while Ronni, DJ and Mena dove for cover. The gun fire was like something out of a movie as glass shattered from the mirrors that used to line the walls and bullet holes plastered pictures and barbicide disinfecting jars. Within seconds, Khadafi found himself the only one with gun power, battling against the unknown assailants on one knee who were both hidden behind a wall near the front door. They'd both taken cover and were now just shooting for the hell of it.

Khadafi, on the other hand preserved his bullets considering he only had two shots left. His goal, one shot; one kill. Suddenly, all fire ceased. Khadafi had taken cover on the side of the soda machine and hoped like hell his last two bullets were enough for him to make it out alive. Things had gotten quiet and no one could really see each other. Wailing sounds were heard beneath the last chair in the shop, but a face couldn't be seen; only cries.

Little did Khadafi know the silence meant trouble. One of the unknown assailants had taken a fresh clip out of his pocket and replaced the old one accompanied by a strong grin.

Out of the blue a voice called out. "Yo, you thought you was gonna give Noble counterfeit money and live?"

All eyes ballooned; especially Ronni's. Although she had no idea that the money she'd given Noble was counterfeit, it was confirmed that they were there for her.

"You gotta be taught a lesson, midget!" one of the gunmen said.

Ronni wanted to break bad, but she was unsure how to handle the situation without her heat. From that day forward she vowed to stay armed. It was now down to life or death and with Khadafi being the only one to have her back, she chose her words carefully.

"Aye, that wasn't me!" she yelled from beneath DJ's station. "Tell Noble we gotta talk. I paid for my shit wit' real money. Whateva happened after that don't got shit to do wit' me."

When Ronni finished explaining, she sighed at the sound of sirens approaching. She wasn't sure if the two dudes had bought her story, but at least help was on the way. One by one, the assailants covered each other and jetted toward the front door hoping to escape the police. With two shots left Khadafi wanted to make them both winners. He leaned out just enough to catch the back side of the taller gunman and fired twice.

Both shots missed as the two men disappeared onto the street. It wasn't clear from the inside if the police out front had caught a glimpse of the two men or captured either one. One thing was for certain; Khadafi wasn't going to be around for the interrogation. Within seconds, he'd rushed toward the back of the shop, broke the lock off the back door and exited without saying a word to Mena or DJ. It all happened so quickly; so quickly that Mena never got a chance to see her man leave.

Before they knew it, the police were inside swarming the place with their guns drawn. Mena, DJ and Ronni had their hands in the air explaining one by one. It took all of five minutes before DJ cleared himself as the owner of Blazin' Kutz and Mena and Ronni as his out of town family. For nearly an hour, the threesome were questioned about the gunmen, what they looked like, what they said, and if they had any suspects in mind.

DJ remained silent with hatred in his heart knowing that Ronni was the cause of his shop looking like the set of a *Wild Wild West* film. It would take weeks to get things back in order and tons of money if the insurance company didn't pay. DJ wanted to say something about Ronni knowing who they were, but couldn't prove it. He remained calm through most of the questioning and just prayed that they would leave soon after dusting for prints.

Meanwhile Mena said nothing, only muffles and cries. She'd cried enough to mop the floor with her tears and no one understood why. The police asked repeatedly if she was hurt or wanted to go to the police station. She simply nodded a negative. Her main thought was Khadafi. What would he think? Would he want to see her again after bringing so much unnecessary bull his way?

Nearly two hours passed before everyone was done and the last officer shut the door. Mena's eyes dropped to the floor as DJ swept up the last dust pan full of glass. *It was always Ronni*, she told herself as she shook her head in pity. Ronni always messed up anything worth having.

"I can't believe you, Ronni!" Mena said staring her down. "You took that unfinished money from our closet, didn't you?"

Ronni tensed up but shrugged her comment off. "What? Don't ask me shit. You blamin' me for this?" she questioned.

Mena got so close to Ronni's face that Ronni could see her smeared mascara from all the crying. "Mmm hmmm…so where'd you get money to give to this Noble guy?" Mena kept blowing fire with her eyes. "You tried to print money?" she yelled.

"Fuck no!" Ronni yelled back.

"Yes, you did!"

"No, I didn't Mena. Now get the fuck outta my face before I slap your yellow ass!"

The shouting match continued until Mena calmed herself a bit massaging her forehead. "You're gonna tell me what you did Ronni. I know you took that money from the closet. It wasn't done, idiot," she exclaimed before grabbing her purse.

"Bitch please, stop whining. Did anybody die?" Ronni asked with her hands spread apart. Her eyes scanned the room zooming in on the bullet holes in DJ's wall. "We gettin' money right?" she asked both Mena and DJ. "And didn't we just have a Forbes meetin' about gettin' more?" She nodded and gave everyone a thuggish look. "Those niggas just jealous. But they gon' pay," she belted then walked out of the shattered glass door.

$Seventeen$

Money was coming in like water through a faucet and everyone drank heavily. Only one month into the business and Counterfeit LLC had come up in a big way. The four person crew had developed a good strategy for producing money on time and had developed a flourishing clientele. Their names rang throughout Charleston, and neighboring towns and states; just as they'd planned.

Thousands had been made; close to the half a million range in just thirty days flat. For Khadafi, that meant stepping things up a notch. Silently, he'd named himself the ring leader. And had a plan for disposing of DJ and Ronni. For the time being, each played their part with DJ and Khadafi completely on sales and Ronni and Mena selling from time to time, but had the meticulous job of producing most of the fake dough. Ronni had some clientele on her own, but not as thick as the others. She dibbled and dabbled in and out of the drug game so her focus was never clear.

For Mena, she was a business woman at heart, grinding day by day, and still never showing Ronni how to completely make the money from start to finish. There were still some trust issues that bothered her, but none which could be discussed. Ronni had been hanging out with a wild crew and some that neither she nor Khadafi approved of. The fact that she'd made amends with Noble after giving him counterfeit money and they were now thick as thieves puzzled them all. Ronni didn't talk about it much, just said, "Hey, I fucked up. But that nigga know

I make shit happen, so he want to be down with anything I'm a part of. It sounded crazy to Mena, and there was that feeling of distrust amongst everyone.

Mena sat at the table in the back bedroom of DJ's apartment like a factory worker rubbing her eyes as she passed a stack of hundreds off to Ronni. Once Ronni did a thorough inspection of each bill, she placed rubber bands around stacks of ten thousand, then placed the finished currency on the floor. Ronni smiled every time she looked at the mounting pile of money that had made it to the window seal.

"I love the sight of doe," Ronni said, wiping her sweaty forehead with the back of her hand.

Mena never took her eyes off the computer. "Who doesn't, especially if you didn't have to work for it."

"Damn, it's hot in here. I need to take a break. We been at this shit non-stop for six hours. It's a Friday night and we in here workin' like damn slaves."

"Look, we're almost done. As soon as we split the money up we can shut down for the night."

"Bitch, I'm shuttin' down now. Fuck this. You not gonna work me to death. I'm goin' to make a grilled cheese sandwich," Ronni said as she made her way toward the door. "You want one?"

"No," Mena said with an attitude.

"On second thought, you don't need one. Your hips look like they spreadin'."

"Fuck you, Ronni," Mena shouted as she left the room.

Even though she hated Ronni's comment, it was true. She had picked up a little bit of weight. But more importantly her breast seemed to swell, and she was always tired. Mena hated to admit it, but she was probably pregnant. She had only missed her period by two weeks, so only a pregnancy test would be the true indicator.

$$$

As half past ten approached, Mena packed her overnight bag just as she'd been doing for the last two weeks, never even missing a night. It was late and unusually cool for a June night, but Mena decided on a off the shoulder, form fitting black dress that stopped just beneath her butt cheeks. She was feeling extra horny for some reason and pleased that Khadafi had promised to take her to a benefit hosted by DeAngelo Williams, a football star with the Carolina Panthers. Mena was geared up for a change in scenery and ready to have some fun for the weekend.

The fact that Khadafi socialized with ballers in the NFL excited her and Mena couldn't wait to meet them all and be introduced as his lady. She'd been told that the Ballantyne Resort Hotel in Charlotte, North Carolina and DeAngelo's event was the place to be and anyone who'd gotten invited were amongst Carolina's *it* crew. Besides that, Mena felt she and Khadafi needed some RFR; rest, fuck, and relaxation. Things had gotten pretty serious between the two; numerous phone calls throughout the day, shopping sprees on weekends and out of town impromptu trips. Life was good and they both seemed to be loving it.

Mena walked over to where she had her clothes laid out on the bed and began stuffing her things into the bag. Ronni stared her down with envy.

"You realize we came out this mufucka together and you haven't hung out wit' me one night without dread boy?"

"Ronni, don't start. Please." Mena's eyes glared at her girl almost begging. "Look, we're doing something special tonight and Sunday we're going to see my mother."

"Isn't that sweet. One big happy family. A non-talkin' Jamaican, a crack-head, and a flunky. I feel sorry for your children," she added sarcastically.

"Ronni, I'm not going to argue with you," Mena said, grabbing her make-up bag off the dresser. "You know the saying, Misery Loves Company."

"Oh, I'm not miserable. You're the miserable one. Have you noticed everyone has been spendin' their money as they please and yours is at Khadafi's?" She paused and shot Mena an even nastier look. "Umph…you even more stupid than I thought," Ronni blurted. "I mean DJ out lookin' for a new house, Khadafi got two new trucks, I got all this jewelry," she said, pointing to a fifty thousand dollar blinged-out chain that lay across her chest, "and you, Mena have nothin' but a bunch of expensive shoes."

"Ronni, I do what I want with the money I've been making. And for your information, I've only bought tons of clothes. I'm saving for my wedding, bitch."

"Sure, Mena," Ronni shot back. "Khadafi is gankin' your dumb ass. Where's the ring?" Ronni paused again, sticking her hands into her two front jean pockets. "That nigga holdin' your money hostage."

Right on cue, the horn of Khadafi's new Range Rover blared. "I'll see you on Monday. Don't eat too much pussy this weekend," Mena sang, throwing her bag over her shoulder and rushing out of the door.

$$$

Later that night, things happened just as Khadafi said they would. They pulled up to The Ballantyne, a swanky hotel just eighteen miles from downtown Charlotte. Off the break Mena became googly-eyed at the Maseratis, Maybachs and six figure cars that were parked out front. She'd seen many extravagant rides before, but all in one place was rare from the places she hung out in Philly.

Khadafi hopped out first wearing a white button down Giorgio Armani shirt, slacks, and Gucci loafers; then made his way around to the passenger side of the truck to greet his lady. Mena was all teeth as he held his hand out for her to grab. It seemed that all eyes were on the attractive couple as they waltzed their way inside.

Once in the lobby, all traffic led to the ballroom to the left of the hotel. It was extraordinary, lit up like the Taj Mahal and resembled wedding-like decor. Everyone was dressed lavishly and the neo soul music that played lightly in the background fit the atmosphere perfectly.

It was clear that the white leather couches and the contemporary furniture had been flown in just for the event. The ballroom had been transformed into a sexy, dimly lit after hours spot and Mena was ready to get freaky with her man. Tons of people covered the main floor dancing seductively to Raheem DeVaughn's song *Marathon* and grabbing glasses of champagne from the many trays being carried around. Mena watched as people made their way through the crowd. It didn't take long for her to spot the NFL player, DeAngelo Williams, and Chris Gamble, the cornerback who was seen on television often. Her intent was to star watch.

Suddenly, a man who looked to be in his early thirties, wearing all black and sporting long, vertical tattoos on both sides of his face stepped in front of Khadafi with ease. He seemed out of place with his hands tucked into his pockets. His skin tone stood out as the darkest and murkiest in the room. Yet Khadafi had no fear.

"My man Khadafi," he greeted, "that was cold," Black uttered then scrunched his face up a bit. "You on some mafia shit now I hear."

"Not the time or place," Khadafi suggested. "Me here wit' me lady." He grabbed Mena's hand as if to protect her.

"I see. At least she can be with her dude, unlike India. She'll never see him again thanks to you."

Khadafi gave Black a hard stare that quickly turned into a deranged expression, one that Mena had never seen before. "Whoaaaa, ya playin' wit' fire baby boy," Khadafi countered. "I think ya need to back up. Let's chomp it up later."

Black stepped aside allowing them to pass, but let out one last comment that made Mena's skin crawl. "All bodies wash up someday, you know? People just don't disappear into thin air!"

Mena cut her eyes at the charcoal looking man as they walked away. Unfortunately, they were approached by another gentleman. She sighed. "Uhhh….not again."

"Is this you, Khadafi?" the six foot six athletic gentleman asked showing his interest in Mena. He held out his fist for Khadafi to hit back with his.

"What'cha ask me someting like dat for? Ya know tis me lady." Khadafi smiled as if he was showing off a trophy. "Tis me Mena, Mena tis Chris Carter. His cousin plays for da Panthers. He's da one me told ya about, the guy who wants ta spend four hundred grand."

"Oh, well nice to meet you," Mena chimed like the trophy girlfriend. She gave up a half-ass smile. Deep inside she was a little disappointed that they were mixing business with pleasure and would've preferred being bunned up in a hotel room with her man. Khadafi had promised her a weekend of fun, sex and love away from the counterfeit rat race. But that seemed more and more impossible by the minute.

After the introduction, Mr. Carter asked Khadafi if he would be ready to see him the following Thursday. When Khadafi nodded, Mena pulled away a little. Just as she moved her body, a familiar face bumped her slightly causing her to frown. *Why the hell is he here? And why did Khadafi make things seem as if we were going far away…alone*? Mena thought.

"Sup, boy?" Khadafi said, pulling his boy in close.

"Look'atcha boy. Ya lookin' like money tonite."

The fact that Skully was there angered Mena even more. For once, he was dressed decently and didn't act like a stone cold killer on site. It surprised Mena that he even owned a pair of black pants and a decent Polo shirt. But he still lacked charisma and caused Mena to frown as she and Khadafi followed him to the left side of the ballroom.

"Where are we going, Dafi?" Mena asked through

clenched teeth as her man pulled her through the crowd.

"Away from all tis whoopla."

"And where is that? I thought we were coming here to spend some quality time."

Khadafi stopped in the middle of the floor and turned to shoot Mena a fatherly gaze. With ease he placed his forefinger across her lips and added a hypnotic stare. "Ya trust me?"

Mena nodded.

"So, bombaclot shut ya mouth," he said softly then took off again.

Mena couldn't believe he'd told her to shut up. Since she'd met him, he'd been nothing but the perfect gentleman, now she wasn't so sure. A frown instantly appeared on her face. She wanted to ask him what that was all about, but didn't need Skully in their business, so she decided to drop it. *Maybe he's just overprotective*, she thought.

Soon, a slight smile appeared on Mena's face when Skully stopped in front of an area up against the back wall with several V.I.P booths that contained black chiffon curtains, circular leather couches and two tables full of champagne and red roses.

"Have fun, me nigga," Skully said as Mena and Khadafi entered their hideout.

Although Mena was happy, she had to ask Khadafi what was up with his boy. "Did you see the way he just looked at me?"

"Who? Skully? C'mon. No worries," he told Mena with a shrug.

"No worries. Hmph. Every time I see him he gives me these deadly looks. I just don't like being around him," Mena uttered as she took a seat.

Khadafi took a seat next to her and placed two red roses across her breast. He bent down to nibble a bit before saying. "He says ya bring trouble." Khadafi laughed. "Me don't believe it. Me don't care."

Mena's eyes enlarged with surprise as Khadafi continued

to tell all that Skully had said and thought about her. He ended with. "Ya me lady and noting nobody say matters. They know to never disrespect ya. Ya safe," he said convincingly. "Now, lets enjoy da night."

At that moment Mena didn't care about Skully or anyone else in the room. It was all about her and her Jamaican lover who smelled like sandalwood and spices; the smell she'd come to yearn. She was mesmerized by the way he paid close attention to her every word and by the way he held her softly as they danced to Anthony Hamilton and every slow cut thereafter.

Khadafi moved from side to side slowly with Mena floating in his arms for what seemed like hours. The alcohol had taken affect and it seemed that everything he said was the right set of words.

"Mena, me want ya to move in wit' me," he said, pulling her close and swinging her a bit.

"Ahhhh, not now Dafi. It's just not a good time. I promised Ronni that we'd get an apartment next month. Living with DJ is played."

"Me know tis. That's why ya should be wit' me. Not Ronni. Let her get her own place. Before long she'll be gone."

Mena's eyes ballooned. "What do you mean?"

"Gone. Somewhere I don't know." He stopped dancing and glared into Mena's eyes. "She plan on movin' wit' us when we get married?"

Mena smiled. "Of course not. But my mother maybe. Just for a little while."

Pulling Mena by her shoulders he confirmed, "Look, me told ya on Monday we're gonna go there and talk to her. Together," he added. "Not to worry, you'll have dat relationship dat ya want wit' ya mother. Ya know all I want to do is make ya happy."

Mena wanted to answer but she couldn't help but notice the strange pair of eyes watching them through the curtain. While difficult to see, it was clear that a body still a ways back with their hands crossed above their waistline watched them closely. With all the crazy talk that Mena had heard while being around Khadafi and the shoot out at the barber shop she became nervous.

"You see that guy over there?"

Khadafi turned quickly. "Where?" He yanked the curtain back and gave Mena a nonchalant reaction. "Me see no one."

"Well, I did. He's gone now. And I didn't like the way he gawked us down."

"Mena, don't me protect you?" he asked, getting back in her face again.

"Of course, Dafi. That has nothing to do with me being a little nervous. I know what I just saw," she added.

"Me lady worries about noting," he said strongly. Khadafi cupped her chin and placed a soft kiss upon the tip of her nose. "Me only concern is for ya to have me babies, and take care of me." He smiled. "Soon, I want ya to put all tis work behind and be a lady. Next week me want ya to show me how to make money. Ya hear me?"

Mena nodded but was extra uncomfortable. She didn't really want to give up all the secrets and technique to making perfect counterfeit money. She'd already showed DJ and really didn't want to show Khadafi, too. It was a skill, and everyone couldn't perfect it the way she had.

"And one last ting," he added, while gripping Mena's hand tightly. "Me gonna give ya two weeks to get rid of Ronni and DJ. Dis me and ya business now."

Mena's eyebrows wrinkled and her heart sank. His eyes proved that she'd have to handle business. She began to speak until forbidden to do so by a touch of Khadafi's finger against her moist lips.

"Hush, beautiful. And let's enjoy the night."

$Eighteen$

Mena seldom got up before nine, but the day she had planned was worth the early morning rise. No one could've ever told her that a Monday morning could've been so bright. With the love of her life by her side and their special mission of the day planned, they pulled up in front of Neiman's at Southpark Mall just in time for the doors to open and for Mena to be the first shopper of the day. Mena hopped out, dressed in a pair of skinny leg jeans, a rhinestone t-shirt and a huge pair of Dior glasses.

Her plan was to return the fur shawl that she'd purchased with counterfeit money just two days ago and receive the real fifteen hundred dollars cash in return. It was her hope that they didn't operate as some of the stores back in Charleston where Mena had to fill out forms and receive a check. The mailing of a check was getting old and as Khadafi had preached, "no paper trail." He urged Mena to stay away from stores that didn't disburse cash on the spot.

She walked with a bubbly spirit, straight through the lingerie department, through shoes, and up the up the escalator headed to customer service. Once upstairs, Mena tilted her shades looking in all directions. Her eyes were drawn to the short, stocky women behind the register in customer service. She seemed to be gazing at a manual when Mena approached.

"How may I help you?" the woman asked when Mena placed the bag on the counter.

"I have a return?"

"No problem, Miss. What was the problem?" she asked with a warm smile.

As the woman proceeded to open the bag, Mena gave some sorry excuse of why the shawl didn't work. Her focus was on getting the cash.

"Here's the receipt," Mena told her before she could even ask.

The woman grabbed the receipt and let off a long hum, "Ahhhhhh, I see you paid cash. We may not have enough cash in the register. May have to do a check."

Mena got pissed. Her mind raced as she thought about what to say next, but before she knew it the woman had wrinkled her eyebrows and kept reviewing the receipt.

"Is something wrong?" Mena asked, placing her hands on her hips.

"Oh, no not at all," she said lifting the receiver on the phone near the register. "Let me check on something," she uttered, while giving Mena a suspicious stare.

Instantly, Mena became jittery. The woman's dirty looks had her so on edge that she thought about leaving the shawl, the receipt, and the opportunity for cash behind. The more she thought, the more chill bumps appeared across her forearms. Mena became cold with worry. Flashes of Trick being led out of Neiman's back in Philly flickered through her mind. Then Mena jumped from the sound of a phone ringing. Everything seemed to move in slow motion as Mena noticed the woman waving someone over near the counter. Beads of sweat formed across Mena's face as she realized it was her cell ringing.

"Not now," she sighed as she looked down at the screen on her cell. Noticing the unknown number she assumed it was Khadafi wondering if something had happened to her. Quickly, she answered.

"Bitch, where you at wit' my muthfuckin' car!" Trick blasted. "You still got my shit like you own it! Like bitch you smokin' or somethin'?"

Mena was quiet, refusing to give Trick the reaction he

wanted. She held the phone to her ear and gave off a phony smile while the woman referred with the sloppy looking Caucasian manager who now reviewed the receipt, too.

"I'ma man of my word, Mena. You'll pay," he added. "I'm out and I won't sleep until I find you."

"Trick, I'm not afraid of you anymore," she belted. "I have a new life." She paused to grin at the manager as if to signal everything was okay. She held her hand over the phone momentarily and asked, "Is everything okay? I really do have to go. My children are in the car."

"Bitch, you hear me!" Trick shouted.

"I hear you," she said calmly. "I'm just trying to have a different life now. One without you," she added, then turned to the manager again with a swift jittery move. "Just give me the shawl," she requested with quick movements with her hand. "I'll have to come back later."

"A new life, huh?" Trick spat with contempt. "Wit' my money, my car, and my equipment!"

"Look, you can have your car. I'll make sure it gets back to you. The money and the equipment your boys probably took that. I never touched it," she said with confidence.

Mena of course lied about taking Trick's money and equipment, but was being truthful about returning the car. It was just more bad news she would have to give to Ronni who thought the car was hers. She'd already been plotting on how to tell Ronni and DJ they were out of the business as of the next day. It was a request by Khadafi and a chance to have a good life with him.

In between thoughts, a slight smile slipped from Mena's lips as she saw the store clerk counting out fifteen hundred dollars. Things still felt a bit eerie so Mena quickly snatched the bills, stuffed them into her purse and headed for the escalator, hoping to make it to the front door without getting locked up. She wasn't sure if they'd realized the counterfeit money had been used to buy something in the store before or if there was an alert for employees to watch for all cash transactions.

Neither here nor there, Trick was on the phone getting real dirty with his words. It had gotten so bad that Mena hung up, placing her phone on silent just before waltzing out of the door happy that she'd made it out safely. Once back in the car, she placed a long wet kiss upon Khadafi's lips as the two kissed and then pulled off going eighty mph. Mena smiled at the thought of what was about to go down. It was her chance at a new life; a chance to make amends; a chance for her mother to love her like a mother should.

$$$

By the time Khadafi's truck had arrived back in Charleston, he and Mena had talked about everything. He'd told her that the following day he wanted to take her around to show her his other businesses. That made Mena feel good. Her boyfriend's occupation was sort of a blur. She had figured out that he did a little bit of this and that, but was really unsure about what had brought the big money in prior to her meeting him.

When the wheels stopped turning and Mena realized they'd stopped and parked in her mother's neighborhood, the same old feelings from before came back. She thought about the way her mother had treated her on the last visit; the way she made her feel unwanted and not worthy of being loved.

Then just a simple touch on the hand from Khadafi eased her tension a bit. "Me goin' wit' ya."

She smiled. "Are you sure? She's a little rough around the edges."

"Me just wanna be here for ya. Tis neighborhood not too good, ya know?" Khadafi caressed her hand while he gave encouragement. "It doesn't matter where ya come from. What matters is where ya end up. And ya wit' me."

At that moment Mena became so emotional that anything sounded good. Khadafi could've won a Pulitzer for that comment as far as she was concerned. Minutes later they had both gotten out of the truck, walked through the scruffy looking crowd and found themselves at Sonya's front door. Luckily, the door was open which allowed the sounds of BET to be heard blasting in the background through the screen door, mixed in with children screaming and an adult cursing someone out royally from inside.

"I don't give a good got damn!" the person shouted.

Mena and Khadafi paused before knocking. It was at that point that Mena noticed a yellow eviction notice taped to the outside of the main door. She wasn't sure how long it had been there, but the texture of the paper told her that it had been rained on and exposed to the outside for days.

Then out of the blue, the loud mouth from inside commenced to talking again. "You know what, Charles, if I had a dick I'd tell you to suck it!" the voice sounded.

Khadafi thought the conversation that he could hear was funny, yet Mena didn't. Although they couldn't see a face, Mena knew it was her mother who cursed like a sailor. Suddenly Khadfai knocked again, this time banging on the torn up screen loudly

"Who the fuck is it?" a strong voice sounded.

Mena's hands shook as an image appeared a few feet away from the door and pranced in their direction. She waited for her mother to open the screen door before she even opened her mouth.

"So, it's you again, huh? And you brought Bob Marley with you this time," Sonya smirked, eyeing Khadafi from head to toe. "Look here girl, I don't have money or nothing else to give you but some food stamps, so stop coming around here wasting my damn time."

"I'm not leaving this time until you at least acknowledge that you're my mother," Mena said like a seven year old child.

Sonya looked at them both like they we were crazy. "I'm not saying no bullshit like that unless you got some crack. But go ahead and tell me why you picked me. I know I look good," she sassed exposing her stained teeth, and missing tooth on the left side. Her short hair was pressed down on her head, packed down with what looked to be cheap, hard gel.

Mena took a deep breath and began. "I was thinking about what happened the last time I left here and decided that I didn't want to live the next ten years of my life without a relationship with my mother."

"Crazy girl, didn't I just tell yo' uppity ass that I ain't yo' mama?"

Mena crossed her arms in confidence and told herself, *no crying today*. She had to be the bigger person. "But you are," she said strongly. "You're Sonya, my mother and Priscilla was your mother, my grandmother. And then there's Catherine who's your sister, who raised me.

"Ain't this some shit!" Sonya belted. She peeped her head around the screen door, refusing to invite them in. "You gone sit here and run down the family tree, huh? You just don't give up, do you?"

"Can we just come in?" Mena begged with her eyes. "I just want a chance to talk to you a bit."

Sonya looked back and forth as she yelled out to one of the neighborhood boys walking by. "Nigga, where my five dollars at for them two boxes of cereal I sold your ass? I want my money, Marcus!"

Khadafi finally decided to speak. "Me saw dat ya screen is fallin' apart," he told Sonya while attempting to mend the torn parts with his scarred hand. "Me send someone ova to fix for ya or just buy a new one."

Sonya wasted no time in responding while still not allowing them into her home. "I'll take a new one."

Khadafi smiled showing his platinum grill. "Here, tis should be enough," he said, passing off a crisp hundred dollar bill.

Instantly, the door flung open and Sonya welcomed them both inside. "Have a seat right here at the golden table," she said, making a joke. The table was lopsided and ready to collapse at any moment.

Mena took a seat and Khadafi stood behind her knowing that if his two hundred and fifty pound muscular frame sat in the seat it would surely fall.

"Listen, I'm just going to be honest," Mena began, "I want us to just spend some time together. I mean who knows, I might be able to help you financially and you may be able to tell me how we got to this point where you're not claiming me."

Sonya turned her eyes away from Mena with guilt. It seemed as though there was finally a break through. She didn't say much, but the shaking of her head and the watering of her eyes told everyone in the room that she was sorry for how things had turned out.

"Don't cry, it's okay. I know things happen in life. I just need to know why you never came back for me," Mena said in a sincere tone.

There was silence. And more silence until Sonya uttered six words sincerely.

"I'm so sorry I did that," she said in a whisper. "I never meant for it to go down like that."

Tears exploded from both sides of the room and Mena's heart pierced, yet life had been given. It was a start just hearing Sonya acknowledge that she was her mother and was sorry she had left her. Khadafi placed his hand on Mena's shoulder as he tried to smooth the situation over a little more.

"Me say we all go out to tis nice Jamaican restaurant in North Charleston. Ya ladies can chat it up and I can handle a little business."

"I'm not dressed for no shit like that," Sonya announced in strong rejection.

"No worries. We'll stop off and buy ya someting," he said, flashing three hundreds in Sonya's face.

"I'll be ready in ten," Sonya quickly said, rushing out of the kitchen. She was back within minutes, with a raggedy purse on her arm, ready to go. Of course she hadn't combed her two-inch hair in place or even thought about fixing up at all.

"What about the kids," Mena asked.

She shoved Mena off with a hand movement. "They'll be fine. They always stay here alone."

"Oh…I mean how old are they?"

"Three and six, but they fine. They know what the fuck to do."

Mena couldn't help but think about the fact that those were her brothers or sisters in the back room. She was dying to see them and vowed to make sure they all had a better life in the near future. For now, the moment to be with her mother filled her spirit.

$ Nineteen $

The bed squeaked and moaning sounds ran wild from Camie's sweet lips. The back bedroom had gone from a money-making home office to a sex sanctuary. And the remnants of chocolate syrup still lay across her succulent breast as she and Ronni continued to fuck Missionary style. They lay ass-naked and their bodies connected as if this hadn't been the first time.

Ronni remained on her knees with her body pressed forward punishing Camie's naive pussy with a black twelve inch dildo that she'd named Rambo. It had a tapered head and smooth shaft that was strapped securely to her waistline by her favorite black on purple harness. The combination had cost Ronni a fortune, but she believed it was necessary when it came to fucking her women right. She worked out like a porn-star while commanding that Camie's legs remain wrapped around her waist as she banged furiously over top of her.

"That's what the fuck I'm talkin' 'bout," Ronni bellowed as she wiggled her ass cheeks attempting to win the *Best Fuck of the Year Award.*

"Ahhhhhhhhhhhhhh," Camie cooed followed by a wincing sound. "Oh—o-oh-my-Goddddd!" she belted.

"Let it do, what it do, baby."

"Damnnnnnnn, Ronni, this- feel- so-good," Camie stuttered.

"See, see, see," Ronni repeated boastfully, "after being wit' me baby, you'll never want DJ's little ass dick again," she commented then slapped Camie on the hip as she continued to grind. "You hear me?"

Camie lay speechless on her backside wondering how a woman she thought she hated could feel so good. She'd always told herself never- never –ever –ever. But it happened. And now she found herself with her pussy high in the air and ass cheeks lifted off the bed wanting Ronni to fuck every crevasse of her vaginal wall.

Ronni felt her orgasm coming and sped up the pace. Her face tightened as she gyrated her hips in quick, circular motions. Quickly, she reached forward and squeezed the perky nipples of Camie's Double D's. She moaned as she plunged the dildo into Camie's tight treasure, back and forth rapidly.

"Oh shit…oh shit!" Ronni called out.

"Talk nasty to me, Ronni…talk nasty!" Camie egged.

"You fuckin' tramp. Get off this good dick!" Ronni belted as she released and watched Camie's eyes roll up into her head.

Camie's juices flowed and her breathing became uncontrollable. She continued to grind her pussy against the toy even though her g-spot had been found and punished. However, Ronni wasn't done. She pulled out, flipped Camie over and slapped her on the ass again.

"Doggi style time," she warned Camie.

Within seconds, Ronni had plunged her way inside as Camie backed her ass up eagerly. She gritted her teeth and let out a victorious yelp! The excitement of feeling the wetness of Camie's pussy made Ronni weak at the knees.

"Oh my Godddddd, Ronni. I love it from the back."

"Damn girl, yous a freak for real. Let me get that syrup again," Ronni said looking near the top of the bed.

"Oooooh, ooooooh, oooooh…fuck me harder," Camie moaned.

Just then the bedroom door flung open and caused Ronni to jump from the bed. Her initial reaction was to dive for her .9mm that rested on the side of the bed near the nightstand.

But when she studied the three faces standing in the doorway, she let out a loud gasp.

"Oh, shit!" she said covering her mouth.

For the onlookers it was strange seeing a dyke completely naked with a harness strapped around her body and a fake dick dangling like it was waiting for a handshake. And it was even stranger to see that Ronni actually had tits. They were small, but nonetheless she had them. Khadafi couldn't stand the sight of Ronni with the dildo on so he turned and left out of the room. Camie on the other hand was in a state of shock as she snatched the only sheet available on the bed to cover her naked body. Tears fell as she processed the look in DJ's eyes.

"Oh my God, DJ!" she shouted, holding the sheet up to her chest. "I never meant for this to happen," she explained.

"No explanation needed," DJ replied pretending, to be calm. Then he snapped. "Get your tramp ass up and out of my spot! Now!" he roared.

"No, DJ, no pleaseeee," Camie cried.

"And you, Ronni!" He paused, then charged Ronni like a defensive lineman.

Mena thought about trying to grab DJ, but it was too late. He dove onto Ronni like his life depended on it, tackling her to the floor. Shit fell from everywhere as Mena screamed not knowing what else to do. She watched as the two of them tussled across the floor. Surprisingly, Ronni fought back as much as she could. It was clear she was still a girl as she took the upper cut to the chin from DJ. Punch after punch she managed to squirm her way from beneath DJ and land on her feet, sweaty but not beaten too badly. Blood dripped from her mouth as DJ called Ronni name after name between breaths. He huffed then puffed showing that he was tired, then he swung again landing a hard one to Ronni's temple. Amazingly, Ronni still returned the punch.

"C'mon DJ, let's talk about this," Ronni suggested. "We gotta all live together," she panted, attempting to catch her breath.

"You're not living in my muthufucking house!" DJ shouted, while remaining in a stance like the incredible hulk. "I can't believe this shit!"

He turned, looked at Camie then rushed toward her. Within seconds, she leapt from the bed, with only the sheet wrapped around her body and jetted past Mena like a runaway slave. At that point, DJ threw up his hands and leaned back against the wall almost completely out of breath.

"You okay?" Mena asked in a soft like tone.

"Ronni, get your shit and get the fuck out," he said calmly.

Everyone had calmed down as much as they could as Khadafi reappeared and brushed past Ronni carrying two boxes that he'd picked up from the UPS shipping store. "Me see everyting bettah now."

All of a sudden DJ snapped and rushed out of the room, calling out for Camie. "I'ma beat yo ass before you leave!"

Things were way too chaotic and Mena couldn't bear to look at Ronni as she asked, "What the fuck is going on, Mena? You movin' or something? What the fuck are these boxes for?" Quickly, Ronni threw a t-shirt over her head which still only covered her upper body and straddled her waistline. "Answer me, Mena."

Mena didn't have the guts to tell her what was really going on. Her heart wouldn't allow her to tell her longtime friend that she and Khadafi wanted to run the business as a duo and that four was a crowd. She kept her eyes low to the ground as Khadafi began unplugging the printers and instructing Mena to pack what clothes were left in the closet. It seemed as if her entire wardrobe had slowly but surely been transferred to Khadafi's over the last month, but the equipment removal had Ronni puzzled. She started to speak on some Ra-Ra, get angry type shit until an older woman appeared in the doorway.

"I know y'all told me to stay in the living room, but I gotta know what's going on in here." She grinned showing her jacked up teeth. "I mean some bitch just ran past me butt ass naked, then her boyfriend runs behind her and slapped the hell outta her." Sonya paused to shoot Ronni the same nasty stare that she was giving her. "Y'all sure you not doing none of that reality T.V. shit? This betta than the crack-house action."

"And who the fuck is this, Mena?" Ronni asked.

"My mother," she answered quickly. "And don't ask anything else about her right now." Her tone was soft as she worried about Ronni's response.

"Ohhhhhh, I get it. So fuck Ronni, huh!" She banged against her chest. "You found your crack-head ass mother and now just dump me!" she blared, directing her comment to everyone in the room.

"Did this lil short, dkye looking bitch just call me a crack-head?" Sonya asked ready to argue.

"Yes, the fuck I did," Ronni shot back. "So, you takin' all the shit, Mena? How are we supposed to keep shit runnin'? Well, I can tell you now, you not takin' the Bentley. Absolutely not," Ronni said, grabbing her pants. Obviously the keys were inside.

Before anyone could say anything, DJ peeped back in the room and told everyone that Camie had left with just what she came with.

Nothing.

"I could've at least given her a ride," Mena complained.

"Sluts need to walk," he countered then gave Ronni an evil glare. "Why the fuck are you just standing there? You need to get your shit, too. You next."

"Shut the fuck up, DJ. I'm not pressed to stay in this bitch. Trust me, I'll leave," Ronni stated.

"Well, well, well…if it isn't Mr. Donovan Joyner. I gotta bone to pick with you boy," Sonya badgered, pointing her finger in DJ's face like a frustrated school teacher.

"What is it, Sonya?" DJ asked.

"The boy who sell me my meat off the truck told me to start confronting everyone who I got a gripe with in life. He's like my therapist…going ova to the college and shit. Anyways, I supposed to tell you that I don't like yo' lanky ass so it'll make me feel better. Gives me new energy he said." Sonya looked at DJ and smiled.

"Fuck you, Sonya," he said then turned and walked away. "I need everyone out!" DJ yelled, headed to his room.

"Sonya, please," Mena said with an added hand movement. "Just wait for me in the living room. I'm almost done." She handed her mother a handful of clothes that were still on hangers. "Take these, please. I need to get my shoes."

Sonya did as she was instructed but not before throwing Ronni a kiss-her-ass smirk. "Dyke!"

Ronni jerked as if she was headed to rumble Sonya until Khadafi's hand stopped her. "Me see no need to fight anymore. The people you need to deal wit' are rych'ere." He stopped to catch eyes with Mena. "Tell 'er, Mena," he instructed in a low tone.

"Tell me what?" Ronni roared, lifting herself on her tiptoes. "I can see that you're obviously a sell out and movin' wit' this sneaky nigga. But what else?" she asked, moving close up into Mena's face.

"The counterfeit money operation is over for the four of us. It's just me and Khadfai now." Mena stopped to swallow hard, then added, "I'm sorry Ronni, but it's just not working out with all this extra baggage."

Mena's words hit Ronni like a Mack-truck. Her feelings were crushed. And just like that Ronni threw a haymaker Mena's way that landed across her temple.

Lights out.

All Mena could see was blackness.

$Twenty$

"I'm out. Be back in fifteen," Noble told Ronni as the door slammed.

Ronni fought hard to open her eyes as she laid back on Noble's grimy looking couch. It had been two days since she got screwed by her good friend and still hadn't regrouped from the betrayal. She'd been up half the night kicking it on the phone with her old crew back in Philly. It had been a hard search, but she was finally able to get Trick's number from a foot soldier who worked the block in North Philly.

It was early, probably too early to wake Trick up, but with the news she had, Ronni figured he wouldn't complain. She'd been waiting to get a moment alone, away from Noble to make the call.

As soon as she started dialing, she threw a pillow over her head to help drown out the sounds of Noble's dogs barking from the back room. It was crazy how they knew Noble had left and all of a sudden were going ballistic. Noble had given specific instructions not to open the door when he wasn't around. The pits were trained to kill and with one bad move, Ronni would be breakfast.

The phone rang three times before a disgruntled voice picked up.

"You wanna know where that bitch Mena is?" Ronni quickly asked.

"Who the fuck is this?" Trick replied.

"This Ronni."

"Like what the fuck you want?" he asked with attitude.

"Whoa…whoa…be easy. I got info you need, nigga."

"Oh, yeah. Like I heard you were with that bitch. Is that true? People ain't seen you since Mena rolled out."

"Maybe…maybe not."

"Where the fuck is my car!"

"I called about Mena big boy, not your ride."

The phone line was silent, all except for Trick's heavy breathing. "Aye, Ronni, don't play with me," he uttered. "Where that hoe at?"

"What's in it for me?" Ronni questioned.

Ronni removed the pillow from her face after realizing the man eaters in the other room had finally calmed down. She took a few seconds to listen to Trick go off about her comment. He cursed and fussed calling Ronni every foul name that had ever been spoken. Then finally said, "Tell me Ronni, cause I will find her. And believe me you don't want to be on my list."

"Nigga, let's get something straight," Ronni blared. "I'm doing you the favor, yamean?" she said, trying to be extra sarcastic. "I'm not scared of you. And if yo' fat ass can't find Mena, I know you won't find me."

Suddenly the dial tone went dead.

Ronni hopped up realizing that Trick wasn't up for her games. She realized she'd played herself and hadn't gotten the information she needed. The information she told Noble she already had. Quickly, she dialed Trick again, but this time when he answered, her tone had changed.

"Mannnnn, I got beside myself Trick," Ronni stated sincerely. "I know that shit Mena did to you was foul. And I'm all for an eye for an eye a tooth for a tooth." She paused. "I'm definitely gonna tell you where Mena is."

Trick said nothing causing Ronni's thick eyebrows to crinkle.

"You there?" she asked

"I'm here," Trick responded, sounding like a psychopath as he blew quick short breaths on the other end of the phone.

"Where is she?" His voice sounded like thunder.

"Here's the deal. Mena told me all about the counterfeit money you been makin'. Give me info on where to get that software y'all use and the right kinda paper and I'll tell you where she at." She paused, hoping that Trick wouldn't blow his top. "And before you start thinkin' crazy, just know that I'm not tryna move in on your territory. I just got some folks ready for action in New York. Cool?"

"Bet. Tell me where she is and I'll help you start yo shit. It won't affect me. I'll think of it as franchisin'. Just hit me off with a little profit sharin' cash every now and then. Now where the fuck is she?"

"South Carolina."

"I shoulda known that bullshit!" Trick shouted. "Her mufuckin' punk-ass cousin live down there. That barbershop nigga," Trick expressed loudly. "Don't call'er and tell'er I'm headed down. I mean that shit Ronni. You know you need something from me," he said as if it was a bribe. "Lemme call my man Felony and I'ma hit you back."

"Aye…wait…"

He hung up right in Ronni's ear just as the dogs started barking again, and Noble strutted back into the run down house carrying a bottle of Colt 45 and a Twix candy bar.

"What the fuck you smiling about?" Noble asked.

"Cuz we about to get paid, nigga," Ronni said, rubbing her hands together. "I'm workin' on something that's gonna have us rich!"

"Let me guess…that counterfeit shit."

"Damn right."

"I shoulda killed your ass when I had the chance for giving me that fake ass money." Noble placed one of the chocolate bars in his mouth.

"Nigga, you still holdin' on to that shit? You need to let that go, move on. We past that now," Ronni said. "Listen, since I know how to make the money, and you got all the connects, we about to take over this muthafucka. We gon' run Charleston! As long as we take that dread head muthafucka Khadafi out the picture, we good."

Noble shook his head. "So, when do you wanna get started because I gotta get my crew together? If we gonna pop Khadafi, we gotta have a plan. You don't just run up on that nigga. Where's the shit to make the money anyway?"

"That bitch Mena took it. It's probably at Khadafi's crib," Ronni advised.

"Well, we gotta find out where that nigga live so we can take that shit."

"Hold fast. I gotta better plan. I got some equipment on the way."

"Bet. Well, I'm ready to do this. Just give me the word," Noble said.

As Noble turned around, Ronni displayed a slick grin. Noble had no idea that she was selling him a pipe dream. *Yeah, I'ma need your ass to help me get rid of Khadafi so I can have this business all to myself. Fuck all y'all niggas. By the time you figure out what's going on, I'll be in another damn state,* she thought

"I need to feed the dogs and let'em go take a shit break."

"Oh hell no. Don't let them muthafuckas out!" Ronni yelled.

"Look, my damn dogs been locked up in that room for two days since your ass been here. They live here...not you. It's not my fault they don't fuck with you," Noble said with a cheesy grin. "Go somewhere. Go out with that Reece bitch you had over here the other night."

Ronni wasn't exactly in the mood for pussy this early in the morning, but leaving the apartment sounded better than being fucked with by Noble's vicious dogs. Slipping on her new Jordans, she grabbed her Sixers baseball hat, then quickly headed out the door. As she ran down the apartment steps, thoughts of how she needed to hurry up and get rid of the Bentley before Trick got to town ran through her mind. Especially now since Trick knew where they were. For all she knew, he might've called the car in stolen. If her plan was gonna work, Ronni had to play her cards right.

Deactivating the alarm, Ronni jumped inside the car and started it up before she began to think about Mena. Every time she thought about how Mena kicked her out of the business without the slightest warning, she got pissed off all over again. Ronni couldn't believe how she'd traveled all the way from Philadelphia to be betrayed by someone she once called a friend. Her love for Mena had now turned to hate.

"That bitch," Ronni said, pulling out her phone.

She'd refrained from contacting Mena ever since leaving DJ's until now. Punching in the number, Ronni turned the radio down so Mena could hear what she had to say. After hearing the phone ring once, it went straight to voicemail.

"Oh, so that bitch hit the ignore button on me, huh?" Ronni said to herself. Her fingers couldn't type fast enough as she sent a text.

That was some foul shit u did Mena. Brought me all the way to SC to do me dirty. U reap what u sow. Remember that bullshit.

Surprisingly, Mena texted back.

I'm sorry Ronni. I neva meant it to go down this way. U should've let me explain instead of punching me in my face. Now Khadafi doesn't want me talking to you.

"Fuck Khadafi!" Ronni shouted as she replied.

Oh, so he rule u now? Another Trick, huh? U left one abusive muthufucka to go to another. He uses u crazy. Watch- he wants u to show him how to make the money then u done. But I'll be here.

That's not true. You're just mad because he made me take the equipment, Mena replied.

Ronni shook her head.

Ok u stupid bitch. You'll see. Oh, by the way some peeps back in Philly said that

`Trick was in SC lookin' for u. Watch ur back!`

After Ronni hit send, she turned off her phone.

$Twenty-One$

Mena stood in the basement near the stairs pacing while she attempted to eavesdrop on Khadafi and Skully's conversation above. They'd been in the kitchen for nearly fifteen minutes discussing some important business, business they obviously didn't want to share with her. For Mena it was a chance to take a break from working. It was crazy how she found herself right back in the same boat just with a different captain; one who wanted to control her life.

For the past two days she found herself on a strict regiment while living at Khadafi's. His rule was to make sure she got fully dressed every morning, looking her best. That included make-up, hair done, smelling good, and no high heels. He'd told her just the night before that the heels made her look slutty and forbid her to wear them again, in or out of the house moving forward.

As the voices above echoed, Mena bit her nails nervously. Things were spiraling out of control and she had no power over anything. The fact that Ronni said Trick was in town had her walking on egg shells. Mena really wanted to talk to Trick. She had called Felony several times but got sent to voicemail. She'd even sent him a text asking if they really knew where she was. Mena knew she would be safe with Khadafi, but couldn't get up enough nerve to tell him about Trick and her past. Surely she didn't want to tell him that she had stolen Trick's business from up under his nose. Besides, the counterfeit game had gotten hot all of a sudden with everyone in town wanting to buy shit loads of cash from Khadafi. It had grown into the new craze with order after order coming in and jealousy building up.

Mena hadn't slept good in two days, and her purplish looking eye still hadn't healed completely from Ronni's powerful punch. Now the Trick situation would keep her from ever sleeping again. It also troubled her that DJ hadn't responded back to any of her text messages. She thought about calling him on several occasions, but knew how strongly Khadafi felt about severing the relationship. That command hurt her the most. DJ had been the only family she remained close with most of her life and now having to stay away from him, hurt. Badly.

Then there was Ronni who of course wouldn't stop. She was crazy and of course seemed to be on some payback type shit. Suddenly, Mena snapped from her thoughts when she thought she heard Skully mention DJ's name. She moved closer to the steps to hear a little better. The voices spoke angrily, but she was still unsure about what they said. The stress was overwhelming.

"Fuck it, I gotta call him," Mena said as she picked up her phone and dialed Trick's number. She knew her voice was the last thing he wanted to hear, but she had to know if he was in town. As soon as Trick answered, Mena didn't hold back.

"I just need to know if you're here," she blurted out.

Just as she thought, Trick went off. "What the fuck do you mean? Am I where? In South Carolina? Is that why you callin'? You got some fuckin' nerve after the shit you did. Yeah, I'm in town, and I'm lookin' for your ass."

"I swear I'm sorry for what I did. I shoulda never took your stuff or set you up at Neiman's, but I just wanted to get you back for killing my brother. He meant the world to me."

Trick chuckled. "Bitch you really do need help. It's obvious that you don't remember what really happened. You killed your brother that night, not me!"

"Stop it, Trick, stop lying!" Mena replied.

"I'm not lying. I know you didn't mean to shoot in his

direction, but it really was self defense. I protected you, Mena," he blasted. "Them niggas tried to rob us, and whether you wanna believe it or not, Donte brought them into our house."

Mena shook her head in disbelief after having flashbacks of that night. She did remember grabbing the gun, but everything else was a blur after that. "Nah, Trick. Nah," she kept repeating. She stood with a blank stare. Had she really killed her own brother?

"Look, you're not gonna put that shit on me!" Trick yelled. "Tell me where you are. I need..."

Mena quickly hung up the phone when a door slammed and Khadafi began rushing back down the stairs to the basement. When he reached the bottom step, Mena was in a complete daze.

"What da fuck ya standin' around for, gurl? Me got people waitin."

Khadafi surveyed the nicely finished basement hoping to see a few new stacks of money. It was hard to tell considering twenty different stacks were scattered about the floor all with a piece of paper on top of each with the client's name written with a black magic marker.

"Me not sure what da fuck takin' ya so long. But tis shit gotta stop. Ya gonna fuck me business up," he told her bluntly.

Mena looked on in disbelief as she continued to bite her nails while clicking the mouse on the computer. She really wanted some time to just talk to Khadafi about a few things, but it was clear by his facial expression that he only wanted to talk about orders.

"Okay. Me now know how to cut the paper up properly. What'cha need to show me next?" he asked with urgency in his voice.

"Ahhhhh…Ahhhh…"

"Answer me, gurl. Ya wastin' time," he scolded.

"Here, let me show you how to line up the security markings before it's time to glue."

While Khadafi held each bill up to the light, he hounded

Mena about her speed. She worked too slow, he complained and wasn't as disciplined as he expected her to be. "And Mena, don't forget, nobody gets a different price. Everyone pays fifty percent. No exceptions."

Mena gave off a dry nod and kept cleaning the bills on the computer.

"Ya call those Columbians back yet?" he asked out of the blue.

An eerie feeling crept up into Mena's stomach. She knew that calling the Columbians back was a no-no. She wished like hell she'd never told Khadafi. Now things were too sticky with Trick looking for her.

"I called. They didn't answer so I left a message."

"If the bloodcots don't call soon, me call them," Khadafi responded, lifting his dreads off his neck and tying a larger rubber band around the ends.

He kept his eyes on the watermarks as he worked on making a perfect bill. "Mena, get ta workin'," he ordered. "We gotta make at least one hundred fifty by midnight."

Mena huffed.

Khadafi froze and shot her the look of death. "Me stump ya in da ground if ya ever do dat again. What da fuck is wrong wit' ya gurl?" He paused. "Dat is some disrespectful shittttt," he hissed like a snake.

Mena's heart thumped and she began to sweat. So many crazy thoughts ran through her mind as she decided to apologize. "I'm so sorry, Dafi. It's just that I got a lot on my mind. Ronni's mad at me, and you don't want me to call the only family member that I been tight with all my life." Her eyes became glassy and begged for mercy as Khadafi stopped working, stood up, and walked over near her chair.

A tear fell which caused Khadafi to grab one of her shoulders. He looked her deep into her eyes and told Mena straight up. "Ya weaker than me thought. That's dangerous," he taunted.

Mena went on a full fledge crying spree hoping he

would feel for her somewhere deep inside his controlling mind. Khadafi never showed any remorse and took things to the next level when Mena ended with dangerous words.

"I heard you and Skully up there, too. What was he saying about DJ? Huh? What was it?" she pressed for an answer while still in a bad emotional state.

Wham! The sound of Khadafi's hand connecting to Mena's face made an eruptive pounding sound. While hard, his hand print remained on her face as he withdrew ready for a second hit.

"What the..." Mena became mute as she held the side of her face.

Khadafi blasted off using all kinds of Jamaican words to curse her badly. "Ya bloodcut no good, bitch! Me give ya nice place ta lay ya head…and all ya want to do is talk back. Me bury people like ya every day, ya know. Ya make Dafi mad…real mad," he preached with his fists balled into a tight knot.

She couldn't believe that the man she thought of as being so loveable toward her just weeks ago had just slapped the shit out of her. There had to be something going on that he wasn't telling her about. Something that would make him flip. He knew her eye hadn't healed from Ronni's punch and now here he stood looking like he wanted to strike her again.

"So, are we ready ta work?" he asked with his fist still balled up.

"Ah huh," Mena sniffled, then sat back down like a trained student.

The tone in the room changed and no conversations were spoken. Only the voices from the television across the room were heard as the two man team worked diligently for the next two hours. No water breaks. No food breaks, and definitely no time for loving. It was all about producing money for Khadafi's new money making business.

Finally, when the doorbell rang it was Mena's cue to escape the rat race of work. She'd asked permission from Khadafi for her mother to stay over for a few weeks while her place was being remodeled. Mena had paid for everything; new appliances, new cabinets, new carpet, etc. You name it, Sonya was getting it, along with all her rent paid up until October. Mena shot Khadafi a hesitant eye as she yawned and stretched.

"Can I go? That's probably my mother?"

Khadafi waved her off as if he were irritated with her work ethics. "Go spend time wit' ya mother. Go. Go," he repeated like Mena's presence was annoying him."And make some food to bring down here."

Mena took two steps at a time rushing toward the constant ringing of the doorbell. It sounded like the chimes were stuck, but she knew it was her mother just being Sonya.

"Hey Ma," she said ,opening the double doors widely and smiling at the two little ones each with a black trash bag thrown over their backs.

Sonya stepped inside carrying close to eight small, white plastic bags, most from different stores, ranging from Target to Walmart. "Where are your bags?"

"Damn, girl, you blind." Her eyes darted down to the white bags full of clothes and the two black trashbags that had been dropped in the middle of the floor. "You must got eyes like yo daddy. Whoever the fuck he is."

Mena frowned and Sonya laughed as she surveyed the living room and made all kinds of crazy sounds with her throat. "Damn, yo nigga went all out on this place," she said, sliding her bare feet and crusty looking toes through the soft carpet. "This place far as hell, too. Long way from the hood."

"Yeah, it is nicely decorated, isn't it?"

"This nigga caked-up!" Sonya's voice erupted with excitement. "We ain't never leaving this mufucka."

Mena laughed. "So, are you going to introduce me to my brother and sister?" she asked, holding her hand out for the three-year old boy to give her five.

"This Ray-Ray and this Shaniqua. And don't ask shit else about'em cause I can't tell you. I think I was high when I had them mufuckas." She paused and looked at the smallest one who had eyes like Mena's. "I hope they mine," she added.

Sonya began scratching her arms like most crackheads did when they needed a fix. Mena watched her as she moved around the first floor of the house gawking at the expensive sculptures and brightly lit paintings on the wall.

Mena picked up the little girl who was in desperate need of a bath and her hair washed. "You hungry, Shaniqua?"

"Yes," Shaniqua replied in a low tone.

"Good, because we gotta plenty of food," Mena said then led them into the kitchen.

For the first time in days, Mena felt good inside. The night they left DJ's place she and Sonya had bonded well. They'd laughed, cried and made amends as best they could. So Mena was looking forward to their week together, all in the same house.

Mena hadn't expected their first night to go so well. Not that she thought it would be a disaster, but she had no idea Sonya would bring her so much joy. After all, her mother was comical and should've been a comedian. For hours they ate, talked, and laughed as Sonya told Mena crazy stories about her past; some good, some bad. Mena kept asking about her father, but that was one question that Sonya seemed to dodge.

"Okay, I have another question," Mena asked in a more serious tone.

"Shoot. What is it?"

Mena's face showed too much emotion for Sonya.

"Okay, none of that Oprah Winfrey shit," Sonya spat. "You 'bout to mess the mood up girl. Just ask me."

"Did anyone ever tell you who killed Donte?" Mena's eyes watered. After listening to what Trick had to say about that night, she wanted to see if Sonya knew anything.

"No. After getting the call about his death, I haven't heard a word." Sonya lowered her head. "I felt so bad. I hadn't seen him since he was six," she said sadly. "Was the funeral nice?"

A single tear raced down Mena's face. "Yes." When Mena felt herself about to break down, she told Sonya that they could discuss it later. "I do have another question though."

"Okay, but this time, nothing sad. I'm just getting to spend time with my daughter." She stopped and grinned, showing that she needed to see a dentist badly.

"Well, DJ told me you are on heroin. Are you?"

"Fuck DJ! And his mama, too," Sonya added. "That's how rumors get started. His mother used to do that shit to me when we were kids and that's why I still throw darts at her mu-fucking pictures now. Hell no, I'm not on heroin," she finally said. She smiled hoping her daughter would fall for her lie. "Now, I got a question for you."

"Go ahead. Ask me?"

"Can that stallion downstairs fuck or what?"

They both fell into laughter until Mena mumbled, "Yes."

Before long, twelve o'clock rolled around, and the ladies were still having a good time. Khadafi still hadn't come up from the basement, so Sonya kept asking what he was down there doing. But of course, Mena shot her a lie. It didn't take long for Mena to show Sonya to her room telling her that she and Khadafi would bring the kids up, who were fast asleep on the couch in just a few.

For Mena, she needed a few minutes to herself in the bathroom to take the pregnancy test that she'd bought the day before. It troubled her that she couldn't pin point the weeks. By her calculation, if the test proved positive, she was probably about anywhere from 6-8 weeks. That was a problem. She'd fucked Khadafi exactly six weeks ago, and Felony the week prior. Under normal circumstances, Trick could be labeled the father too, so Mena's situation was far from normal.

Within seconds, she pissed and held her hand over her heart. Her adrenaline pumped while waiting for the results. All sorts of thoughts swirled in her mind. The what if's…the how do I's… and the big question…

All thoughts stopped when Mena glanced down noticing

the pink line.

Positive. *Damn, I'm pregnant.*

$$$

Once Sonya heard Mena and Khadafi's bedroom door shut, she quickly got out of bed and put on her tennis shoes. She'd tricked Mena into thinking she was in her nightgown, and even had the comforter pulled up to her neck every time Mena walked by the guest room door. Knowing this was new territory, there was no way Sonya was going to bed without checking out the place.

Slowly creeping down the steps, Sonya made sure to keep checking behind her as she quietly made her way downstairs. Her first stop…the kitchen. With the refrigerator open for some light, Sonya gently opened all the drawers hoping she would find something for keeps.

Every damn body got a junk drawer in the kitchen Sonya thought as she continued to search. By the time she'd made it to her fifth drawer with no luck, she started to become a little frustrated. *Shit. Do they even have any loose change around this mufucka*?

Giving up on the kitchen, Sonya closed the refrigerator then made her way into the living room. Seeing how neat and clean that area was as well, she began to think that investigation might turn up empty when thoughts of the basement instantly made her smile.

I almost forgot about the basement, Sonya thought as she made her way to the basement door. Not wanting to fall, she took a chance and turned on the light leading downstairs before looking back one last time. When everything seemed clear, she walked downstairs and quickly surveyed the big open space. Not giving a damn about the pool table or the six seat bar, it wasn't long before Sonya marched over to the office area.

She didn't even get within two feet of the desk before she saw several stacks of money laying around. Sonya's eyes became two sizes larger as she walked toward the cash like a zombie. Holding her hands in the air, she did a little happy dance before looking back at the cash to make sure she wasn't dreaming.

Damn, this nigga really is caked up, Sonya thought as she quickly peeled off five hundred dollar bills and stuffed them into her pocket. She thought about taking more, but didn't want the stolen cash to be too noticeable. *I'll borrow more later.*

With a pocket full of cash, Sonya made her way back upstairs and out the front door. There was no need for a formal goodbye.

$$$

When Mena thought she heard the front door close, she jumped up out of bed and looked at Khadafi.

"Did you turn on the alarm?"

"No, me forgot. Go turn it on," he replied.

Shaking her head at his dumb move, Mena got up and made her way over to the key pad that was in their room. Luckily, she didn't have to go all the way downstairs. After punching in the four digit code, she decided to see if Sonya was asleep. Hoping the sound hadn't startled her as well, Mena wanted to make sure Sonya was comfortable in her new temporary home.

When Mena got to the guest room and realized her mother wasn't in the bed, she looked in the bathroom and in the room with her brother and sister before calling out her name. When Sonya didn't answer, Mena checked downstairs. Once every room had been searched, Mena finally realized that Sonya was gone. Trying her best to only entertain positive thoughts, she slowly made her way back upstairs hoping that her mother would return.

$ Twenty-Two $

Two different Glocks pointed at DJ's head as he continued to scream out in agony. "Ahhhh mannnn…c'mon mannnnn. Why me?" he cried out.

"C'mon, fake-ass nigga. You know why. Give up the info and we'll let you go."

DJ dropped his head in defeat realizing there was nothing he could do to break free from the tight rope wrapped at least four times around his waist. He was being held hostage as he sat tied to the fold-out steel looking chair. It was almost unheard of to be detained against your will in your own place of business. But Blazin' Kutz had gone from a barber shop to a crime scene.

He and his attackers all sat cooped up in the supply room in the back of the shop as pain pulsated from his cheeks. Even though he tried to hold it in, every now and then he shouted out hoping something would help the throbbing sensation. He could feel his skin peeling from the chemicals infiltrating his skin. But nothing would prepare him for the greenish color that now spread across his face. Little did DJ know that he resembled a beast with craters in his face.

"You keep screamin' like a bitch! Come on country boy, where she at?"

Trick looked around at Felony crazily, giving him the go ahead to pour more acid onto DJ'sface. Quickly, Felony grabbed the gasoline can containing the acid and splashed at least a quart of fluid onto DJ's burning skin.

"Ahhhhhhhh…shit! Mu-thu-fu-cka!" DJ fought to get out. "Man, just go head and shoot me man. Go ahead man…I can't take this shit!"

"Cause you a punk-ass nigga. I got a few young jawns back at home who can take more pain than you."

"Just shoot me man, just shoot me."

Felony approached DJ quickly and pressed the tip of his Glock up against his temple. "Oh so you'll die for Mena, huh? You rather take yo mufuckin' life than tell us where that bitch is?"

Trick celebrated quietly as DJ screamed out in agony once again. This time they could've sworn he was in labor. No one understood the excruciating pain except someone who'd been stung by a massive gang of killer bees.

"Be a man, baby. Be a man," Felony teased while dancing around real kiddy-like. "You wanna keep secrets do you? Shit gon get worse, dawg. This Philly style, baby!"

"Where the fuck Mena at?" Trick added coldly. He was tired of playing games with DJ and hoped that he didn't have to leave the barber shop with another body on his gun.

DJ knew the moment that he told him where Mena was they would kill him. But it was getting to the point where he would rather die than take any more torture. They had already shattered the glass of all the mirrors behind the stations out front and now talked about ways of ruining his life if he didn't snitch.

For DJ he was broken; mentally and physically. For the second time since Mena had been to town his shop had been trashed, shot up, and in need of another insurance check. He'd had enough and contemplated giving up Mena's whereabouts. DJ could feel Trick's eyes staring him down and knew more drama was coming. He began to pray as Trick pulled his chrome Beretta from his pants with a frustrated grin.

DJ gritted his teeth and held his breath until he felt Trick stick his hands in his pocket pulling out everything but the lint. DJ was puzzled. He didn't know a lot about Trick, but from what Mena had told him in the past, the brother was paid. So why did he need to rob him of his money.

He watched as Trick studied the bills carefully, signaling that he knew something was strange. Unfortunately for DJ, it was money that he had made while in training with Mena, and money that he would use when dealing with people in the streets. It was also money that had imperfections; imperfections that Trick could spot instantly.

Within seconds, Trick had knelt down making sure he was eye to eye with DJ as he spoke.

"DJ, my man, we got a problem homey." He tugged at his beard. "It seems like you got some counterfeit money in your pockets."

DJ said nothing, simply squirmed in his seat.

"Now see, I know you been with Mena. And I know y'all grimey muthafuckas been printin' fake money." Out of the blue he slammed his fist into DJ's jaw causing his mouth to fill with blood. Remaining calm, he continued. "Now, the way I see it, Mena got my muthafiuckin' equipment and came down here makin' counterfeit doe on my damn behalf. That was my operation, yamean?"

He kicked the chair in anger, flipping DJ and the chair onto the floor. Even though DJ landed on his side and was in pain, he refused to get up…or even move for that matter.

"Now, I came here for one reason only, yamean?"

DJ lay on his side sniffling like a bitch. "Um huh."

"Now tell me where Mena is before I cut your fuckin' dick off." Trick whipped out a two inch blade while Felony cosigned from the background. "Kill his ass!"

DJ's eyes grew wide. But he still lay speechless, afraid to even talk.

Felony laughed. "Naw, fuck dat shit. The nigga don't even look like he get no pussy so cuttin' his dick won't do him no good. The nigga cut hair for a livin' so let'em cut wit' nubs." Felony shrugged his shoulders. "Let's see if he talk after I chop the fingers off he need to work them clippers."

There was no reaction from DJ at all. He was thunderstruck.

Just like out of a mob movie, Felony grabbed DJ's left hand while Trick inched the knife toward his hand. Before DJ could even react, Trick had quickly chopped off three fingers. Luckily, he wasn't married because his wedding ring would've been on the floor.

DJ let out a terrifying scream as the pain shot through his entire body. It felt like he was going to pass out as pools of blood oozed onto the floor.

"That's what the fuck I'm talkin' 'bout!" Felony boasted. "You ready to talk nigga!"

In the midst of all the action, Trick's cell rang, causing him to look at the screen. He hoped it was Mena calling back to return the threats he'd made to her after she hung up on him. He wanted a fight and was ready for war. With his adrenaline pumping he answered only to hear Ronni's nagging ass voice. He had promised her that he would help her get some equipment, but was all of a sudden feeling disrespected. Somehow he had a crazy feeling that Mena, DJ and Ronni were all involved somehow with trying to take over his industry, so he asked bluntly.

"Yo, I'm here. Thanks for the tip," he told her. "But I gotta question for you. I hear Mena been making counterfeit dollars out here. You know anything about that?"

"Oh, naw…I haven't heard no bullshit like that, but yo, when we gon' meet up so you can fulfill your part of the bargain?"

Trick knew Ronni was a liar and her tone gave herself away. But her next set of words took his mind off of Ronni's deceiving bullshit.

"You know she with Khadafi, right?"

"So I heard," he said with a balled up face. "A whore will always be a whore, yamean? I can't change that," he said pretending not to be bothered by this new guys name. "You know where the nigga lives?"

"No, but I can find out." She paused, "Do what you supposed to do for me and I'll take you to the spot where he hangs out from time to time."

"Bet."

"I'll call you in the morning and tell you where to meet me. Let it do, what it do," she ended feeling like things were about to get profitable for her in no time.

As soon as the call ended DJ attempted to speak again. It was clear that he was losing too much blood as his body shook and his eyes seemed to roll toward the top of his forehead.

"So Ronni, put you up to this," DJ uttered hardly able to get any words out. "She's in on it, too," he managed to say. "She got your Bentley and been showboating around town." He paused to catch his breath. "And she the one who gave me the counterfeit money."

Trick's face crinkled for seconds wondering why Ronni would try to play him. Then he thought about the guy Khadafi who Mena was supposedly staying with. Everything seemed to bother him and everyone was a potential enemy. Just like that, Trick aimed and fired twice, causing DJ to drop like a boxer who just got knocked out in the ring.

"Let's ride," he told Felony who'd already taken the keys to DJ's Porsche. "Mena and Ronni got some explaining to do."

$Twenty-Three$

Mena pulled onto the side of the Shell gas station and hopped out of the Range Rover with puckered lips. It was obvious she didn't want to be there, but had a job to do. Thoughts of her leaving her brother and sister in Khadafi's care troubled her. Her head hurt like hell, yet the two Advils she'd popped before leaving the house hadn't helped in the least. An older gentleman who pumped gas nearby watched in admiration as she used her hand to press the wrinkles from her high waist Marc Jacobs skirt and scoop neck, cream-colored shirt that exposed her neckline. Within seconds, she'd slipped her Gucci aviator shades onto her face and thrown the stylish looking green backpack onto her shoulder.

Mena shot her admirer a plastic smile, slammed the truck's door, and strutted a few blocks down the street headed to the drop off spot. It angered her deeply that Khadafi had her doing the job of an employee; and so early in the morning at that. Counterfeit LLC was supposed to be her baby, and had essentially been snatched away from her. She was mad at herself for allowing it all to happen. The fact that she thought Khadafi was the one for her and that his initial kindness and loveable behavior had faded, tore her up on the inside. How could she have been so dumb, she wondered.

Everything seemed to be going wrong. Now that Mena knew she was pregnant, she badly needed to get to the doctor. And the one person who now brought her joy had disappeared…left her home without saying a word. Mena still hadn't figured out why Sonya left abruptly, or why she hadn't called back to check on the kids. Thoughts about her whereabouts swam around her head as she crossed the street and entered the Hot Wheels parking lot.

A skating rink was the last place she expected to meet some baller wanting to buy fifty thousand dollars in counterfeit money. It wasn't how she would do business, but then again, she wasn't in charge anymore. The whole deal seemed foul and Mena just prayed she wouldn't get locked up. The fact that Skully was the only one who knew the people she was waiting to meet had her on edge.

Mena leaned against the brick next to the front door of the rink and crossed her arms impatiently. Quickly, she whipped out her cell after a sudden thought to call DJ. She still hadn't heard from him and wanted to set some things straight. Her guilt ate her up inside at the way things were done. He'd lost his girlfriend because of Ronni, and had his counterfeit business ruined because of her. She wanted to make it up to him, even if it meant giving him some of her proceeds from all the money she and Khadafi were making.

Just as she was about to call DJ, Mena got angry. It was twenty past nine and still no sign of anyone. Khadafi needed to know. She punched the digits roughly into the phone and waited for him to pick up.

"Khadafi, I'm still here. I can't believe this! You sure this is the right spot?" she asked, looking around at the old looking building. "I mean…you said this would be a piece of cake, but I'm feeling kinda weird."

"Ya tink me feelin' weird," he shot back with speedy words. "Me got t'ree people me gotta see, ya know; all within the next hour. Tis ting gettin' big, ya know, Mena. People talkin' about tis money shit all ova da city. Me got eighty thousand dollars to deliver over the next two days," his voice deepened and he spoke with venom in his tone, "and ya fuckin' talkin' about ya feelin' weird!"

"But there's nobody in this parking lot at all," Mena complained. "Nobody. And they're late," she added, showing she was salty about even having to meet them.

"If Skully said they'll be there, then they'll be there. Be patient," he warned. "They're just a little late. But with da amount of money dat these boys wanta buy, me know they'll show up."

Mena huffed.

"Ya told me ya want to live good, right?"

"Mmm hmm," she responded dryly.

"So wait," he told her. "Tis is bizness," Khadafi preached like Mena was a child being told to wait at the bus stop no matter how long it took. "What'cha gonna do when we got customers comin' from other states?"

"I'll be ready."

"Well, get'cha thong out ya pussy, gurl. Every person who is somebody in tis city wanna get wit' us right now, so be happy."

"Okay, fine," she sulked again. "But I don't know why you said Skully is getting such a big cut off this deal. He's done nothing but brought us the connect. He shoulda been the one out here at nine o'clock in the morning meeting these people."

"Stop it!" he shouted strongly. "Now shut ya bloodclot mouth, Mena! Ya hear me?"

"Yeah, I..."

When Mena heard the dial tone, tears welled up in her eyes. At that moment she missed Philadelphia badly. She missed her quiet home in the suburbs where she slept as long as she liked, shopped, and got dick on a regular. She would probably give anything to get back there. Her head thumped on each side, signaling that a migraine was near. She just needed Skully's folks to show up, fast.

Out of the blue, her phone made a noise, indicating that a new text message had come through. Mena glanced down seeing that it was Ronni. *More drama*, she told herself before even opening the text.

Out of the corner of her eye she could see a white cargo van approaching, so she pulled herself off the brick and stepped toward the curb, waiting for the van to get closer. She could see two men in the front with eager grins on their faces, even though the van crept at a slow pace.

"Come the fuck on," she said out loud as her phone sounded letting her know there was another text.

With one click of the button, Mena made an annoying sound and sucked her teeth. Her frustration showed as she read the words across the screen.

"Ugghhhh, Ronni…Stop it!" she said to herself after seeing her first text.

`Oh, so u just fucked me wit' out a condom and now won't even call a bitch!`

Mena clicked the button again to read the next message. Suddenly, she felt her heart skip a beat. Her temples pulsated at the thought of the message being true. Mena kept her head downward as she gasped for air, attempting to digest the words.

`Trick is here. He knows where u r. Watch your back.`

Before Mena could even lift her head back up, the sliding door to the white cargo van opened. Two men jumped from inside while the driver and passenger remained straight-faced in the front. Mena attempted to catch a glimpse of them all as she knew the deal had gone sour. She panicked after glancing at the mean mug on the tallest guy's face. He had a black patch over his right eye which made the whole scene even scarier. Her eyes bulged and her temperature rose. She didn't seem to be able to think fast enough as the tallest guy's fist connected with the left side of her face, knocking her out coldly. The other spread his arms to catch her fall, and tossed her limp body inside the van.

"Just like the fuck we planned!" the men shouted victoriously as the van sped out of the lot and onto the main road.

"Yeah, I'ma bad boy," the shorter guy with a southern accent announced.

"Aye, stop all the fucking cheering back there," the

driver called out. "Where to now?"

"Club Rain!" the guy with the patch shouted back. "Didn't you get paid to drive and have all this figured out? Nigga, I need yo' pay."

"Fuck you!" the driver spat.

"Aye. Everybody, shut da fuck up. Me tired of erring ya rant and rave. Ya act like little children," the passenger announced, speaking for the first time. His Jamaican accent seemed to take reign over anything anyone else said.

Unfortunately for Mena she was out cold, spread out across the hard floor of the van, and didn't hear where she was being taken. Her backpack had been taken off her shoulder and thrown to the front near the cage-like divider that separated the front passengers from the back. The van must've been some type of delivery van from the looks of the shelves that lined the wall and the posters plastered about.

Suddenly, the passenger pulled out his phone and hit the number one on his key pad activating the speed dial.

"It's done," the passenger said as soon as someone picked up. "We'll meet ya there."

$$$

An hour later, Mena moved her body slowly attempting to come back from her sleep-like comma. She wasn't sure if it was all a black-out, or if she'd really been knocked unconscious. Her jaw ached and her side hurt from the fall she remembered taking inside the van. Everything else seemed to be a blur, even her present visibility.

Still blindfolded and hands tied tightly behind her back she could see nothing. For her, that was a sign that her kidnappers would possibly let her live. In a frenzy, she squirmed to break free from the ropes, just wanting to make sure nothing else had been done to her. The thought of being raped worried her most.

Mena moved her feet around the floor, patting the area

beneath her to get a feel for where she was being held. Her body seemed to lay against a couch or some lounge-like type furniture actually feeling comfortable to her back. Finally, she was able to stand and made her way around the room as best she could.

A get-away seemed impossible without the ability to see. Eventually she rested her body against what felt like a door. Soon, she began to cry wondering, why her? She'd done nothing terribly wrong to anyone in life who didn't deserve it. And now she was being dealt blow after blow. While the tears flowed, Mena could hear movement in the next room. Her adrenaline pumped as she had to decide whether to scream out for help or remain silent.

Just as she played different scenarios in her head, voices blared in the next room. It was as if three to four people had just walked in, throwing items onto a table that made loud, piercing sounds. Everything scared her from the voices, to the sounds, to even the corks being popped from what sounded like Champaign bottles.

"Here's to you," one guy said in a low tone.

"No you," another chimed.

"No, you, nigga. You got us the van, and you drove that shit."

Mena tried to remain still so she could listen as best she could to the voices. The dialect wasn't a hundred percent understandable, but the louder voices could be heard clearer than the others.

"So, listen here rude boy," a strong voice sounded. "Get'on da phone and let Khadafi know we got his gurl, and his cash. Tell da nigga, we want t'ree hundred grand to get her back. Counterfeit, or real."

As they all laughed, Mena began to cry silently even more.

"What about four hundred?" the country sounding tone asked.

"No need. Me not tryna take his everting. Me just want my fair share. Ya see, tis the first time we not share in da profits together. Khadafi just let tis bitch come ere and she try'ta separate us. After he pay, I'll go back to him feelin' even. He'll never know I was involved and I'll convince him dat he needs me as a partner. Of course for protection."

"Word?" someone commented.

"Now, seriously," the Jamaican accent continued. "Call Khadafi. Use da fake-me-out phone I gave ya. Tell him if ya don't get da money by nine o'clock tonight, his bloodclot, bitch, Mena dies."

Mena wasn't a church going girl, but she began praying instantly. And vowed to seek God if He ever got her out of this situation. She sat on the floor with her knees pulled up to her chest, crying like a two year old who'd lost her parents. Of course she was shocked to hear Skully's voice in the other room. And to know that he would go that far to get money from Khadafi amazed her.

Crazy as it sounded, Skully really did feel like he'd been left out of the business and had some right to be a part of it. Mena could tell from day one that he never liked her much. And she also knew that he'd been plotting things lately and was up to no good. But his jealously issues were now affecting her life.

Suddenly, the voices stopped, footsteps sounded in all directions, and some walked toward Mena. She scurried from the floor with speed, patting her way like a blind person back to the couch. Within seconds the door opened. Mena trembled in fear hoping there would be no torture.

"Why am I here," she spoke softly.

"Because we need money," a country sounding voice fired back.

He rushed over to Mena, alarming her in the process and snatched the blindfold off of her eyes.

Even though he had a bag over his head, Mena could tell from his physique that it was the same tall guy that had hit her and knocked her out. "You're not going to kill me, are you?" She sniffled a bit, then tried to loosen the grip on her hands.

"Not yet. We just want the money. My boy is making a

call to your man. If he comes through, you're good." He hunched his shoulders. "If he doesn't, you're short."

As he laughed loudly, all kinds of gruesome thoughts about her death bounced around Mena's head. She realized that she'd entered into a treacherous world where it was easy to get with the in crowd, and just as easy for them to betray you. She hoped like hell Khadafi really cared for her, and that she would make it out alive.

$ Twenty-Four $

2:15 p.m.

Ronni walked hesitantly. But not with her usual strut. It seemed she didn't want to go through with the plan. Even though she hated Mena for what she'd done, the payback was too deep. It was too brutal and just plain, grimey. But there was no turning back now. Noble was on Ronni's heels as they entered the Bridgeview Village housing projects.

The rain all of a sudden began to pour as they neared Sonya's with their heads down using their hands as umbrellas to duck the rain. The sky was cloudy, almost dark, like a major thunderstorm was coming. Noble wasn't concerned at all. It could've been snowing for all he cared. He had an agenda, one that would soon make him rich. For now, it was all about turning Ronni against Mena.

Noble walked even faster feeling familiar with the area. Unfortunately, nobody was out because of the weather and wouldn't be able to give out any fist pounds or shot outs to those who had bought from him or his crew before. He had however gotten the call from one of the boys in the hood; the call he had been waiting on to let him know that Sonya had returned. No one could understand why she was so important to him…but didn't really care either. For Noble, his goal was to help Ronni get revenge…and Ronni in return needed to live up to her word. They had to get the right equipment to insert themselves into the counterfeit game.

"You sure about this?" Ronni stopped to ask Noble, not

caring that they were getting soaked.

"Come the fuck on!" Noble snapped. "Scared ass lil nigga. This the house right here. I thought you was a soldier? Now you comin' with this paranoid bullshit."

"Nigga, I am a soldier," Ronni barked back.

"Act like it then, and knock on the muthafuckin' door," Noble responded as they stood outside Sonya's front door.

Ronni resented the paranoid comment. But she knew she had been acting a little shaky since the call she got from Trick on the way to Sonya's. His questions puzzled her. Scared her too, and made her feel like something shady was up. He wanted to know if she knew Mena had been making counterfeit money, and who'd been helping her. Ronni couldn't think fast enough; especially when Trick asked if Ronni had been driving his Bentley. Of course she told him, no; and that Mena had been driving it all along.

Sonya on the other hand was inside, stretched back with the music blasting and couldn't hear Ronni's first knock on the door. She had gone through the early morning without her fix, and struggled like crazy as the late afternoon approached. The club-like atmosphere had her in a daze. She smoked the last cigarette in the pack of Kool's hoping to fight off the urge of more heroin. She tried everything to keep her mind off the drugs. She'd ran through the five hundred she took from Mena's in less than a day and sat scratching, wondering where her next hit would come from. Her thoughts spun rapidly inside her twisted mind while another pound sounded at the door.

Her first, thought; *I'll sell my children to Mena since she wants them around so bad*. Sonya had to laugh at herself. Her second thought, *Fuck, I should just go back to Khadafi's house and steal me some more money, even more this time. Shit, what them dumb mufuckas gone do*? she asked herself, seriously.

Sonya's next crazy thought was interrupted by what sounded like the police. Loud, hard knocks told her the person at the door wanted to get in badly. She flew from her chair wondering who it could be. She had fired the Mexicans Mena hired to renovate her place as soon as they showed up for work in the early hours of the morning. So, she was sure it wasn't them coming back. If it was, she had some *knock down, make you wanna cry* type words ready for them.

"Y'all taco-eating mufuckas might as well hit the fucking road, cuz I'm busy!" she yelled out.

Then she thought about Poochie, her crack-head friend who she had gotten high with just ten hours ago. Maybe he'd sold the Prada sunglasses she had slipped into her bag when leaving Mena's, and was back with the profits.

"You betta have my damn loot, you ugly mufucka!" she shouted, hallucinating that she actually saw Poochie from the peep hole.

Before Sonya could open the door, the loud knocking started again. She didn't bother to fix her messy hair, or care about the fact that she smelled like spoiled milk.

"Who the fuck is it?" she shouted. "You gone tear down my got damn door! And I will sue your ass!"

"It's Ronni. Mena's friend. Open up!" she hollered over the music.

"Ronni, the fuck who?" Sonya snapped. "And what do you want, dyke?" she added, snatching the door open like she was ready to rumble.

"C'mon now," Ronni greeted with a devilish grin. She studied Sonya from head to toe noticing her dirty, torn t-shirt and raggedy sweatpants that were rolled up to her knees. "Let's put the other day behind us, Miss Sonya," she said from the other side of the screen door. "I came with a gift just to show you that I'm sorry. For real," Ronni added.

Sonya's wild looking eyebrows crinkled. "A gift for me?" she asked.

"Yeah you." Ronni hit her with a hard nod. "And this my man Noble right here."

Sonya gave them both suspicious glares. But said nothing while Noble held his mean grimace without even saying hello. He just stood letting Ronni do all the talking.

"So, I started thinkin', Mena my girl in all so I want us to be cool. Noble works this area a lot and we tryin' to drum up new business. We lookin' for taste testers, and someone to spread the word about his product. And it's a paid gig."

"How much?" Sonya asked quickly.

Ronni flashed a hundred dollar bill in her face. "Cash plus product."

Sonya frowned showing that she was confused, but reached for the money anyway. Unfortunately, Ronni flipped her hand backwards keeping her from touching the crisp bill.

"Let us in first," Ronni suggested.

The door flew open and Sonya led them in. "Look, my new furniture not here yet so tell your boy there's nothing to steal," Sonya remarked still giving Noble the suspicious eye. Her eyes were blood shot red and appeared watery as she offered them a seat in the living room on the couch covered by a paint splattered, white throw cloth.

"Excuse the mess. I'm renovating," she joked. "My painter did this shit. Them mufuckas owe me," she joked. "So, sit down, and tell me a little about this test shit. And what kinda product?" she added with a snappy tone. "I don't smoke weed."

"Nah, this not weed, baby. This that beast!" Ronni explained.

"The Big H?" Sonya inquired.

Ronni shook her head. "Damn straight."

Sonya's eyes grew to the size of watermelons. The heroin she had last night was potent and had her feigning for more. Quickly, she took a seat across from them in her favorite lounge chair, ready to hear what they had to say. She saw Ronni glancing at the paint buckets that lined the wall and the white and blue throw cloths that covered almost everything in the living room and kitchen area. She kept scratching at her arms as she became angrier by the minute.

"You fucking looking down on me?" she asked Ronni in a war-like tone? "I mean you eyeing my shit like you got a problem with how I'm living."

"Nah..nah, like I said, I'm here on business," Ronni said calmly. "Let me explain."

"Ummm hummm," Sonya hummed sarcastically.

As Ronni began to talk, Sonya interrupted. "Listen, run me that hundred first, then finish," she told Ronni, "you said that shit was a gift. Now are you a liar, or what? Produce baby…produce."

Sonya kept her forefinger moving back and forth rapidly letting Ronni know that nothing else would be discussed until she got the money. Her antsy behavior would have been puzzling to most, but not Noble, or Ronni. They had spent countless hours around drug users and could identify with Sonya's twitches, and jittery moves she made while they talked. For them, they knew the sale to Sonya would be a piece of cake.

By the time Ronni gave a blow by blow account on how they were paying people to test the heroin, Sonya was already rolling up her sleeve. It sounded like a good time to help somebody else out. Poochie hadn't showed up with shit anyway, and she wasn't about to let some free heroin waltz out the door.

"Shit, so I'm like one of those surveyors at the mall. I test the shit, tell you if it's good, or what it needs to be better?"

"Right," Ronni agreed.

"So, what if I can't quite figure it out on the first try?" Sonya questioned.

"Then you get another try," Noble chimed in.

"Damn, I like this shit!" Sonya scrambled to her feet and spread her arms wide, as she listened to the rain land harder on top of the roof. "So where is it? I'm game," she told them both.

Noble gave Ronni the evil eye. Cautiously, she pulled the small, white plastic bag from her back pocket then stood up, standing face-to-face with Sonya. "This is it," Ronni announced, passing the bag to Sonya. "They're two syringes in there. The shits inside."

Sonya smiled like a welfare chick on the first of the month. "So y'all staying?" she wanted to know.

"Hell yeah," Ronni announced. "We gotta ask questions.

That's the whole point. What if the shit not good. We need to know," she added.

"Ummmmmmm," Sonya commented, pretending to still listen to Ronni. She had already ripped through the bag, ignoring their small talk, and had the first syringe in her hand ready to get right on the Big H that she loved so much.

Before they knew it, Sonya had grabbed everything she needed, and was back in her favorite chair searching for a vein. She kept popping at her skin vigorously, talking shit to herself like she was the only one in the room. Ronni began pacing the floor wondering if she should've paid Mena back in some other way, or if Noble's concoction was after all the best plan. While she paced in deep thought she saw Nobel's eyes light up with victory. Swiftly, she turned back around in just enough time to see a huge grin spread across Sonya's face. Within seconds she was all teeth while the potion pumped into her veins.

"Damn! Who the fuck is yo' chemist," Sonya blasted.

"You like?" Ronni questioned.

"Hell yeah! I love the way this shit makes me feel."

As the seconds passed, Sonya's pupils dilated more, almost popping from her head, and her grin turned in a frozen piece of art. With each breath she took it became harder to breathe. Her arm moved slightly as if she wanted to ask Ronni a question, but her jaws kept her from speaking.

"You still like it?" Ronni badgered. "Or should we change anything?"

Sonya's face turned a purplish color signaling that something was deeply wrong. Her facial expression told Ronni and Noble that she wanted to say something, but instead of helping, they were all smiles, watching Sonya overdose on some bad heroin.

Sonya struggled to get her words out. "H-h-h-e-e-e-e-l-l-l-p…"

"You say something, Sonya?" Ronni pulled on the back of her ear with a smirk. "Help you, Sonya. Is that what the fuck you tryin' to say?" Ronni stooped low, and got close to Sonya's frozen-like body.

Her lips were dry and cracked as Ronni shook her head just two inches from her face. “Your daughter is a cruddy bitch, Sonya. You hear me?”she asked, smacking Sonya across the face. “When you do bad, you know it comes back, right? So thank your daughter for the good liquid,” she ended.

Sonya wasn’t responding to anything. She couldn’t. Then just like that, lightning struck. The loud sound ironically hit at the same time that Sonya took her hardest hit. The Big H had stolen her soul. Stolen her life. Just like that, Sonya threw her head back, allowing her discolored face to brush against the couch.

Noble stood up. “The bitch dead,” he said calmly. He hadn’t moved from his spot the entire time, and seemed to watch it all unfold live a movie buff at the theater.

“Nah, not yet,” Ronni said in a low tone. “I think she’s still breathing.”

“Let’s go. I told you the old bitch dead.”

Noble’s tone was now more ruthless. He didn’t give a damn about Sonya, or Ronni for that matter. It was all about being able to insert himself into the talked about counterfeit business. And whatever it took to make that happen, he would do.

As they walked toward the door, Ronni attempted to look back at Sonya’s lifeless body until her cell rang. She didn’t recognize the number, but figured it could’ve been Trick again. While she answered, Noble had a cloth wiping down fingerprints off the door just in case they were ever considered suspects. He didn’t do jails, so didn’t want to take any chances.

“Talk to me,” Ronni answered, walking back out into the rain.

She listened for a few seconds until her jaws tightened and her mouth fell open. “You shittin’ me?”

“No, me very serious. The bloodcot muthufuckas got Mena,” Khadafi reported. “They call me, ya know. Say they want money.”

"Who?" Ronni questioned intently.

"Me not know." Khadafi paused to get his thoughts in order. "Fuck, fuck, fuck!" he shouted out in frustration.

"Look, me and Mena cool, but I don't have no money, dawg. You cut me out the business, remember?"

"Me got money. Me just need some back up. Dat's all." He paused to clear his head. "Me can't get Skully," Khadafi said with anger in his voice. "Fuckin' don't know bombaclot where he's at!" He paused to breathe again. "And me don't know what kinda fire power they got or how many there are. Can ya help me get her back, Ronni?"

"I don't know about that," Ronni said with uncertainty in her voice. "I mean…."

"Look, me know ya still a little upset about her leavin' and movin' wit' me , but she need us both right now, ya know. So what'cha say?"

Ronni let out a long pause. "Where they got her at?"

"Some Jamaican club. Me neva heard of it. Ahhhhhh, it's Club Rain."

Ronni gave another long pause as she made it back to Noble's truck. "Bet. I'll meet you there. When?"

"Hold tight. Me need time to gather da money and get some more help. Stay by da phone. Me call you in thirty."

$Twenty-Five$

3:45p.m.

Trick had personality like honey. He'd only been in town less than twenty-four hours, and like bees, niggas flocked to him wanting to be in his presence. At first glance, some thought he was Rick Ross when he strutted into the Palm Tree Lounge on Old Folly Road. His intent was to get a feel for the movers and shakers in Charleston and a location on where the ballers hung out.

Everything he had found out from DJ troubled him. The fact that Mena, DJ and Ronni had been running his business in the south was foul, so Ronni and Mena would both have to pay. He wasn't certain about Khadafi's involvement; or how much he knew. But he was definitely going to find out. From what Ronni and DJ had reported, he was Mena's new love.

Trick paid the guy at the front counter for rental time, and instructed Felony to grab some pool sticks from the back wall. Back at home he would've never been caught playing with house sticks. Trick was good at his game, but this time he was simply scouting out anyone who knew information.

It took about fifteen minutes before he ran the table on Felony. He bragged loudly and ordered a drink noticing a few stares from nearby tables. Trick asked one guy if he wanted next, and made small talk with another fat guy with a low cut fade. It didn't take long for them to start kicking it like they'd been boys forever. By the time Trick asked if they knew his boy Khadafi, news started swirling through the pool hall like a gossiping hair salon.

Everyone was amazed that he and Khadafi were boys and wanted to know if he had access to the counterfeit money. Trick cringed inside wondering how Khadafi had made a name for himself that quickly. From what the guys had told him, Khadafi's name buzzed through the streets. He had become the King Pen of Counterfeit in the area and Trick couldn't understand how. It was too fast. Too perfect. It had taken him nearly nine months to get a decent clientele back in Philly, yet Khadafi seemed to have South Carolina on lock within two months.

"That nigga only charge half for that fake money too, so I need to get my hands on some," the fat guy stated.

Trick's eyes bulged. *Half? Damn, and I was only charging a forth*, he thought. "I haven't seen my boy Khadafi in a minute and I think he moved," Trick said as he put chalk on the tip of the stick. "I lost my cell phone so I don't even know that niggas number by heart. You know where he live at?"

When the fat dude looked at him with a confused expression, Trick knew he'd taken a risk by asking that type of question, but it was worth a shot.

"Oh naw man, I don't know where he live at. I mean I see him riding around town a lot cuz the nigga got about four different cars. But I'on know where he lay his head." He took a sip of his Heineken. "But what I do know is that the broad he be with is fine as hell. Somebody said she not from around here, and I can tell. These bitches down here don't look like that."

Trick bit the inside of his lip and glared at Felony as the guy continued to rave about Mena. The thought of how she'd stolen his business and was now sharing it with another man, made him furious. He was actually kind of hurt by the fact, but refused to show any signs of weakness in front of his boy, or a stranger for that matter. He couldn't wait to find her so he could put an end to her betrayal.

As Mena continued to invade his mind, Trick's cell phone rang. As soon as he looked down and saw that it was Ronni's number, a quick grin appeared on his face. He was determined to find out where she, or Mena was before they hung up.

"Talk to me," he answered.

"Yo, I got some good news, nigga," she responded.

"Oh yeah and what news is that?" Even though Trick knew Ronni was up to bullshit, he couldn't let her know what DJ had told him about his car or the counterfeit money just yet. *I wanna wait until I see her little bitch ass in person,* he thought.

"I finally know where Mena is."

Trick's ears seemed to perk up like a Doberman Pinscher. "Really. So, where is she?"

"Not so fast big boy. I got a business proposition to talk to you about first," Ronni quickly replied.

Trick was so tired of Ronni and her games. "Hell nah! No more talks, no more propositions. Like, the business I started is boomin' in this town. I need to find Mena."

At that moment Ronni wanted to confess to helping Mena and Khadafi build the business. She wanted to shine and boast just like she loved to do, and take credit for someone else's work. But then she thought about how things would play out if she told the truth.

"This shit is simple," she began. "You know what a franchise is, right?"

"Ronni, when I see you, I might just shoot you for GP. Like, you know I know what a franchise is."

"So, I was thinkin'… instead of me gettin' equipment and setting up shop, you set me up the right way. Show me everything. I'll run shit in other states, and give you a percentage of the money."

"I'll think about it," he responded dryly. "Where's Mena?" His voice deepened.

"She gone be at Club Rain in about an hour or two. It's on Grey street. Stay by the phone, I'll let you know when she's almost there," Ronni said before hanging up.

Trick felt like he'd just hit the jackpot as soon as he hung up. He wondered why Mena would be going to a club so early in the day. Maybe it was some type of special event, he thought; a baby shower, or fashion show. Hell, he didn't know. He figured country people rolled differently than people up north. Right before he could turn to tell Felony the good news, his phone rang again. It was another Philly number, but this time he had no idea who it was.

"Talk to me," Trick answered again.

"Is this Trent Fowler?" a man asked.

"Yeah. Who this?"

"This is Officer Moyer from the Philadelphia Police Department."

Trick started to become nervous. He had no idea what the officer could've wanted. "Okay."

"Mr. Fowler, I'm calling from the Auto Theft Detail division. You recently called your 2010 Bentley Continental in stolen, correct?"

"Yeah, that's correct."

"Well, Mr. Fowler we received a call from the Savannah, Georgia Police Department this morning, and it appears as if they found your car completely vandalized and abandoned in some type of trailer park."

Trick couldn't help but shake his head. He knew Ronni was behind this, and couldn't wait to make her pay.

"Mr. Fowler, are you there?" the officer continued. "Would you like the address to where the car was located?"

"Look, I can't talk right now, yamean? If I need anything else from y'all I'll be in touch," Trick said before hanging up. Throwing the pool stick on the floor, he looked at Felony and said, "Let's roll." He was tired of playing Mr. Nice Guy. It was time to handle business.

$$$

Twenty minutes later, Trick's Escalade pulled back in front of DJ's Porsche truck; the truck that Felony had driven to the back of an abandoned shopping center earlier. Time was key, so

Trick knew he had to hurry. His plan was to make it to Club Rain before he even got the call from Ronni saying that Mena was on the way. Shockingly, he would be there to surprise them both.

Felony had a mystified look on his face. "Why we back here at this nigga's truck again?"

"We not gone drive my shit to the club," Trick spat. "If some shit pops off, let this nigga DJ's tags get traced."

"Right, right. Good move."

Trick thought about how he pressed Felony to roll with him to South Carolina. He was confident that he would need help finding Mena and getting his equipment back. He felt he needed a soldier ready for war. But now everything had changed. It seemed that getting to Mena would be easier than he originally thought. It was now time to handle a new problem.

They hopped out, leaving Trick's truck next to the big blue trash can in the back of what used to be a Marshalls. Trick stepped with an extra gangsta walk and scowl on his face, getting ready for his showdown with Mena. He snatched his nine millimeter from the back of his pants as he opened the passenger door to the Porsche. Once inside, he asked Felony if he had his gun.

"You know it," Felony bragged, sticking DJ's key in the ignition.

"Man, did you hear that shit them niggas was saying back there about Mena?"

"In the pool hall?" Felony laughed. "Damn, nigga, they was just complementin' her."

"Oh yeah. That's it," he asked with a deeper scowl. "You think she look good? You wanna fuck her?" Trick grilled.

"C'mon man, where you goin' wit this shit," Felony asked, backing the truck up slightly.

"You fucked Mena, didn't you? The streets talk, nigga."

Before Felony could respond, one bullet released into his chest. When Felony slumped over and pressed his head against the dash board, Trick smiled. His job was done.

$ Twenty-Six $

5:00p.m.

Mena got lucky. Finally, she'd gotten the babysitter who didn't give a damn if she saw his face or not. Even though her blindfold had been removed, tears still dripped from her eyes every now and then. She didn't know if he had been one of the original guys in the van or not, but he remained mostly quiet without the exception of asking Mena where she was from.

"Philly," she answered softly, between sniffles. "Look, I don't feel too good. I think I'm pregnant," she added, attempting to get a little extra sympathy. "Can you loosen these ropes on the back of my hands? Or at least my feet?"

"I don't think so light-skin."

Mena sulked, then got teary eyed again. "Can you at least get me some water?"

"I'ma get you some water," he responded dryly, "but you going too far, light-skin. I already turned the T.V. on for you."

"Thanks," she said as he got up from the table, and walked toward the door. "Don't try nothin' stupid," he added, lifting his shirt, and tapping the gun on his side.

Mena knew he had a good point. No one else had been that nice. When he removed her blindfold at the start of his shift, she realized that she was being held in the green room of a club. It was the area where celebrities hung out before a show, or club employees chilled from time to time. A forty-two inch plasma hung on the wall and three couches, and a big conference table filled the room.

She was comfortable and at least not beaten or raped. That had been her biggest concern. She wanted nothing to ruin her chances of delivering a healthy baby. Mena gave off a big sigh when the frail guy with moles all over his face walked back into the room with a water bottle. He handed it off to Mena, then stared at the breaking news report that flashed across the screen.

Mena's eyes quickly followed and her face suddenly froze. DJ's barber shop had made the five o'clock news. The T.V. showed police swarming the entire street and yellow caution tape blocking off the entrance to the shop. Mena's anxiety tripled as she hoped DJ wasn't involved. It only took seconds for the reporter to give a quick account of what had been found in the back room. When DJ's full name was spoken, Mena's face turned into an ugly cry.

"Oh my God! Whyyyyyy!! Khadafi, why!!!!!"

In her heart she knew that her man had killed her cousin. She couldn't understand how one man could be so greedy that he would kill off one of the few family members she had left. Then her mind switched to her little brother and sister which completely sent her over the edge.

"Ohhh…uhhhhh," she moaned and cried all at the same time.

The guy with the mole watched Mena for a few seconds then bounced, locking the door behind him. That was too much drama for him. He simply wanted his cut of the money from Skully. "Who the fuck was that who got smoked at the barber shop?" he asked himself.

Hysterically, Mena shouted, "Noooo, Nooooo, Noooo!"

Her eyes were glued to the television when DJ's body was brought out on the stretcher and the camera gave a quick glimpse of some of the guys who worked at the shop standing nearby. She held her stomach tightly, feeling like she had to vomit. Suddenly, her body dropped to the floor as she rolled from side to side on the cold, black, painted floor. This was all too much to bear.

$$$

5:10 p.m.

By the time Khadafi stuffed three hundred grand into an old gym bag it was already a little after five. Time flew. And each second counted. He found himself rushing up the stairs from the basement, taking two at a time trying to remember if he had everything. The Spanish maid burst from the living room, fussing, and complaining about having to stay to watch the children. Quickly, he peeled four hundreds from his back pocket, throwing the cash onto the granite countertop.

His eyes filled with worry as he moved rapidly from one area of the first floor to the other. His dreads swung back and forth wildly as he talked to himself, laying out the plan. His final stop, the hall closet. Khadafi reached in and pulled the black gun case from the top shelf which held his .380 and a chrome Beretta. Neither had bodies on them. And he hoped like hell by the end of the day he wouldn't be a suspect in a murder case.

Within seconds, he'd darted out of the house, hopped in the Benz and jetted through the neighborhood. He picked up his cell to try Skully one last time. One last effort was all he had time for. It was crazy how Skully still hadn't called back. Crazy thoughts began to swirl through his mind. If Mena had been taken, maybe someone had Skully too. *Maybe tis was all an attack on me*, he thought to himself. After the fourth ring, he knew there was no chance of Skully calling back, or rolling with him to trade off the money for Mena.

Khadafi sped along knowing that he was breaking a sacred rule. He never rushed into a hostile environment without his boy, Skully. He was the rugged enforcer and always carried three guns at one time. But for now, Khadafi would have to rely on his own firepower and whatever help Ronni would bring. At that moment he thought about Ronni. The car swerved slightly as he dialed.

"Ronni," he said when she answered. He took his hand from the wheel for a brief second to wipe the sweat from his forehead. "Me on da way. Meet me there," he added hurriedly.

"How long," she replied.

"Now. Me should be there in less than twenty."

"Bet."

Ronni's next set of words were a complete blur for Khadafi when he noticed a black Suburban following closely behind. He hit the pedal, increasing his speed to nearly eighty miles per hour. But as fate would have it, he got caught at the light. The Suburban was no match for the Benz, but the vehicle still sat four cars behind, seemingly waiting for Khadafi's next move. As soon as the light changed, Khadafi cut somebody off, then swung a hard right, cutting in front of a large Deer Park delivery truck.

It was clear, Khadafi had lost his follower, but he continued to speed like a race car driver making sure the truck never caught back up with him. His heart raced as he had flipped through possibilities of who it could have been. Then it hit him. Maybe it was Mena's kidnappers. Without delay, he grabbed his cell from between his legs and scrolled back to the call back number that had called him earlier. Unfortunately, there was no answer. He simply told the voice mail, "Me got da money…and on da way!"

5:20 p.m.

Ronni obviously didn't waste any time calling Trick. As soon as Khadafi hung up from her, she called her new friend. "She on her way there now," she told Trick with a smirk. "I'm on my way, too. Don't forget what we talked about, nigga."

"Yeah...yeah..."

Trick was fed up with Ronni. He hung up without waiting

to hear anything else she had to say. Little did Ronni know, he was already pulling into the parking lot of the club. It wasn't quite what he expected. The black awning had the name written in cursive letters and the brick that faced the building had wild graffiti writing sprayed along the edges. It also puzzled him that there was only one other car in the lot besides his.

Trick sat patiently for minutes, thinking about how he would handle things. He already had enough blood on his hands for the day, and hoped no one else had to die. He wanted what was his and simple answers from Mena; especially about Felony. Even though he was dead, he needed to know everything, so that niggas in the street couldn't laugh in his face.

The fact that Felony had been betraying him all along made his insides boil. Something in his gut had been telling him that Felony had a thing for Mena for months; especially the way he protected her when Mena had Trick locked up. A part of him thought he'd gotten soft because it was his girl. Then after reading a text message just two days ago that Mena had sent Felony, it became clearer. It hurt. Bad. But Trick knew that he hadn't been faithful to Mena, so she would go with a slap on the wrist, or a punch to the face. Maybe even an ass beating. But Felony he would never forgive. *That punk got just what he deserved,* he told himself, stepping from the truck.

Trick made his way to the front of the club, walking with his normal swagger. Seconds later, he knocked hard, wondering why the door was locked. *Maybe this the nigga Khadafi's club, and him and Mena inside,* he thought. His thought pattern changed to a more hostile disposition. He wanted someone to answer the door. Immediately.

Finally, a frail guy unlocked, and opened the door widely. "We don't open on Wednesdays," he said with a tightened face.

"Nigga, I know," Trick shot back. "The owner told me to come up. We got business to take care of."

The mole-faced guy stepped back, frowned, and led Trick into the dimly lit club. "Sit tight. Lemme try to get him on the phone," he responded with attitude.

While he dialed, Trick observed the open floor plan of the two thousand square foot club. Everything could be seen from the front counter where he stood; the DJ booth, the three bars, dance floor, and the rooms off to the side that lined each side of the wall.

While Trick surveyed the area, the mole faced guy kept nodding and saying, "Yep, ummmhuh."

Things seemed strange, but Trick held his composure waiting on a response.

Suddenly, the guy removed the phone from his ear. "You Khadafi," he asked harshly.

"Yeah," Trick responded.

$Twenty-Seven$

5:35 p.m.

Trick remained near the front door of the club while listening to the frail guy with moles talk uneasily to his boss on the phone.

"Yeah. That's what I said...that's what I said," he repeated speedily; almost in a stutter. "It's Khadafi, man. C'mon!" He tensed up while staring Trick up and down.

He couldn't believe he'd been left alone, and now Khadafi stood before him with a suspicious look on his face. *What if he tried to retaliate without giving up the money now that he knew he was single-handedly in control of his girl*? He had his gun on him if anything kicked off, but it was only a .38. Besides his skinny body, and lack of courage was no match for the hefty man before him.

"Yo, hurry up," the frail guy pressed, noticing how Trick's frown had intensified.

Trick could tell he was afraid. He just wasn't sure why. "How much longer," he asked in a stern voice, making it seem like someone was really expecting him.

"Nah, I don't see it," the worker spoke into the phone. He paused, checked Trick out again and asked, "Where the money at?"

Luckily, Trick was quick on his feet. "In the truck." He played along with confidence. "I'll wait on the big dog before I go get it."

Trick wanted to see how far things would go. He assumed this was a counterfeit transaction set up by Khadafi. Without being able to produce any big money he realized it wouldn't go far; but was hoping Mena would show up with Khadafi in the meantime. His thoughts went wild as the guy's phone conversation ended. He wondered how much cash was involved. And of course couldn't wait to get a good look at the infamous Khadafi; the man who had stolen his business and his woman.

"They'll be here in less than five," the guy told Trick fretfully. Beads of sweat formed across his face as he tried not to give Trick eye contact. The club was silent until Trick said, "Nice spot."

No response was given. Only stares as the mole faced guy watched the front door like a hawk. He was scared shitless and didn't know how to process Trick's behavior. Just as he was about to speak, a black Suburban sped through the lot and parked right out front, curbside.

Two men, one six feet tall with a patch over his eye, and the other, a short Jamaican, hopped out with killer faces. It was clear to Trick that trouble had just arrived. The glass front door swung open and the shorter guy with craters all over his face spoke first.

"Yo, why ya got'em standin' at the fuckin' front door?"

"Ahhhh…I don't know," the soft worker said, backing his way deeper into the club area.

"And where's da money?" The Jamaican turned to bark at Trick after seeing no bags or sign of cash nearby.

Trick shot them all suspicious looks.

The two rugged men returned the hard stare. They'd never seen Khadafi before, but expected him to be Jamaican since Skully, who hired them said he was his boy. They'd heard that Skully hung with Jamaicans, but figured at this point nationality didn't matter. And the fact that Skully hadn't planned to show his face until after the transaction was complete made things even crazier.

"You gone go get the money?" the tall guy asked, tapping on the butt of his gun.

Trick remained silent. His eyes simply did another quick dance around the club. He wasn't afraid of patch boy's gun. He had Felony's tucked down his pants. And was ready to use it if anything popped off. Something was up. He knew it. He sensed it. He felt it.

"What? You wanna see your girl first, nigga?" the guy with the patch questioned? "She still alive."

Trick's adrenaline pumped. *Were they talking about Mena?* "Yeah," he finally answered followed by a nod. "Where she at?"

"Bring her out, Marc," the tall guy instructed, followed by a head nod.

Just like that the guy with the moles all over his face, who Trick now knew as Marc rushed off to the far right corner of the club. It was about six yards from where they stood, but he could still see the door to the room being opened. It didn't take long for two bodies to reappear, and the sound of a woman, saying, "Where are we going?"

Trick took a few long steps in the direction of Marc and the woman he tried to make-out. The sound of the voice told him that it was Mena. But it hadn't been confirmed since they hadn't made it into the light yet.

His initial plan was to confront Mena about his car, his money, his equipment, stealing his business, and the nigga, Khadafi. But when he laid eyes on Mena being led out with her hands tied in front of her body, he paused. Trick's eyes bounced from the Jamaican, to the guy with the patch, and finally to Marc and Mena.

His eyes asked the question, *What the fuck is going on*?

But when Mena called out, "Oh my God, Trick, help me!" Trick went for his gun. He stood away from the door, but in between Mena and Marc, and the two guys who had pulled out two black .45's and inched their way toward Marc also.

"Yo, who the fuck are you?" the taller guy asked with wrinkles in his forehead. "We just want the money. And you can take her."

"You a'ight?" Trick asked Mena.

She sniffled, then responded softly, "Yes."

As much as she hated to admit it, Mena was glad Trick was there. Whatever she had done to him, she hoped he would forgive. For now, he seemed to be her way out.

"Look, where's the fuckin' money?" the Jamaican guy repeated, only this time, spitting his words more strongly.

At the same time, the faint sound of a door shutting from the back startled them all. Each of the men held the guns steadily while turning from right to left unable to stand in one place. The moment was tense. It was obvious someone else was inside.

"King, who the fuck is that?" the guy with the patch asked his Jamaican boy frantically. He never took his eyes off Trick. Or his gun.

So much for me not knowing who they are, Trick thought. He now knew two out of three names.

"Be easy," King replied. "It might be Skully. "Hey, is dat you Skully?" he called out. "Nigga, stop playin' games!" he shouted in his thick accent.

Out of the blue, Ronni, Noble and Khadafi could be seen stepping from the darkness near the back of the club. All three inched along with guns drawn like three cowboys coming to a gun fight. No one could've imagined what was about to go down. Nor, how bad it would get.

They inched forward slowly, analyzing the situation. Khadafi held the bag of money on his arm as his eyes rotated across the floor. He could see that Marc had Mena gripped tightly by the arm and that on the surface she seemed okay.

Trick recognized Ronni when they were almost eight feet away from each other. It was weird how they all ended in a circle-like stance with Khadafi being the closest to the back.

"Ronni!" Mena shouted. "I shoulda known. Why are you here?" she called out. "You had something to do with this? You and Skully?"

"I'm here to meet your man, Trick," she announced slyly. She pointed the .357 Magnum held tightly in her hand toward Skully's three goons.

Quickly, Khadafi frowned. *Trick? Mena's guy?* It was all too much to comprehend. He'd already heard the guy call out Skully's name, and now with Mena saying it too, it was clear Skully was involved.

"This all your fault, baby girl," Ronni taunted Mena. Her posture told everyone she was ready for whatever came her way. "See, this is what happens when you betray people." Quickly, she moved the position of her gun, and pointed it directly at Mena. "You don't give a fuck about nobody, do you? Go 'head and tell Khadafi how this fat nigga here is really your dude, and how you ran off wit' his shit."

"Stop it! Stop it! Ronni," Mena screamed. "Your payback is coming!"

"Yours already came, baby." Ronni paused to give a sinister grin while noticing that the fellas were annoyed. "Sonya's dead!"

Mena didn't respond at all. She remained next to Marc with a blank stare. Her body shook and chill bumps covered her arms. Everyone she loved was potentially dead. Her mind flashed to DJ, and how she assumed Khadafi had killed him. She wanted to be shot right there. There was no way she would leave with Khadafi.

Skully's boys didn't want to hear anymore. They were there to get paid. "Throw that bag of money over here," King told Khadafi, "and everybody will walk outta here alive."

Noble's face balled up like one of his pits. He had other plans. He'd decided he was the one leaving with the money. Just like that, he opened fire. "Bulls eye!" he cheered, leaping from his feet as his Desert Eagle ripped through King's face. Within seconds the club shook from all the gun shots popping off at one time. Everybody fired; even Marc. So much heat spread. It was like the devil had joined them all.

One by one they all got off shots, firing at anyone they

thought were shooting at them. Mena hit the floor, after taking a hit near her abdomen. And unfortunately Noble fell beside her. He had just put two slugs into the right side of Marc's head, when three bullets caught him, mid-air.

Mena was an emotional wreck while pressing her hand firmly against her wound. The pain shrieked through her body but the sight of blood caused her to lose control. As shots continued to blast off above her head, she watched Noble's eyes roll to the back of his head, as blood gushed from his temple. She began screaming like a frantic child, "Ohhhhhh myyyyy Goddddd! Somebody help me!" she sobbed, crawling to grab Noble's gun off the floor.

Suddenly the fire stopped. It seemed like they were all police practicing at the range. The dry wall had been splattered from parts of the walls and bullets were lodged into anything solid. All three of Skully's guys lay stiff in a pool of blood. From where Mena sat she could see that Trick, Khadafi and Ronni were all still standing.

Ronni had been hit in her left leg, but still managed to hold her .357 in her hand. Why? Mena wasn't sure because all the kidnappers were dead. She watched from the floor as Ronni limped over near King's body to make sure he was dead. When she saw that his chest was covered in blood, a sly smile crept on her face. "We did it," she told everybody, hoping to break the ice.

Khadafi didn't lighten-up. Neither did Trick.

"So Mena, ya want to tell me about tis guy here?" Khadafi asked with his eyes glued to Trick and the .380 lowered by his side.

Only sniffles could be heard coming from the floor. Mena was distraught, and also afraid of Khadafi. It was crazy how she didn't know who to trust. A part of her felt like Ronni would shoot her on the spot if given the chance, so she held onto the gun tightly and rested it between her legs.

"Ya hear me, Mena?"

"There's nothing to tell," Trick finally spoke up. "That's

my girl. She took my equipment, and my counterfeit money." He shrugged his shoulders like it was nothing. "I think you know the rest," he barked. "You took over. So now you got my equipment?"

"Dis gurl here took your equipment," Khadafi said, pointing to Ronni.

In a blink of an eye, Trick raised his gun and shot Ronni in both arms causing her gun to fly away from her body. Like something out of a movie, she fell beneath the counter with the cash register on top. Her body formed in a curled position as she fought off the pain with wailing sounds. Finally, Ronni had been shut down. Her only hope was to stay alive as she heard faint sounds of sirens in the background.

Khadafi's eyes darted back to Mena. "Gurl, didn't me tell ya when we first met, ya die if ya double cross me?" Each word he spoke seemed to have venom inside.

Mena continued to press down in between her pelvic bone and the bottom of her belly searching for the actual gun-shot wound as blood oozed from inside. The pain…unbearable. She felt light-headed. She wasn't about to respond to Khadafi.

"So, it's me and ya, big boy," Khadafi barked.

"What you wanna do playa," Trick shot back. "I just want what's mine. And let's do this quick. Sounds like we got company comin'."

"Look, da equipment is mine. Da counterfeit business is mine. And Mena is mine," Khadafi said firmly. "Ya forget ya in my town?" He paused with a strange grimace. "Let's go, Mena," he ordered.

Trick couldn't react fast enough when Khadafi raised his gun and fired two shots his way. Both were meant for the head. Trick dove quickly, dropping his gun in the process. Like an attacker after his prey, Khadafi advanced on him, hoping his last shot would kill him dead.

Then another shot rang out. Then another...and another. Khadafi had been hit from the back all three times. The deadly bullet was to the head. Trick hopped up in search of another gun. Anybody's gun, when he noticed Mena still on the floor with the Desert Eagle clutched tightly between her hands. She shook uncontrollably as the tears flowed. She had actually killed a man.

$ Twenty-Eight $

Trick sat on the floor with his arms wrapped around Mena's upper body, shaking his head. He tried to make her understand that everything would be okay and that she would live. He had cleaned her prints from the gun the best he could with his shirt, and had even thrown the pistol across the room before the police swarmed inside. The fact was, she had saved his life.

Ronni had already been taken out on the stretcher, and rushed to a nearby hospital. It was told that her chances were fifty-fifty. That news troubled Trick. Who knew what she would say if she made it to see another day. Another group of paramedics had already checked on Mena's abdomen and rushed back out to the ambulance to bring in a stretcher and supplies to treat the wound on site. They made it clear that she too was in danger, and would have to go to the hospital.

Club Rain now resembled a three ring circus. The area buzzed with dozens of police and paramedics all trying to figure out, what left five people dead, and two wounded? They wondered from the way the bodies laid out who fought against who? And the biggest question, how did Trick make it through it all without a single hit? He had already had his hands in the air when police barged inside, saying, "He and Mena had gotten robbed."

Mena just laid back and sobbed uncontrollably, unable to answer any questions. For the moment, the police allowed Trick to remain on the floor to console her seeing that she was distraught and headed for a breakdown. They needed answers. And witnesses were the key. Mena, Trick, and Ronni would all be questioned at some point. That was made clear by the big, muscular officer who walked around encircling the area, and scratching his scruffy chin.

Finally, with a quick chance to talk alone, Trick wiped Mena's face with his two largest fingers. "Like, you know we gotta get our story together, right?"

Mena looked up into his face as emotions filled her again. "Trick, I just don't know what to say," she cried. "I killed a man," she spoke softly. "I can't believe this!"

"Shhhh," he warned. An officer nearby knelt down drawing an outline of Noble's body with chalk. "It was self defense," he told her. "But for now, just remain quiet. Act like you're in shock, unable to speak. Yamean? Let me handle everything."

For Mena, It was just like old times. Trick was by her side taking control. She was glad he had come to South Carolina even though she'd done him wrong. "Look, I'm s-o-r-r-y for what I-I –I-I-I d-i-d," she uttered, wincing from the pain.

Just then two paramedics rushed back in and asked Trick to move aside. Quickly, one opened a box and began working on Mena's gunshot wound. "This not looking good," they reported to Trick as he knelt on the sidelines with a blank stare.

"Mena," he told her after she screamed out from the pain caused by the movement of her arm. She didn't respond, but he kept talking anyway. "We going back to Philly, baby, and we gone be partners, okay?" Trick knew he hadn't fully forgiven Mena for all she'd done; especially fucking his boy. But for now, he had to front just in case she didn't make it. Trick knew he had secrets and so did Mena.

Mena shook her head, closed her eyes and gritted her teeth as a solution was blotted on her wound. "Oullllll," she screamed.

"She's losing a lot of blood," the head paramedic blasted.

"Get her to the ambulance," another medic who looked to be in his thirties uttered with a worried frown.

"Where do I go to get our stuff back?" Trick asked as

they lifted her from the floor, onto the stretcher. He knew he would probably have to remain for questioning. "Where Mena?" he begged as they began moving Mena speedily toward the door.

For Trick, he figured they had come too far and it was time for them to shine. Making money had proved to be lucrative and he wouldn't stop just because some dread head had tried to take over his business. He vowed to make things work with Mena so no one would ever invade their hustle again.

Before Mena could answer Trick, another paramedic asked her question after question, then hit her with the last two, "You allergic to any kind of meds? Are you pregnant?"

Her eyes lit up. She looked at Trick before answering hesitantly, "Yes."

Immediately, his facial expression changed. He thought about Felony, then Khadafi. "Who's baby is it?" he quickly asked while on the move. Trick tried his best to keep up with the fast pace of the paramedics.

"Look, sir, she's losing too much blood. We gotta hurry," the thirty something year old pressed.

Trick took one last look into Mena's glassy eyes. He knew she had no idea if he was the father. "You dirty bitch!" he shouted as the ambulance doors closed tightly.

Money Maker Part 2

Coming Soon

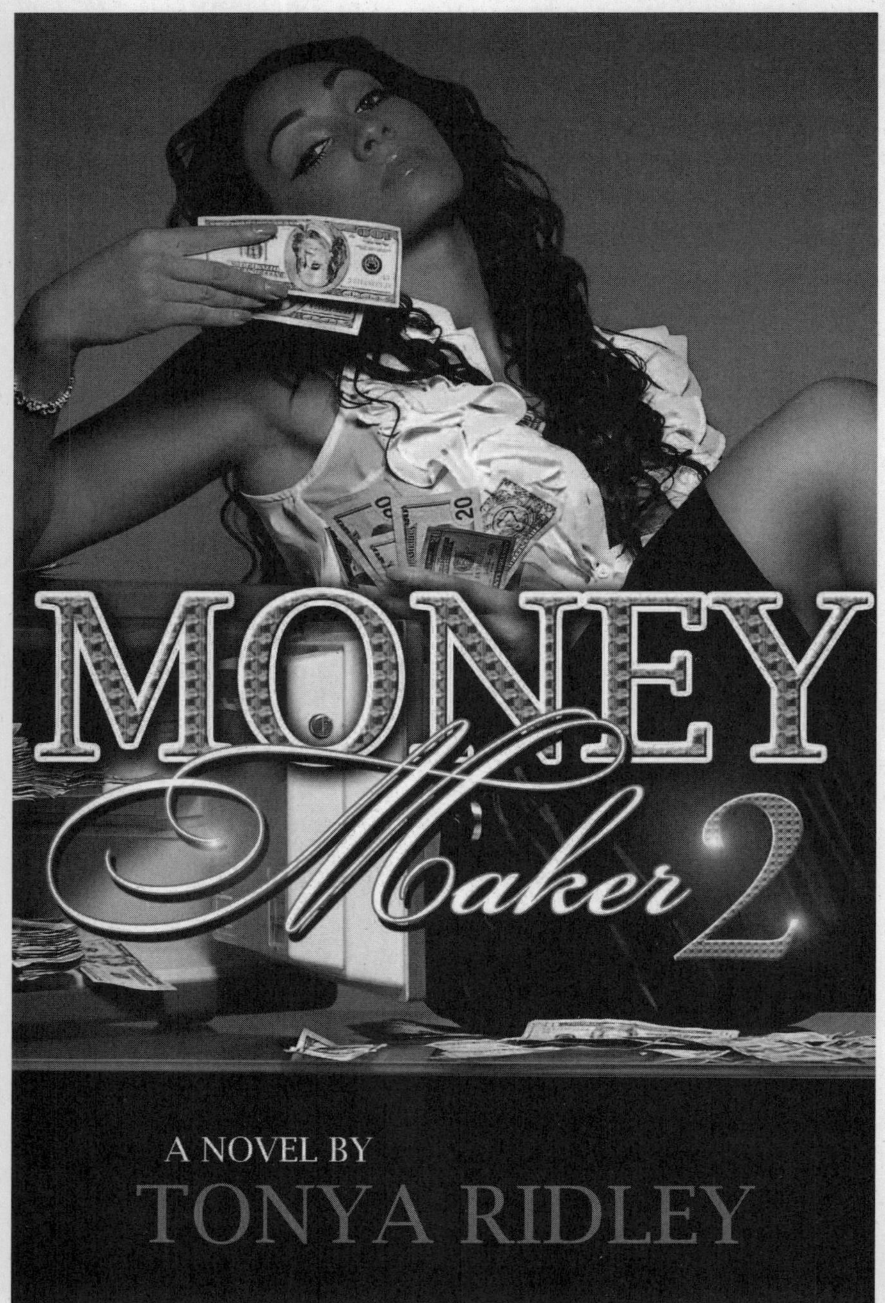
MONEY
Maker 2
A NOVEL BY
TONYA RIDLEY

COMING NOV 2010

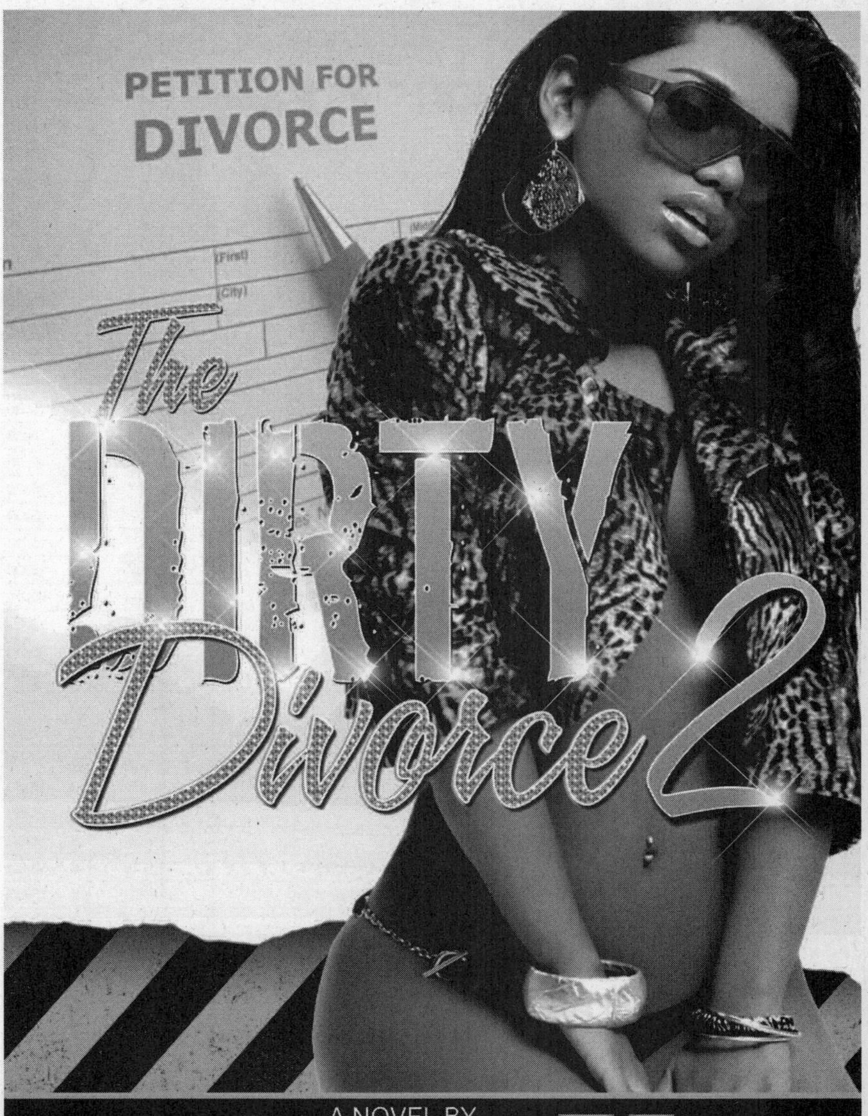

ORDER FORM

MAIL TO:
PO Box 423
Brandywine, MD 20613
301-362-6508

FAX TO:
301-856-4116

Date:	Phone:
Email:	

Ship to:	
Address:	
City & State:	Zip:

Make all money orders and cashiers checks payable to: **Life Changing Books**

Qty.	ISBN	Title	Release Date	Price
	0-9741394-5-9	Nothin Personal by Tyrone Wallace	Jul-06	$ 15.00
	0-9741394-2-4	Bruised by Azarel	Jul-05	$ 15.00
	0-9741394-7-5	Bruised 2: The Ultimate Revenge by Azarel	Oct-06	$ 15.00
	0-9741394-3-2	Secrets of a Housewife by J. Tremble	Feb-06	$ 15.00
	0-9724003-5-4	I Shoulda Seen It Comin by Danette Majette	Jan-06	$ 15.00
	0-9741394-4-0	The Take Over by Tonya Ridley	Apr-06	$ 15.00
	0-9741394-6-7	The Millionaire Mistress by Tiphani	Nov-06	$ 15.00
	1-934230-99-5	More Secrets More Lies by J. Tremble	Feb-07	$ 15.00
	1-934230-98-7	Young Assassin by Mike G.	Mar-07	$ 15.00
	1-934230-95-2	A Private Affair by Mike Warren	May-07	$ 15.00
	1-934230-94-4	All That Glitters by Ericka M. Williams	Jul-07	$ 15.00
	1-934230-93-6	Deep by Danette Majette	Jul-07	$ 15.00
	1-934230-96-0	Flexin & Sexin Volume 1	Jun-07	$ 15.00
	1-934230-92-8	Talk of the Town by Tonya Ridley	Jul-07	$ 15.00
	1-934230-89-8	Still a Mistress by Tiphani	Nov-07	$ 15.00
	1-934230-91-X	Daddy's House by Azarel	Nov-07	$ 15.00
	1-934230-87-1-	Reign of a Hustler by Nissa A. Showell	Jan-08	$ 15.00
	1-934230-86-3	Something He Can Feel by Marissa Montelih	Feb-08	$ 15.00
	1-934230-88-X	Naughty Little Angel by J. Tremble	Feb-08	$ 15.00
	1-934230847	In Those Jeans by Chantel Jolie	Jun-08	$ 15.00
	1-934230855	Marked by Capone	Jul-08	$ 15.00
	1-934230820	Rich Girls by Kendall Banks	Oct-08	$ 15.00
	1-934230839	Expensive Taste by Tiphani	Nov-08	$ 15.00
	1-934230782	Brooklyn Brothel by C. Stecko	Jan-09	$ 15.00
	1-934230669	Good Girl Gone bad by Danette Majette	Mar-09	$ 15.00
	1-934230804	From Hood to Hollywood by Sasha Raye	Mar-09	$ 15.00
	1-934230707	Sweet Swagger by Mike Warren	Jun-09	$ 15.00
	1-934230677	Carbon Copy by Azarel	Jul-09	$ 15.00
	1-934230723	Millionaire Mistress 3 by Tiphani	Nov-09	$ 15.00
	1-934230715	A Woman Scorned by Ericka Williams	Nov-09	$ 15.00
	1-934230685	My Man Her Son by J. Tremble	Feb-10	$ 15.00
	1-924230731	Love Heist by Jackie D.	Mar-10	$ 15.00
	1-934230812	Flexin & Sexin Volume 2	Apr-10	$ 15.00
	1-934230748	The Dirty Divorce by Miss KP	May-10	$ 15.00
			Total for Books	$
			Shipping Charges (add $4.25 for 1-4 books*)	$
			Total Enclosed (add lines)	$

*** Prison Orders- Please allow up to three (3) weeks for delivery.**

Please Note: We are not held responsible for returned prison orders. Make sure the facility will receive books before ordering.

***Shipping and Handling of 5-10 books is $6.25, please contact us if your order is more than 10 books. (301)362-6508**